MW00975377

SHATTERED LOYALTIES

ELLEN W. MARTIN

*Thank you
for keeping me
moving!
Hope you enjoy
my new book. My son
did the cover!!
Hugs,
Ellen
Martin*

BookLocker
Trenton, Georgia

Print ISBN: 978-1-64719-830-5
Ebook ISBN: 978-1-64719-831-2

Published by BookLocker.com, Inc., Trenton, Georgia, U.S.A.

Printed on acid-free paper.

The characters and events in this book are fictitious. Any similarity to real persons, living or dead is coincidental and not intended by the author.

BookLocker.com, Inc.
2021

First Edition

Library of Congress Cataloguing in Publication Data
Martin, Ellen W.
Shattered Loyalties by Ellen W. Martin
Library of Congress Control Number: 2021918788

OTHER BOOKS BY ELLEN W. MARTIN

DEDICATION

I dedicate SHATTERED LOYALTIES to my son, "Pepe" Martin, who is an inspiration on so many levels.

At hour zero, he made time in his busy schedule to do the artwork for the cover of this book — and, did so while working 12-hour shifts following Hurricane Ida's rampage through the city of New Orleans. He is truly a gift from God, and the pride and joy of my life.

ACKNOWLEDGEMENTS

First and foremost I want to acknowledge my son, Pepe, who lives and works in New Orleans — the very setting I chose for *Shattered Loyalties*. He helped me with so many facets of this book. Not only was he able to advise me with NOLA police procedures, but also shared mystical stories from his personal knowledge of the city, the people and the unique culture. When he isn't keeping the streets of New Orleans safe, he is an artist creating folk, pop and street art, and, also, does assemblage and painted wood art that capture the soul of the Crescent City. I'm proud to say he designed the cover for this book.

Check out this talented artist's work at https://pepemartinstudio.com. Follow him on Instagram and Facebook.

As always, I cannot write an acknowledgment without mentioning my husband, Jim, who has never wavered from his continued support, encouragement and willingness to help me over the rough spots. I don't know what I would have done without his valuable suggestions that aided in the storyline of all four of my books — particularly during the early stages of plot development and continued until the day I typed the words THE END.

Stay tuned. My next novel will also be a suspense thriller located in New Orleans. The plot is still developing and untitled, but my hope is it will be completed by next year.

ABOUT THE AUTHOR

Ellen W. Martin

A proud wife of a retired Air Force officer, mother of one son and grandparent of three grandchildren, Ellen, didn't start writing until retirement years, and even then, she considered writing a hobby. She spends her free time playing Pickle Ball, likes to bake for her loved ones, and enjoys a good laugh with friends. Ellen loves reading (and writing) suspense thrillers and mysteries laced with unsuspected twists and turns in the plot.

In 2017 she reopened old computer files of the three books she'd written between 2000 and 2010, wrote and rewrote them, and finally, published *BOOK I -SONS OF CUBA – Prelude to Revolution* and *BOOK II - SONS OF CUBA - Homecoming* — a historical fiction that is a two book series. Both books were released in the fall of 2019. The reasons she wrote about Cuba, in the first place, is a story in itself.

Even though she thoroughly enjoyed writing the historical fiction, her heart belongs to the suspense thriller genre. In the fall of 2020 she released, *INTO THE DEVILS DEN - Snared by Their Own Lies.*

During the spring of 2020, while COVID-19 was wreaking havoc throughout the United States and around the world, she spent the boring time in quarantine writing *SHATTERED LOYALTIES.*

The Martin's call the snow-white beaches and emerald waters near Northwest Florida home.

Website: https://www.booksbyellen.com

CHAPTER 1

BURT HARRISON stood next to Sarah Carlton, first lady of the United States. His arm was wrapped around her grief-stricken shoulders and forced back his own tears. They both stood frozen in time, willing the medical monitor to return to the steady beep indicating President Carlton's heart was still beating — instead they were left with the squeal of the flat line signal.

Only moments ago he and Sarah had been pushed into a corner to watch the medical staff work with frantic, but skilled, precision to try and beat the inevitable. God's will had spoken. Post mortem tasks would now wait. It was time for the doctors and nurses to stop hovering over the president's bed and allow the first lady to adjust to the fact that her husband of fifty-two years was gone. They both needed time to adjust to the reality the United States was left without their Party's nominee with only weeks left before Election Day.

As soon as the medical team left the hospital room, Sarah walked to her husband's bedside, and placed her hand on his silent heart. "Why Michael? Why now? I can't lose you. I need you. This country needs you more than ever." Only the hiss from the oxygen machine answered back. Sarah sighed, leaned down, and kissed his lips. "I'll miss you, my love. How will I go on without you? This is all too much...too soon for me." Once again her body quaked with grief along with a flood of tears.

Burt reached to take her into his arms and comfort her, but Sarah pushed him away and blew her nose into an embroidered handkerchief.

"The country is in big trouble," she said as she brushed away a latent tear. "Michael was needed at the helm *now* more than ever.

With a lump still caught in his throat and unable to speak without giving in to his own grief, the campaign manager nodded his head in agreement. Michael had been his best friend, his mentor for over twenty years, and had begged him to return as his campaign manager for a second time. Despite his own cardiac issues, there was nothing he would refuse his friend, much less the president of the United States.

Sarah clasped her hands beneath her chin; she furrowed her brow. "Say something," she said to Burt. "*Anything* that will assure me the Party will find a suitable replacement for Michael." She looked up, her eyes wide with anxiety. "*Please* convince me Dylan Randle won't be the Party's choice to replace my husband on the ticket..."

Burt knew exactly how she felt and started to speak, but Sarah continued her rant. She needed to vent all the pent up anxiety and fears she had held inside so bravely for the last several hours — Dylan Randle the III became her target.

"I'll never understand why Michael chose that skirt-chasing son of a bitch to be his running mate the first time, much less for a second term," she continued. "How does that sweet Céline put up with him and his shenanigans?" She narrowed her eyes. "My gut instincts tell me that man is capable of more than just philandering."

Burt remained quiet. There was nothing he could say...nothing he could do. The replacement choice for the presidential candidate was beyond his and Sarah's control — particularly this late into the campaign. Politics was politics. Those in power had their ways and means to twist the dialogue into whatever direction worked to their advantage and what *they* considered was the best direction for the country — regrettably, too many times, it was in contrast from the desires and needs of the voting public.

"Burt, are you listening? Sarah asked, her voice an octave higher. "This is important."

"Yes ma'am, of course. Unfortunately," he said with as much empathy as he could muster, "there is a political machine in place, always has been, that control these matters. In the old days they called them *'King Makers'*. Whether you and I like it, *'they'* are still around and have the last word."

"Ridiculous," the first lady spat in disgust, and then released a deep, melancholy sigh.

Resigned to reality, Sarah plopped on the edge of the hospital bed and took her husband's cold hand. Without looking back at Burt she said, "I believe you have phone calls to make, meetings to arrange so that the Party," a sneer twitched her cheek, "can quickly nominate a new candidate. Time is obviously of the essence."

"I've already contacted the Party Chair," Burt said. "All the necessary protocols and preparations have been set into motion. We'll have a new nominee by the end of the day."

"Good," she said without looking at Burt. "Michael would expect nothing less. The last thing this country needs right now is Allison Benson and her unconventional platform winning this election. Let's just pray the Party makes the right choice; someone who'll carry on Michael's good work." She turned her attention back to her dead husband. "Now if you don't mind, please allow me some last moments alone with the love of my life."

"Of course," Burt said. "If you're sure there isn't anything else I can do for you, I'll be on the next plane to Washington." He walked over, leaned down, and kissed the top of Sarah's head. "I take to heart *every* last word from the president's dying wish," he said. "I promise you I will personally do everything in my power to influence the Party's final decision for the new nominee and his running mate. This country must not fall into the hands of the wrong people."

CHAPTER 2

AS THE sun crawled above the rolling hills of Eastern Montana, a brisk steady wind whipped the grassy plains as a herd of bison grazed two hundred yards in the distance. Dylan Randle the III climbed out of the Jeep. The hunting guide handed him a Remington 700 and two 300 Winchester magnum shells.

"Are you sure you don't want more cartridges?" the guide asked. "It could take three or four shots to bring down a big bull."

"*God Bless America*" chimed on Dylan's cell phone. He reached into his pocket, ignored the message and switched to silent mode.

"Don't you think you should get that?" the guide asked. "It could be important. You *are* the vice president of the United States in the middle of an election campaign."

Dylan loaded two cartridges into the rifle's magazine. "President Carlton made it perfectly clear who was running the show when he was *forced* to accept me once again as his running mate," his voice tinged with scorn. "I'm right where he sent me...well close proximity anyway." He smiled and said, "With one minor detour."

The guide shrugged and ignored the text messages blowing up on his phone. "No skin off my knee," he said. "You're paying the big bucks for the kill. I'm just here to accommodate your wishes and put food on my table."

Dylan shrugged. "I don't know what everyone is so worried about," he said. "Vegas is only a puddle jump flight from here. That crackbrained cowboy *will* get his Rodeo Championship buckle on time and the people in Nevada will get their bullshit political speech, a look at my pretty face and plenty of kisses for all the babies." *Preferably with one of those gorgeous, Vegas' show girl babes,* he thought with a mischievous grin. *Too bad he'd been ordered to behave.*

A gust of icy wind shifted into Dylan's face. *Everyone wanted a piece of him,* he thought as he zipped and then lifted the collar on his down jacket. *Not this time. Not before he got his rocks off staring a trophy beast in the eye and show him who was boss — who was in control.*

The guide nodded to Dylan the wind direction and the bison's position was primed for his best chance for a clean kill.

Dylan lay on the ground and elbow-crawled to the top of the knoll. His thoughts continued to swirl like an out-of-control dirt-devil speeding across the plains. He still couldn't believe the party chose Michael Carlton to run for a second term and not him. That old man looked like walking death and needed to retire. With the old man's medical issues the grim reaper had to be lurking around the corner, Dylan thought with a roll of his eyes. At least President Carlton had the good sense to keep me as his running mate — just in case. Dylan peered through the rifle's scope and adjusted the focus. *After all, everyone knows I'm the best choice for VP and the future of American politics.*

A sharp rock dug into his belly. Dylan readjusted his position and tried to find a more comfortable spot to shake the growing ire that threatened to ruin his perfect day. More memories from the time leading up to the Convention continued their unwanted march into his thoughts. How dare the Party even suggest dropping him from the ticket... and replace *him* with Callie Summers! There was no way she had more to offer than he. The people loved him. He was without question the wisest choice to remain the vice presidential nominee. Not even the president of the United States gathered more supporters at rallies than he. After all, if it hadn't been for him on the ticket, Michael Carlton wouldn't have won a first term, much less have any chance of winning a second term.

The guide lay next to Dylan; touched his shoulder and whispered, "There, one hundred yards to your left. That monster bull must weigh over two thousand pounds and stand over six feet high. What a trophy, man. Go for it."

Dylan forced his indignation back into the memory vault promising he would never forget who his political enemies were. Someday, some way they all would regret their treachery. He had the means, and most definitely the desire, to destroy them all without a blink of an eye.

He slid a live-round into the chamber, slowly swept his Remington to the left, and then adjusted his Leopold scope until he stared at the broadside of the animal. The massive beast turned and faced him. Their eyes locked. Dylan slid his finger onto the trigger, hesitated for a brief moment. If he didn't know any better, he would have sworn that bull dared him to pull the trigger. Dylan grinned. *You don't think I'm capable of killing you, you magnificent beast? Well, just watch me.* He took one last calming breath, slowly released the air ——

"*Stop!* Mr. Vice President." Two pairs of hands grabbed Dylan under his arms and swept up his six foot two frame from his prone position as easily as if he were a child.

"What the fu——," the rest of the word stuck to the roof of his mouth. He was surrounded by a group of secret service agents in dark suits, all grim faced.

They snatched the Remington 700 from Dylan and handed him an iPad. A headline emblazoned with bold lettering announced: *President Michael Carlton dead at the age of seventy-eight leaving the country without a president and a nominee just weeks before Election Day.*

Dylan, still shaken from the interruption, glanced back and forth at the two Secret Service officers holding onto him. He was both pissed and confused. "Wha...what does this mean?" he barked.

"It means you need to be sworn in as quickly as possible as president of the United States of America."

CHAPTER 3

ENGINES rumbled; the ferry vibrated as the passenger boat eased away from the Algiers Point Ferry Terminal. The large barge fought against the fast moving current of the Mississippi River; dodged errant logs that bobbed and dipped below the surface, only to pop up again and continue their serpentine path toward the Gulf of Mexico.

As the ferry headed into the open water, Penelope "Pepper" Mills guided her bicycle to her favorite spot at the bow of the boat. She rested the rusty contraption, which had seen better days, against the protective railing that surrounded the lower deck. She leaned forward, held both arms out straight, shut her eyes, and listened to the melodic swish from the ferry's wake. The river's mist and the cool, late October breeze brushed against her skin as the early morning sun kissed her cheeks.

Leonardo DiCaprio was holding onto her waist, she fantasized. His soothing voice whispered promises into her ear. Once again the engines rumbled; the barge bounced off pilings and jolted Pepper from her daydream as they pulled into the New Orleans Ferry Terminal.

So much for my daily date with Leonardo, Pepper sighed with a shrug. Pretty sad her happiness had been reduced to a short ten-minute ferry ride across the Mississippi River twice a day. Not ideal, but definitely an improvement after hop scotching from job to job for over a year, left broke, depressed, and without purpose.

Pepper hooked the strap of her oversized faux Gucci Bag across her chest and wheeled her bike over with the other commuters who waited to exit the ferry. *New Orleans really wasn't so bad,* she thought as she watched the ferry crew secure the mooring lines. Admittedly, she would be enjoying this city a hellava lot more if it were under different circumstances. Having been reduced from high-profile Washington correspondent to writing obituary blurbs was a long way to fall.

The crew dropped the chain and all the passengers crossed the gangway, scattering to points unknown. Pepper maneuvered her way with the crowd down the steel-plated walkway, and then headed for the Mississippi Riverwalk and Café Du Monde for fresh Beignets and Chicory coffee. *Definitely an acquired taste,* she thought with a smile *and a must if you hoped to persuade the Crescent City to accept you as one of her own.*

She suppressed a laugh. *So far so good for me.* If folklore were to be believed many had come to live in New Orleans from all over the world, but eventually moved away because bad things repeatedly happened to them. Unlucky? Or, was New Orleans nudging the unwelcome to go and live elsewhere? She wasn't superstitious; however, the city did have a colorful history with plenty of ghosts from the past that had a mind of their own.

Pepper biked along the Mississippi Riverwalk, turned off the trail, and headed straight for Café Du Monde. After she ordered her breakfast to go, she walked her bike to Jackson Square and found an empty park bench — an easy feat since it was early morning and the tourists weren't out.

This was her favorite time of day when the Square woke up with its kaleidoscope of characters. T-shirt peddlers and other arts and craft vendors were vying for premium spots, while mule-drawn carriages lined up on the Decatur side of Jackson Square offering leisurely city tours. Just watching the local artists display their latest creations of Folk Art depicting the French Quarter, the Superdome and other popular scenes of New Orleans, lifted her melancholy and gave her hope she would once again have a career she could be proud of.

Pepper broke off pieces of her last Beignet and tossed them to the pigeons. The squatty birds scrambled for their meager share. A wave of sadness returned and washed through her like an unsuspecting undertow. She knew exactly how those little foragers felt. She, too, had become a scavenger, with New Orleans being her last chance to succeed as a serious journalist. *More like survive*, she huffed under her breath.

It had been less than six years, but it felt like a lifetime since she had personally interviewed heads of state from all over the world. How quickly those sweet memories had faded since she was the rising star and the envy of her colleagues.

A taste of venom mixed with resentment and regrets soured her mouth and blackened her thoughts. Her life would be forever tormented, scarred because of that ill-fated encounter with the golden boy of Washington D.C. ... a sexual predator... heir apparent to become a future leader of the free world.

She had her chance to exposed him at the time, but she was too naïve and blamed herself. For ten years, she had swallowed, no, buried the shame... her pride... her bitterness toward Mr. Dylan Randle the III and focused only on her career. Even when the "Me too Movement" spread across the nation, she remained reticent to speak out against him. No one in their right mind went against the currents of political power and lived to tell the tale —

particularly a Washington D.C. correspondent who wanted to hold onto their rising career.

And then, five years ago, Dylan was being vetted as a potential vice presidential candidate. Pepper could no longer keep silent — the public needed to know what kind of man was vying for the second highest office in the country. She, in her new status as star reporter, felt invincible and full of herself. She believed in her hard-earned credibility and the power to influence political opinions. Obsessed and unwilling to turn back, she seized the moment and attempted to expose the underbelly of Dylan Randle the III.

Pepper sighed. The moment she made public her accusations against him, it was jaw-dropping how quickly her friends, her colleagues, the Washington elite abandoned her — how quickly her opportunities dried up. To this very day, it still baffled her how the public could believe that... that lecherous womanizer — even when other women came forth with their accusations. How easily all the claims against him had been nipped in the bud and did so without a moment of consequence.

Unlike the other women, and much to Dylan Randle's ire, she refused to let go of her accusations. Unfortunately, the end result was that *she* became toxic, unreliable, and labeled a crackpot who was obsessed and resorted to unsubstantiated and sensationalized stories. She was accused of slandering the fine reputation of the darling of Washington politics.

Once the political inner circles of D.C. hung the unwelcome sign around her neck, her prospective job opportunities fell faster than a zigzagging line of dominoes. For almost a year after her downfall, she was left unemployable with only seven-hundred dollars in her once fat bank account.

Pepper bit the bottom of her lip and tried to contain the rising bitterness she had hoped she'd permanently put to bed; she tried to silence the paralyzing obsession she thought she had come to terms with after two years of intense therapy. But the flood gates had opened and now all the unwanted memories began to spill over the dam.

The one person she thought she could count on was Washington's top anchorman, Mark Saderfield. Even though she didn't know him very well, they enjoyed a casual flirtation while attending the same parties. Unlike her other so-called friends and colleagues — the very ones who scattered like roaches when the lights turned on, Mark continued to believe her about Dylan's unwanted advances. Mark convinced her he was on her side. Pepper furrowed her brows. He promised he would do everything in his power to help repair her reputation and reset her career. *But he, like the others, abandoned her when she most needed a friend.*

Nine months into her exile from Washington and completely out of the blue, Mark sent a one line text message with a prospective job opportunity at the New Orleans Advocate. It was obviously a pity apology for bailing on her. No, make that more a cruel joke. *Did he actually believe he was doing her some big favor?* She scoffed under breath. What better way to keep the trouble-making reporter under wraps than to get her a job writing obituaries far away from Washington? *After all, dead people don't talk back, do they?*

Stop fixating on the past, Pepper screamed in her head. *You're spiraling out of control.* She pressed her hand against her chest and tried to calm her racing heartbeat;

she took a deep breath and slowly exhaled. She had vowed never again to let Dylan Randle consume her thoughts and destroy her hard fought well-being.

Today should be a time to focus on the positive and concentrate on how she'd been given a second chance. A second chance that took a lot of cajoling, begging and pleading to convince her editor she was a reformed woman. *Remember,* she reminded herself, *you promised Delacroix you had learned your lesson. You promised you would not allow personal feelings to ever again contaminate your objectivity.*

Pepper closed her eyes, inhaled, exhaled and then repeated the controlled breathing exercises the doctor had given her. *Today is about new beginnings,* she nudged her thoughts. This is *your long-awaited return to the real world of journalism.* As Pepper's old demons reluctantly slithered back into the dark side of her memories, her heart rate slowed to a normal pace.

She leaned back against the bench and straightened her posture. She inhaled one last deep cleansing breath and once again scanned the morning activities buzzing about Jackson Square. With renewed determination, she soaked in the positive vibes released by all the creative people humming around the Square. Each of them was there today with renewed hopes and dreams for their future. So must she.

With all signs of negativity flushed from her system, Pepper welcomed her rejuvenated spirit now bursting with confidence and a willingness to succeed against all odds. Today promised to be the best day she had had in four years. Today she had landed an interview with Harley Durham — one of New Orleans most colorful and controversial characters.

This interview was to be *the* opportunity that finally dragged her out of the past towards a new and promising future. This long-awaited assignment was the avenue to write more meaningful articles, and once again, become the true professional she needed to be — the one she wanted to be — the one she knew she could be. And yet, she still had one major hurdle standing in her way. The very man she would face today just happened to be a close personal friend of the campaigning presidential candidate, Dylan Randle the III.

CHAPTER 4

PEPPER boarded the St. Charles streetcar bound for the posh neighborhoods of the Garden District that oozed with nostalgia from times gone by. As the tram rumbled away from Central City and around the track past Lee Circle, she glanced over at the sixty-foot pillar now minus the statue of Robert E. Lee. The once iconic landmark, like so many other Old South memorials, had been warehoused in some unknown location. *I know how you feel, General,* Pepper whispered under her breath. *I, too, was removed from where I should be. With a little faith and a whole lot of luck, maybe, someday, both our reputations will be restored, and we can come out of hiding.*

As the wood and steel streetcar rattled along the track, Pepper surrendered to its rhythmic sway and enjoyed the scenery. A medley of small hotels, restaurants, churches and schools rolled by; Mardi Gras beads, errantly thrown from parades past, dangled precariously from the branches of live oak trees clustered along St. Charles Avenue.

The closer Pepper neared her destination the calm she had enjoyed at the beginning of her journey melted away and ignited into full-blown jitters. She tried, but she couldn't shake the urge to cut and run at the next streetcar stop and return to the city. Were her instincts warning her she might be walking into a trap? The longer she thought about it, the more she wondered why her editor had picked Harley Durham, of all people, as her first serious interview in over four years — particularly with Dylan Randle's campaign stop arriving in New Orleans in only a matter of days.

Nothing added up. In the past when it came to anything that connected her to Dylan or anyone he was acquainted with, every major news outlet would react like she was ground zero and as uncontrollable as Covid-19. Her breath caught in her throat. What if the plan was to lure her to Harley Durham's house so he could finish the job Dylan started?

Pepper pressed her hand against her racing heart; fought against the flood of crippling memories rushing to the surface. *Get over yourself, Penelope. You're being ridiculous and paranoid, again*, she reasoned as she slowly regained control of her breathing. It was obvious she was giving herself way more credit than she was worth. Four years was an eternity in a news cycle. Mr. Durham probably didn't even remember or care who she is or was. She was going to do just fine as long as she maintained her cool and reminded herself she needed this break as much as the air she breathed.

The next scheduled stop flashed across the streetcar reader-board. Pepper pulled the cord above her head, and then reached into her oversized purse for a compact mirror. She checked her teeth for lipstick smear, and then fluffed her short, curly blond hair with her fingertips. When the St. Charles streetcar squealed to a stop, Pepper stepped off the tram and walked the half block toward what may be her last chance to revive her fading career.

Moments later she arrived at the massive mansion protected by a hedge and wrought iron fencing. The name "DURHAM" was scrolled across an iron arbor announcing the entrance into the compound. Pepper opened the gate and walked along diamond shaped stones to the marble steps leading up to an etched-glass French door. She took a deep breath, and then exhaled fluttering a wisp of blonde curls resting on her forehead. The doorbell chimed.

A black woman with wiry, snow-white hair opened the door. "Yes? May I help you?" she asked.

There wasn't a stain on her white uniform and her scuff-free black patent shoes shined as if she had just polished and buffed them. Pepper smiled. "Hello, my name is Penelope Mills with *The Advocate*. I have an appointment with Mr. Durham."

"Of course, Mr. Durham is expecting you," the woman said and stepped to the side so Pepper could enter.

Even though the floor to ceiling windows were draped with heavy brocade, light streamed in; the wood plank floors glistened. From the antique French provincial furnishings, the ornate oriental carpets to the grand piano and harp in the music room, the entire house screamed stinking rich. The small amount of research she had been able to find on such short notice indicated Mr. Durham's fortune was anything but old family money.

Pepper brushed a fingertip across the top of the dust-free ebony piano. How did this man crawl out of the backwoods of a Louisiana swamp into a place like this? She raised an eyebrow. When she was back on top, maybe she'd dig a little deeper into Mr. Harley Durham.

Stop this, she scolded under her breath. Every time she got too curious and dug too deep, trouble latched onto her like suckerfish onto a shark. Today she had one mission and one mission only — to focus wholly on Harley Durham, the business man and the philanthropist. If she was lucky, maybe she could persuade him to verify some of his best known colorful, sometimes dubious escapades.

Pepper continued meandering around the room admiring Ming vases and knockoff Renaissance masterpieces hanging on the walls. Framed photographs of various sizes were placed at a diagonal on top of the fireplace mantel. She picked up one photo and then another.

"That's a picture of me and President Randle when we played football together at Tulane," a voice said from behind her.

Pepper spun around; the photograph slipped out of her hands. "Mr. Durham, I...you..."

Harley, a bear of a man with a belly that spilled over his belt, caught the photo just before it hit the floor. "It seems a hundred years ago my lineman skills were protecting Randle's sorry ass," he smiled showing tobacco-stained teeth. "Looks like I'm still his protector in some small way."

He replaced the picture back onto the mantel and picked up another. "This one was taken when we were on African safari. That big 'ol bull elephant refused to die that day. Probably wasn't Dylan's proudest moment. But, once that stubborn son of a...," Harley glanced at Pepper. "Pardon me, I mean my old friend, sets his sights on a trophy of sorts, nothing seems to stop him from possessing or destroying his...the target." He captured Pepper with his eyes for a brief moment.

Every muscle in her body seized. *He knows...he remembers who she is.* Her breath caught in her throat; her hands and fingers tingled; she felt dizzy, but refused to give in to his subtle move to catch her off guard.

Harley clapped his hands together and said, "Before we start, may Ruby Jo bring you a beverage?"

"A...a glass of sweet tea would be nice," Pepper managed to say as she regained her composure.

"Ruby Jo," Harley yelled to the back of the house. "Bring a pitcher of sweet tea for the lady. "I'll have my usual."

Harley offered Pepper a seat on the French brocade settee. She opted for the Queen Anne chair that was across from the small sofa separated only by a large glass-top coffee table.

He shrugged, sat on the sofa and stretched his arms across the back. "Where would you like to begin?" he asked.

Pepper took out her cell phone. "With your permission, I'd like to record our interview," she said, and then placed the phone on the table in front of Harley.

He shrugged, "Of course. We *certainly* want the article to be accurate. There's nothing worse than twisted facts getting out of hand," he winked. "'Old Harley needs all the glowing reviews he can get these days."

Pepper steadied her hand, picked up the iced tea the maid had set on the table. With as much calm as she could muster, she took a sip and avoided eye contact. She knew if their eyes met one more time, she would lose control and melt into a pool of vulnerability. She placed her glass on the coffee table and asked her opening question.

"Tell me about your family and what it was like growing up in the swamplands of Louisiana." Her voice denied all signs she was ready to jump out of her skin.

"I'd rather not," Harley said. "Most of those days were unpleasant memories. I prefer focusing on the new psychiatric wing I'm building at Tulane Hospital. A much more pleasant conversation, I assure you."

"Of course," Pepper said. She glanced at her notebook. "I understand you recently received the Presidential Citizens Medal."

Harley cocked an eyebrow. "Thank you for mentioning," he said. "A lot of folks around here believe giving me that award was a joke...that I'm a joke."

"I doubt that," Pepper said. "Your contributions toward the betterment of mental health are renown not only in Louisiana, but throughout the U.S. You must be very proud."

Pepper chanced a quick glance at Harley and asked a follow-up question. "With so many charitable options to choose from, why have you focused on mental health?"

For the next twenty minutes Harley raved about all his accomplishments and his plans for future projects. Not once did he hint what prompted his interests on that particular subject. He skirted her questions by bragging how he, not the Governor or either of the State's Congressional Senators was chosen to introduce President Randle at the forthcoming reelection campaign rally. When he finished blowing his own horn, he stood, and gulped down the last swig of Dos Equis.

Harley glanced at his watch. "Any other questions?" he asked.

Pepper closed her notebook. "May I ask you one personal question?"

Harley tucked his chin and raised an eyebrow. "I'm game," he said, "but only one." He grinned playfully.

Pepper turned off the recorder and slid it into her purse. "Is it true you marched in an Endymion Parade during Mardi Gras with your pet alligator on a leash?" she asked.

Still laughing, Harley escorted Pepper to the front door. "It's true...it's true," he said finally able to speak. "It was a good day. That eight foot carnivore showed his compassionate side during the parade. He only ate one whinny child and two yapping dogs for a change."

***

Harley stood on the front porch and watched the well-portioned, spunky reporter walk away. *Nice ass*, he mused with a sly grin. *A little short for his taste, but according to Dylan, a real fireball. Do ya suppose she brought that spirited passion into the bedroom?* He raised an eyebrow. *Perhaps he should have invited her to stay.* He shrugged. *Maybe next time.*

"Ruby...Ruby Jo," he yelled. "Bring a double Scotch and a cooler of Dos Equis out to the pool. I'm a bit overheated and feel like a swim."

Harley yanked off his collared shirt and pulled down his trousers and underwear. He stepped into the swimming pool buck-naked, sank into the cold saltwater pool up to his neck. As he treaded water, his mind reeled with questions. With all the reporters Buford Delacroix had on *The Advocate* staff, why in the hell would he assign Penelope Mills, of all people, to interview him — particularly with the presidential campaign arriving in New Orleans in just a few days? With Mills' and Randle's infamous run-in four years ago, it seemed like even a backwoods news-hack, like Delacroix, would know better than to link those two together in *any* way. He shook his head. *Yep, looked like a potential catastrophic collision course to him.*

He ducked under water and swam to the edge of the pool. Harley took a sip of the beer Ruby Jo had left him in the bucket of ice. You don't suppose this was Delacroix's payback to him for screwing his wife after the Mardi Gras Rex Ball last year? He laughed. *Bold move, you dumb bastard.*

Harley narrowed his eyes. *Be careful my old "friend", this little game you're playing might well backfire on you. When Dylan Randle discovers you not only hired Penelope Mills, but also sent her to interview me, your little news rag will be reduced to a local advertising blog — and that's if you're lucky.* Harley tipped the beer to his lips and drained the bottle. *No one walked into the Dylan Randle minefield without protection, and even then they rarely came out unscathed.*

Harley climbed onto a floating raft, rolled onto his stomach, and rested his head on folded arms. The nap he hoped to catch eluded him as his thoughts continued to roam. Perhaps he shouldn't be wishing ill-will on the one person who was putting *him* in the spotlight for a change. When he thought about it, Delacroix was actually doing him a favor by giving him positive front page coverage for a change. What had Dylan or his campaign manager, Burt Harrison, done for him lately? Nothing, but ask for money and give him grief when he occasionally colored outside the lines. Maybe this was *his* turn to share some of the glory that his 'ol buddy assumed he owned. *Dylan wouldn't be where he was today if it hadn't been for me and my ability to keep secrets —— and man, oh man did he know a lot of secrets.*

Harley slid off the raft and climbed out of the pool. He wrapped a towel around his waist and pulled a Dos Equis from the ice chest. *Life had been so boring lately*, he thought as he took a swig of beer. He missed the good old days when his free spirit could fly. He was tired of other people monitoring his behavior because of who he once was instead of who he became. He, too, had a life to live.

A mischievous grin played at the corners of his mouth. Why not have a little fun shaking up his friend's in-the-bag campaign? Maybe allowing Penelope Mills a peek back into the world of politics through him was just the ticket he was looking for. It could be fun stirring the pot and make this boring campaign more interesting. It was either that, or regress to wrestling alligators for sport again. What could possibly be the harm in playing a little prank? There were only a few weeks left before the presidential election and Dylan's poll numbers were through the roof and still rising. No way would his old friend lose this election. How could he? His opponent was a woman.

Harley leaned back on the chase lounge and savored the memory of how Pepper reacted while looking at those pictures of Dylan. Her glare burned hotter than the fires of hell. And yet, if he had touched her, she would have crumbled into a pile of dust. Who could really blame her? His "dear" 'ol friend, without an ounce of guilt, did destroy that young woman's career, and most likely, just as she claimed, assaulted her to boot. He shook his head. *Some things never changed.*

Harley finished his beer and opened another. If he had learned one thing over thirty years of "friendship" with Dylan, was that the Randles were the last family you wanted to cross. *Unless you knew you could get away with it*, he mused with a grin.

Harley took his cell phone out of his pants pocket and punched in the number for *The Advocate*.

"Buford, Harley Durham here. Just wanted you to know your girl reporter just left. A real professional. Liked her a lot...Uh huh...Uh huh...Be sure she gets an invitation to the campaign cocktail party following the presidential rally...Then give her yours...I know it's your ass on the line...Uh huh, uh huh...I'm well aware of the circumstances. I'll handle President Randle. You leave the worrying to me. Okay? It's time that little gal was given the opportunity to redeem herself...Yeah, I'm sure. In fact, I'm willing to bet she has learned her lesson and wouldn't dare allow history to repeat itself."

Harley roared with laughter after he ended the call. He dropped the towel from around his waist and dove back into the pool.

CHAPTER 5

"DYLAN...Dylan...Dylan...."

Dylan Randle the III rocked back on his heels. He closed his eyes and inhaled the roar of the crowd. Their spirited chants and stomping feet pulsated inside the New Orleans Superdome that was filled to capacity.

Harley slapped Dylan on the back. "Told you D-Rod. They love you in Louisiana. Aren't you glad I talked you into coming to NOLA? No way can Benson win this election. You're too popular and your war chest too deep."

"Yeah, she may have kicked my butt at the last two presidential debates," Dylan said over the noise. "But this, this is what it's all about...the people. Her pretty words and hollow promises mean nothing compared to this."

A sharp pain shot through Dylan's knees. He winced and tried to muscle through the growing discomfort. *Damn old football injuries*, he mumbled. This stop in New Orleans was exactly what both he and Cèline needed. After weeks on the campaign trail, his body and enthusiasm were beginning to wane. Right now, all he wanted to do was climb into Harley's hot tub with a Johnny Walker in one hand and a Cuban cigar in the other.

Dylan shifted from one foot to the other trying to relieve the dull ache moving into his arthritic joints. He could cope with his pain, but his wife's attitude lately was a different story. He'd like to blame this grueling campaign schedule Burt had put them on as the reason she had become more irascible and uncontrollable than usual.

His brows pinched together. But, it wasn't everything. Something else was going on. Céline hadn't been herself in weeks. She'd even requested separate bedrooms when she joined him in Chicago and Dallas. He furrowed his brow. *A man has needs, after all.*

Harley whispered into Dylan's ear. "Where's your wife? Shouldn't she be standing here with us?"

Dylan whipped his head around trying to locate her. The crowd had been so exhilarating he hadn't even missed Cèline. Harley was right. Where in the hell was she? His so-called better half *should've* been by his side, smiling with admiration and pride, acting like she actually cared about him and this campaign. But once again, his darling Cajun queen had chosen an inopportune time to defy him. *Would it really be so hard to show some semblance of support for her husband*? He grumbled under his breath. *Particularly in front of her hometown crowd.*

Harley nudged Dylan in the ribs, and then motioned with his head. "Down there," he whispered.

Dylan couldn't believe his eyes. His "adoring" wife was at the foot of the stage laughing and joking with his running mate, Callie Summers. The two of them were surrounded by a group of media vultures all jockeying for their attention; multiple microphones were being shoved towards them; the flashes from all the cameras mirrored a fireworks show on the 4th of July.

His eye started to twitch. Why weren't those television cameras focused on him? Those reporters should be scrambling to hear what *he* had to say. He was the one running for president of the United States not the vice presidential candidate Callie Summers — and most definitely not his wife.

The longer he watched the two women getting all the attention, the more the veins in his neck pulsed; heat crawled to his cheeks. This campaign was supposed to be about him. This would have never happened if the Party had chosen a man instead of a woman to be his running mate. Since when did a presidential candidate lose the privilege of choosing their own vice president?

I presume President Carlton's bitchy widow, Sarah, played a large part in that deal, he thought. The small spasm that plagued his eye now moved to his cheek. Well, he had news for them all. *He* was now president of the United States. Yes, maybe for only a measly month, and only because that old bastard Carlton dropped dead in the middle of a presidential campaign — but nonetheless president and one who expects to be reelected. If everyone would just leave him alone and be more supportive, he'd show them all he could win *this* election on his own merits. He didn't need some female on the ticket to sweeten the deal.

"Hey Mr. President," a group of men shouted from the stands and waved, "Great speech...we're with you a hundred percent, man. You'll bury that bitch Allison Benson in November."

Dylan flashed a forced smile and gave two thumbs up, but he still bristled inside knowing Callie and his wife were getting more media attention than he. Where was his campaign manager? Burt should have broken up that little tea party long ago. Didn't his running mate have somewhere else to be?

Dylan clenched and unclenched his fist, resisting the urge to march down the steps onto the football field and "encourage" his wife to join him, but luckily for her he had his image to preserve.

The longer he watched Callie and Cèline the angrier he became. *My darling wife, you'll pay for this blatant show of disloyalty.*

***

Burt Harrison dropped his head into his hands. He knew it...he knew something like this would happen the minute the first lady insisted Callie Summers join them in New Orleans for the Superdome rally. For weeks now he had purposely and successfully kept the vice presidential candidate campaigning at opposite ends of the country from Dylan – until now. He shook his head, heaved a deep soulful sigh as he watched the president's joyous mood turn sour and grim the moment he caught a glimpse of his running mate getting all the media attention.

Burt glanced at his watch. Callie had a plane to catch to the West Coast. Why wasn't she moving? She should have been headed to the airport ten minutes ago. His heart pounded until he thought it would blow through his chest. If Callie didn't leave these premises soon, Dylan was going to have a complete meltdown in front of everyone.

Weariness like he'd never known swept through Burt like an old dog seeking a place in the woods to crawl and die. With each passing day he regretted more and more accepting the responsibility to become Dylan Randle's campaign manager. He swiped a hand across his mouth, glanced toward the ceiling. How do you argue with your best friend and mentor when he is on his deathbed? Even today he could still see and feel the faith radiating from Michael's eyes assuring him that Dylan Randle would come around and become an acceptable presidential candidate — but not without Callie Summers as his running mate.

Burt furrowed his brow. What a chaotic nightmare this entire process had been. With President Carlton's untimely death just weeks before the General Election, a bomb had been dropped into the lap of a bunch of polarized decision makers. To make things worse, most of them argued against Dylan Randle being on the Party's ticket as Carlton's running mate in the first place. When Dylan suddenly became the presumed presidential candidate, it was almost a deal breaker. *Their* "brilliant" plan was to shake up the entire ballot by offering two completely different choices. He rolled his eyes and shook his head. It was ludicrous to think they'd even considered that lame option so late in the game. Time for quibbling had run out.

A throb thumped against his temples. If the Party had taken that road, it would have spelled disaster with no hope for holding onto the White House. Thank God, and just in the nick of time, the powers that be wilted like fragile flowers on a hot summer day. He released a long sigh. But the only reason they caved was because Dylan finally agreed to accept Callie Summers as his running mate.

He took off his horn-rimmed glasses and pinched the bridge of his nose. *I'm trying Michael; I'm trying to keep my promise.* In his heart he knew he should have faith in his old friend's judgment and do the job he was hired to do. But...

Burt rubbed his hand across his brow. This job was getting more and more difficult with each passing day. He'd been reduced from campaign strategist to a glorified babysitter for an egotistical child with no moral compass.

He chanced another quick glance at Dylan. For the time being his boss seemed once again engaged with the crowd. As hard as it was to believe, many people *did* believe, wholeheartedly, Dylan was the right choice for president. The crowds here and at every other campaign stop even made him believe that Dylan had more to offer as a presidential candidate than he gave credit.

Maybe the real problem was with me, Burt reasoned. After all, he *was* still grieving over the loss of his friend who had been one of the most beloved presidents in years. Perhaps, the real reason he harbored doubts and allowed them to overshadow any smidgen of faith in Dylan was because, in his mind, there was no one good enough to hitch a ride on the coattails of Michael Carlton. It wasn't fair that just *anyone* would be allowed to claim his friend's accomplishments as their own — particularly men like Dylan Randle the III.

Burt rubbed his eyes with the heel of his hands. He needed to stop with all the pessimistic thoughts. But it was hard. Even though the campaign still enjoyed double-digit poll numbers over Allison Benson, they needed to consider the negative results of the recent disastrous debates. In just the last week alone her popularity and numbers were surging faster than a tsunami rushing toward a crowded beach in July. The one small factor that gave him hope for a positive outcome in this election was that the Benson woman had very little experience in national politics. Statistically speaking, she had no chance of winning against a popular incumbent administration. But — and it was a big but — Dylan's victory was *only* assured if time and Allison Benson's luck ran out before Election Day — a mere two weeks away.

One problem at a time. Burt sighed. Right now his biggest headache was separating the vice presidential candidate from a president who looked like he was about to eat somebody alive.

Burt weaved his way through the crowd to Callie. He leaned over and whispered into her ear. She smiled, hugged the first lady, and thanked all the people still gathered around her. Escorted by her Secret Service detail, the vice presidential candidate left the Superdome with a small group of media still trailing behind hoping for one last word.

The moment Callie exited the Dome, the first lady politely slipped away from all the media attention and headed back up the steps to the platform. As Cèline reentered the stage, Burt felt his blood pressure begin to drop within a normal range.

***

What the hell, Cèline? Am I invisible? Dylan's jaw fell slack as he watched his wife reenter the stage, sit down in a chair, and open a bottle of water. The earlier resentment he worked so hard to suppress returned poker-hot; his nostrils flared. *Put down that damn water bottle and get your butt over here*, he thought resisting the urge to scream into the microphone. But Cèline remained seated and sipped her water.

He couldn't figure out what was going on with her, but he'd had enough of his wife's inopportune defiance. He was sick of all their little spats. They had become too frequent and at the wrong time testing his resolve beyond his tolerance level. It was time for her to start remembering who the president of the United States was *now* and *would be* in just a few weeks — she needed to start acting like a first lady and not a spoiled brat whose feelings got hurt much too easily. What happened to that mousy, subservient woman he married? That was the woman he needed to be his first lady. Not this defiant one with a disrespectful mouth.

He casually walked over to Cèline, reached down, grabbed her hands, and pulled her up from the chair. He wrapped his arm around her shoulders and squeezed, hugging her close. With his free arm he continued to wave at the retreating crowd.

"What the hell, Cèline?" Dylan whispered through a forced smile now sticking to his teeth. "What's going on with you? You're supposed to be supporting me. *Me* and not that bitch Callie. I'm the one running for president of the United States, not her."

The first lady planted a smile on her face and stared up at him with fire in her eyes. "You're the one that has the problem," she said. "I'm surprised you even allowed Harley to stand next to you. You've made it perfectly clear you hate sharing the spotlight." She shrugged. "Callie and I were just honoring your wishes and staying out of your way during one of your never-ending ego trips." Her sarcasm slashed through him like a finely sharpened sword.

A brass band marched onto the football field and formed a second-line parade. A gangly leader twirled and spun a red, white and blue umbrella as Dylan Randle supporters waved white handkerchiefs and pranced onto the football field. They all were chanting Dylan...Dylan...Dylan.

The president narrowed his eyes, forced his wife into a dance position. "Dance, my darling, dance, this is a celebration."

Cèline tried to shake free from his iron grip, but Dylan held strong and then waltzed her to the edge of the stage until he could feel her teetering on the rim. He clutched her body close and then slowly released a little pressure and hissed through clenched teeth, "Don't you *ever* embarrass me like that again." He pulled her close and kissed her lips.

***

Burt cringed. He and everyone else knew better than to interrupt Dylan during one of his temper tantrums, particularly when his wife was the target. He'd come to realize a long time ago Dylan was capable of a lot of repugnant things, but this...this....my God, he almost let Céline fall from the stage. Sweat rolled down his face. His stomach turned sour. What if someone else witnessed what just happened, or saw the threat glowing in Dylan's eyes...?

Burt mopped his brow with a handkerchief. Would this campaign ever end?

His breath caught in his throat. *Oh God, he had forgotten.* At this very moment Penelope Mills was possibly somewhere in the Superdome. If anyone was capable of catching Dylan in his bad moments, it was she. It took almost four years and her being shamed out of Washington before the gossip and innuendos against Dylan finally stopped.

Panic zipped through Burt like an errant Fourth of July rocket. Of all the reporters in the world to let slip through the cracks during this New Orleans stop, Penelope Mills wasn't the one. Tonight was not the night for their past history to collide. If anything or anyone was capable of derailing this campaign, it was Penelope "Pepper" Mills.

Burt quickly texted a message to the press secretary and asked him to be on the lookout for that one particular *Advocate Reporter*. He had to do whatever he could to stop her at the door and politely withdraw her press pass and party invitation. This ticking bomb needed to be nipped in the bud before it exploded into a full-blown catastrophe. His stomach twisted into double knots. It was getting more and more difficult to cover things up whenever Dylan unleashed his inner demon in public.

With as much composure as he possibly could, Burt nodded to the secret service agents it was time to move the president and first lady to their next destination. As he watched the first couple being escorted from the building, Burt silently prayed Dylan wouldn't screw up again tonight — particularly after this victorious evening with the Louisiana base; a night just weeks away from the election.

CHAPTER 6

A CHILL zipped through Pepper. She tried to stand, but her knees had turned to jelly. The blood in her veins felt as if it had crystallized and made it impossible to move. She was numb —stupefied, as she watched the first lady's head thrash back and forth, her feet searching for solid ground.

Watch out! She's going to fall! The voice in Pepper's head screamed. *Move her away from the edge! Somebody help her!*

As hard as she tried to shout out, the more she remained petrified in time, caged by painful memories catapulting her back into that living nightmare from ten years earlier. All she could see, all she could feel was Dylan Randle tearing at her clothes and forcing her against her will. She fought him, broke free, but fell to the floor and crawled. He yanked her up, but she escaped once again and rushed out to the balcony. He caught her, lifted her up, and ripped off her thong until she was teetering against the edge of the railing....

Stop, stop! The anguished thoughts were trapped in her mind. *Don't go there.* You were the one who had been star struck by the handsome, charming, and very rich Dylan Randle the III. You were the one seeking the most sought-after interview with Washington D.C.'s most intriguing, but elusive and upcoming political figure.

After the media party, no one forced you to accept his invitation to go to his Georgetown Townhouse alone. Don't you get it! Your accusations failed! Everyone had made it perfectly clear that *if* he in fact attacked you, you should have thought twice about going to his apartment after midnight in the first place.

Pepper fought the repressed anger, the guilt, and the regrets that weighed heavy on her soul. She'd tried so hard for so many years to move on and forget that night ever happened — she often prayed that loathsome night would never haunt her again.

Now, here she was at a presidential campaign rally, years later, actually witnessing the same intimidation and the same abusive behavior she herself had experienced. This time she wasn't the victim, it was the first lady of the United States.

Pepper released a sigh of relief when she saw the president pull his wife close and kiss her. Dylan's campaign manager stepped onto the stage and appeared as if everything was normal. Mr. Harrison whispered into the president's ear, and then he and the secret service detail escorted the first couple off the football field.

What was wrong with her? She must be nuts dredging up past history and that soul-damaging nightmare. She wasn't even sure what she thought she saw had been real. More than likely, it was her keen imagination in overdrive that flooded her memories with the past.

No presidential candidate, in their right mind, would openly abuse their wife in front of thousands. She needed to think rationally. The first couple was just dancing and unaware of the close proximity of the stage's edge. That was all. Hadn't her fixated obsessions done enough damage to her life and career? It was time she quit beating herself up.

Pepper glanced at her watch. She had less than thirty minutes to get to the Marriott Hotel for the combined press conference and cocktail party hosted by the presidential campaign. She needed to get a grip and not let her editor down. Mr. Delacroix had just told her again today she had written an excellent article about Harley Durham, and he looked forward to giving her more opportunities to shine in the future. If Buford was kind enough to go out on a limb and give his own personal press pass and invitation to her, the least she could do was respect his judgment and show she wasn't a loose cannon. Neither Mr. Delacroix, nor the newspaper needed or deserved an encore performance from her past here in New Orleans.

Pepper shouldered her purse and fell in line with the crowd shuffling their way out of the Superdome. The crowd pressed closer together as they inched their way through the doors into Champion Square.

She reached into her faux Gucci bag to quiet the text messages blowing up on her cell phone. She scrolled the growing list and stopped, her eyes not believing the name that had popped up on the screen. *Mark Saderfield.* Why in the hell would Mark text her after all these years? What could he possibly want? She had made it perfectly clear she wanted nothing to do with him — or at least she thought she had. She tried to resist reading his message, but her eyes disobeyed and scanned the text.

"Hey "Penelope". What did you do THIS time? Why is the president's press secretary looking for you?"

Pepper's hand shook; she wanted to scream; stomp her cell phone under her foot. Those were almost the exact words Mark had used when he stopped supporting her claims Dylan Randle had assaulted her. After her "friend" abandoned her the first time, she swore she'd never trust Mark again – much less talk to him. She tossed her phone back into her purse, but the out-of-control messages continued their never-ending, irritating buzz.

Ignoring the persistent ringing from her cell phone, Pepper continued to tailgate the retreating crowd. Perhaps she should check her phone to see if her editor had sent her a message. He certainly would know why the press secretary was looking for her.

A moment of panic swooped in and sucked her breath away. *You don't suppose they want to retract my press pass,* she wondered. Why would they want to do that? Unless...no, no that was a stretch. She wasn't even sure what she saw was real. Or, was it?

Penelope pushed her way through the massive crowd. The more she thought about it, the more old wounds opened and spilled dormant anger and the desire for revenge.

They might try to take her press pass away, but just let them try, Pepper thought with a sneer. She was more resourceful than they gave her credit. She wouldn't allow them a second chance to bury the truth. This might be her last opportunity to get even with Dylan Randle the III. A man like him *did not* deserve to be elected president of the United States.

CHAPTER 7

ANDRÉ BÉLAIR opened the armored limousine door for the first lady. As she ducked to step into the car their eyes met for a brief moment. André forced back a conspiratorial smile as he shut the door and stood by waiting for the motorcade to proceed to the designated destination. Finally, the slow moving convoy of vehicles, with a waving president, the governor of Louisiana, the New Orleans mayor and several fat cat contributors, pulled away from the Superdome and weaved a route along Poydras to Loyola to Canal Street.

As he jogged along Canal Street beside the first lady's car, one hand touching the "Beast", he couldn't shake the uneasiness nagging his thoughts about the events that were inescapably going to unfold; his mind whirled out of control. What if someone made the connection? What if they were caught? What would happen to the three of them? He shook his head, inhaled and chastised himself. None of that mattered. Céline's safety was number one priority. Enough was enough. They just needed to get through this election the best they could and figure it out from there. Nothing was going to go wrong. They had everything planned to a "T". Their ruse worked perfectly in Dallas and last month in Chicago. Today was no different. If anything, they had ironed out the kinks. He stumbled and quickly caught himself, but not before he caught a disapproving look from his supervisor. André nodded that everything was under control, and then continued his pace beside the first lady's car.

The motorcade pulled in front of the Marriott Hotel. TV cameras whirled, reporters yelled for attention, cell phones flashed and blinked faster than bursts of lightning during a Florida electrical storm. André opened the limousine door, offered the first lady his hand, but avoided her eyes.

CHAPTER 8

PEPPER stepped out of the UBER and elbowed her way through the swarm of Dylan Randle fans that were grouped along the palm-lined Canal Street all the way to the Marriott Hotel. Rainbow colored confetti rained down from above and caught in her curls. She shook her head trying to free the shards of paper clinging to her hair. A reveler shoved a beer can toward her; she pushed it away and kept moving. *At this pace I'll never make it in time*, she huffed under her breath. *Thank goodness the motorcade was moving at a snail's pace.*

She crossed Canal Street and hustled along the street car tracks trying to avoid as much of the festive mob as possible. She hated big crowds. Navigating through this army of supporters was the last thing she needed right now. High-spirited crowds were a fact of life in the Crescent City. One got used to them or stayed home.

When she neared Royal Street, Pepper traversed Canal and raced a half block past the Palace Café and a corner liquor store. She crossed Royal and elbowed her way the remaining two blocks to the corner of Chartres Street. She marveled at the sea of enthusiastic supporters. They were jammed so closely together at the front entrance of the Marriott Hotel that the color of their clothing blended like the swirled-pattern of a tie-dyed shirt.

When she reached the side entrance of the Marriott, she ducked between groups of guests who openly complained about the crowd blocking their way into the hotel. She chuckled. *Just my kind of people*, she thought. *Not big fans of Mr. Dylan Randle the III either.*

After she entered the hotel, Pepper slipped past the guests, turned right and walked by the bell captain's desk. She stopped for a moment and admired the chic soulful décor of the Marriott lobby which was a perfect balance of utility and contemporary style. The blocks of tan and beige terrazzo floor sparkled underfoot as the large group of people hustled toward the elevators to get up to the Riverview Ballroom to await the arrival of President Randle, the first lady and their entourage of secret service agents, special guests and key personnel.

She glanced toward the sleek front desk pods with frazzled employees trying to both check in guests and direct confused people to their proper destination. The more she thought about it, there was no doubt in her mind that the president's press secretary and that overzealous campaign manager would find any reason to revoke her press pass — particularly when they discovered who she was. Her dilemma was if she waited for the public elevators, she'd risked being seen and losing an opportunity to make Dylan Randle squirm.

At the moment, her biggest problem was finding an alternate way up to forty-first floor before the presidential entourage arrived. The longer she stood contemplating how she was going to accomplish this challenging goal, the more her chances slipped away without detection.

She took her iPhone from her bag, scrolled through her contacts searching for Jamey Jones. *God, she hoped he was working the kitchen tonight and in a giving mood.* He was her only hope of accessing the service elevator up to the ballroom. She punched in his number, listened as the ringtone droned over and over again. *Come on Jamey.*

Answer your damn phone, her mind screamed. Pepper punched off the call, opened her message display and quickly typed a text. *"Need a favor."*

Three little dots blinked back indicating an answer. *"Busy. Big night tonight. Another time."*

Pepper text back, *"Extremely important!!!!!"*

"Sorry no can do."

"You owe me big time."

Seconds rolled by, but no response from Jamey.

"Crowds crazy. Need ride on service elevator to 41st."

Finally, a message flashed across her screen. *"You crazy? Secret Service everywhere."*

"Have official press pass," Pepper typed. *"Imperative I bypass crowds."*

Minutes ticked by without a message. More and more people poured into the hotel lobby. Every nerve ending pricked inside her with gut wrenching anxiety. Each passing moment meant her chances to face off with the president were dwindling.

A message popped up on her screen. *"Agent in kitchen gave okay nod. Must have official credentials in hand."*

Elation and relief buzzed through Pepper like the day she discovered she had actually graduated with honors instead of flunking out of LSU — *Go Tigers*, she smiled.

Pepper made her way into the hotel kitchen. When she reached the double stainless steel doors, a secret service agent protecting the entrance met her and asked, "Penelope Mills?" She nodded and handed him her press pass and other official credentials. He then checked the contents of her purse. Finally, the agent gave her a quick pat down, then handed back her credentials and personal belongings.

"I suggest you leave the big purse with your friend," the agent said, "or you'll be searched all over again once you get up stairs."

Pepper nodded a thank you and pushed through the double doors. Jamey grabbed her elbow and whispered in her ear, "Promise me you're not going to get me fired. The chef just told me he recommended me for culinary school. This is my big chance and I don't want anything to screw it up."

"Culinary school! That's great news," Pepper congratulated.

He pushed the service elevator button. "Can the phony rhetoric," he warned. "We both know the trouble your big mouth can cause. Don't make me collateral damage."

"Come on, Jamey. I won't. I promise... at least not intentionally." Pepper grinned as she dug into her purse for her phone and pulled a couple of twenty dollar bills from her billfold. She held out her purse toward him. "Will you put this in your locker?"

Jamey glared at her with both hands on his hips.

"The Secret Service guy said..." She pleaded with doleful eyes.

Jamey snatched her purse just as the elevator arrived. When the doors opened a crew of waiters pushed empty food carts out and wheeled in a fresh supply of warm, fragrant replacements. The delectable mix of aromas waft passed Pepper as she crammed between the carts.

"Thanks, Jamey, I owe you big time," Pepper yelled as the elevator doors slid closed.

"No kidding," he yelled back as the large stainless steel doors began to close.

***

Just as the service elevator doors opened onto the 41st floor, Pepper tucked her press pass inside her blouse and slipped her phone into her pants pocket. She stepped quickly out of the away as wait-staff frantically pushed the fresh food carts into the preparation zone. As quickly as personnel efficiently prepared multiple serving platters with a variety of hors d'oeuvres, a line of waiters and waitresses swooped up the readied trays and rushed them into the Riverview Ballroom.

"Why are you wearing blue pants?" A man dressed in a black tuxedo yelled. "Staff was specifically told to wear black." The maître d' shook his head. "You'll have to do. Tonight of all nights, we're shorthanded."

Pepper stood dumbfounded.

"At least your blouse is white," he barked handing her a tray of canapés. "Now get out there and be invisible."

Amused and with gold-plated tray in hand, Pepper pushed through double doors into the opulent ballroom. As she stepped into the large room with high ceilings, her shoes seemed to melt into a sea of blue and gray. Embossed cloud-shaped patterns, outlined in white, were scattered across the multihued carpet. The floor to ceiling windows wrapped around the ballroom and opened the area to river vistas as far as the eye could see. For just a moment Pepper felt weightless as if she were flying over the city. A barge loaded with shipping containers glided along the Mississippi River; the city's first evening lights winked on one by one signaling that the party in New Orleans was about to kick off.

"Those canapés aren't going to serve themselves," a gruff voice barked from behind.

Pepper stumbled, almost dumping her tray, caught herself, and then moved through the crowd offering hors d'oeuvres. Along with state and city dignitaries, there was a mixture of local and national journalists from all over the country and various other media outlets, but mostly there were big time campaign contributors. If she hoped to pull this off, it was a must she stayed away from any of the White House staff or journalists who might recognize her.

As she passed around the canapés, she scoped out the room trying to decide where the best place would be for her to position herself — not too close where she would be conspicuous, but not too far where she wouldn't be able to confront Dylan if the opportunity presented itself.

The podium, where the president would give a brief speech and then answer questions was placed near a window with a backdrop of the massive Crescent City Connection Bridge and New Orleans' West Bank. Some of the White House staff busied themselves shuffling papers, adjusting the microphone, and setting a couple bottles of water on a small table next to the dais — whatever made them look useful and important.

The White House team had arranged three rows of chairs in a semicircle in front of the podium specifically for POTUS's pet journalists; the ones he deemed fit to ask the "proper" questions; the questions that wouldn't make Dylan Randle the III squirm like a clutch of newly born hatchlings.

Pepper sighed. *Because of her past history with the now president of the United States, she wouldn't be sitting in any of those seats of honor... tonight or any other night.* A wave of rejection and melancholy swooped through her like an unwelcome splash of ice-cold water that had just been thrown in her face.

She frowned. *Way to snuff out that fire in your belly, genius. You're here for one mission and one mission only.*

She managed a slight smile. *Plus she had half a tray of hors d'oeuvres that still needed to be delivered.*

"Canapé?" she asked offering her tray to a nearby group, then continued to weave through the crowd constantly on the lookout for anyone who might recognize her.

She did a quick scan of the room for Mr. Tuxedo — he was nowhere in sight. Pepper passed her empty tray to a retreating waiter and pulled out her press identification hidden beneath her blouse. She fluffed her blonde curls with her fingertips and headed for the bar.

"A double Sazerac neat," she said, and then moved toward a laughing cluster of guests. At that same moment the double doors leading to the hall swung opened, loud conversation slipped to a low hum and then united with the crackling sound from the PA system. Moments later "*Hail to the Chief*" blared through Bose speakers.

***

On the other side of the double doors Dylan Randle heard his name shouted through the microphone, and on cue his favorite anthem resonated throughout the Riverview Ballroom on the forty-first floor of the Marriott Hotel. Whoops, cheers and clapping melted in unison with the melody, followed by the chants, "Four more years...Four more years...Four more years."

The president held his head high, planted a smile on his face and gently forced his wife's arm through his. He held her wrist tight with his other hand and whispered, "Act like you want to be here. We'll talk about your behavior at the Superdome later."

Just before the doors opened for him and the first lady, Dylan caught a glimpse of his campaign manager and press secretary talking in frantic hushed tones.

Dylan frowned, whispered in disgust through clenched teeth. "For God's sake, you two, what in the hell is wrong?" he snapped.

Burt rushed over, took Dylan by the elbow and whispered in his ear, and then stepped away as the music ended.

Dylan jerked his head around; his eyes blazed with fury as he quickly skimmed the room, and then he caught a glimpse of Penelope Mills near the podium; cowering in the corner; trying to hide from him.

"Get her out! Get her out now," he spat in as low a voice he could muster. "Do it before she ruins everything."

Dylan regained as much composure as possible under the circumstances and moved into the ballroom with his wife on his arm greeting those he past. Out of the corner of his eye he kept watch over Pepper Mills. *How in the hell did that...that...fuh...menace resurface?* He frowned. *What part of "disappear" don't people understand*? A slow fury burned in his gut. *When I find out who is responsible for her being even within a hundred mile radius of me, heads will roll.*

***

Burt nabbed the nearest secret service agent and ordered him to accompany him and quietly escort the reporter out of the room. The campaign manager nonchalantly walked over to Pepper, smiled and said, "I'm sorry miss, you're not welcome here. Please accompany this officer out of the room."

Pepper straightened her five-foot-two frame, held her head high and raised her voice. "I beg your pardon. Are you speaking to me?"

Burt reached out his hand. "No need to cause a scene," he said hoping the guests were too involved with the president and first lady's entrance and personal greetings to notice. "Please just follow the secret service agent."

Pepper stood her ground. "I have every right to be here," she said flashing her press pass. The secret service agent grabbed her upper arm and held firm, urging her to take a step.

Burt glanced over his shoulder, and then cringed. His worst nightmare was unfolding before his eyes. Attention moved from the president and first lady and now focused on the secret service agent escorting a reluctant reporter from the room.

Pepper yanked free, turned to the crowd and yelled, "Mr. President, your poll numbers have dropped five points. Allison Benson is breathing down your neck. How does it feel?"

Three New Orleans police officers rushed over to assist the secret service agent trying to control the wreathing, unruly, determined petite young woman.

"Why did you try to push the first lady off the stage at the Superdome today?" Pepper yelled over her shoulder as she was dragged from the ballroom. "Is she the latest casualty on your vengeful hit list?"

Burt avoided Dylan's eyes. There was no need to confirm his boss' ire. What he needed to do was damage control, and he needed to do it fast. He raced to the podium, grabbed the microphone, and started singing loud and off key, *"Who let the Dogs Out? Who, who, who, who?"*

The crowd turned their attention away from the scuffle and pointed at Burt, and then started laughing. The normally buttoned-down campaign manager was singing, dancing, and flaying his arms. Everyone started clapping their hands and joined in on the fun.

CHAPTER 9

DETECTIVE Marty Sullivan parked his 2012 red Charger in front of the 8th District Police Department on Royal Street. The massive wrought iron fence surrounding the police station beckoned him to get off his butt, go inside, and take care of business. But no matter how many times he reached for the door handle, his butt remained firmly planted in place. *The way I'm acting,* he thought with a shake of his head, *you'd think I'd just shot my own mother with my service pistol and came here to fess up.*

What he should do was switch on the ignition and head to the nearest bar. He had no authority getting involved in a situation like this. This was federal business — not his business. Any local yokel in their right mind would never allow themselves to become entangled in a personal dispute involving the president of the United States. "This must be *the* dumbest career busting decision I've ever made," he said with a shake of his head.

Detective Marty reached for his "On Duty" sign and placed it on the dashboard. He breathed one last deep breath, swiped his mouth with a hand and opened the car door. This was absolutely the last time he was going to let loyalty and friendships interfere with his better judgment.

As he climbed out of the car, he mused at the foot-traffic flowing in and out of the ocher colored building. It was business as usual on a Saturday night as police officers ushered their latest arrest from the wild festivities that swarmed the streets of Canal, Bourbon, and Frenchmen. *It never failed*, he thought. *Each time a special event occurred in New Orleans, the balancing scales of justice tipped toward the wrong side of law and order.* But, when you mix a devoted crowd of presidential supporters with a bunch of LSU and Alabama fans in for the big game, the city turned into a ticking time bomb.

Marty walked up the steps through the columned entryway and pulled open the pane-glass double door. He caught a glimpse of the etched gold crescent of the 8th staring back at him; the very emblem that was the essence of not only the city of New Orleans, but the NOPD. Was this his last warning that what he was about to get involved with had consequences? Then, a flashback from BUDS training triggered his memory. He sensed himself sinking down, down into the Pacific depths. Suddenly hands grabbed him under the arms, pulled him to the surface and breathlessly whispered in his ear, "Die now, sailor, or on the field of valor."

He opened the door and walked toward the huge desk that faced directly in front of the entrance and wrapped around the room in a half circle. Adorning the façade of the large counter were individually small framed paintings depicting scenes of old New Orleans. Elongated, wrought iron chandeliers hung from the high ceiling. Their multiple globe lights lit up the room and highlighted the latest lawbreakers caught in varying degrees of crime. Marty smiled to himself. It was hard to believe these genial surroundings temporarily housed NOLA's latest offenders.

The desk officer, hands clasped beneath her chin, stared at a computer screen, and then glanced up. "Hey, Sullivan, it's not your shift. You got a case brewing?"

"Evening, Vivian" Marty said and gestured to the benches behind him. "Looks like you might have a full house tonight."

"No kidding," the desk officer said. "This is going to be a night the devil himself is prowling the streets." She stood, stretched her back. "Anything I can do for you?"

Marty scratched the back of his head and said, "No thanks. My business is with Lieutenant Jackson."

"He's on a long-distance call at the moment," Vivian said.

Marty rolled his eyes. "Trust me, I'm in no hurry."

The desk officer lifted a brow and smiled. "Not in trouble again, are you?"

Marty shook his head. "Nothing I can't handle." He walked over to the three vending machines against the wall, fed one the desired currency and waited for his Snickers to drop into the bin. He quickly scoped the benches holding the detainees. At least a half dozen or more perps were handcuffed to the holding cable stretched behind the benches reserved specifically for those unlucky souls awaiting their fate. Not one of them was a curly-headed blonde woman. The good news — if it was possible in this situation — she was probably being held in one of the interrogation rooms waiting for the Feds to pick her up. It would be unusual that she had already been sent to Orleans Parish Prison at Tulane and Broad. The wheels of justice just didn't crank that fast on such a busy night.

As the detective tore open the wrapper on his candy bar, Lieutenant Jackson walked into the lobby. He nodded at Marty. "Come on up," he said.

The detective tossed his untouched Snicker into a trashcan and followed his boss up the stairs.

The lieutenant ushered Marty into the small office and shut the door. He offered a chair directly across from his desk and told the detective to sit. Still standing, he leaned forward, fists on the desk and started talking. "How in the hell did you get mixed up with Fed business — Fed business concerning the president of the United States?" His normally pallor complexion was now tinged a glowing red. "Why me? Why my house?"

"Not really my choice," Marty said."

The Lieutenant peered over his half glasses as he sat behind his metal desk. "Come on, Marty, everyone has a choice. Some just make bad ones. That's what keeps us in business."

"Please spare me the lecture, Sir. Trust me. This decision wasn't an easy one for me." Marty swiped his hand across his mouth. "I know I'm asking for a big favor."

"Favor?" the Lieutenant asked. "You're asking for the moon."

Marty leaned forward in his chair. "I'm only here because one of my classmates from BUDS needed... Well, someone *he* works for insisted the reporter, Mills, stay out of jail at all costs." The detective hesitated, cocked his head. "You, also, know the guy who asked for *the favor*." Marty paused. "He graduated from the same Police Academy class we did."

Jackson raised an eyebrow; his mouth dropped open. "You don't mean...?"

"The same."

"Holy crap," Jackson said. "I like the hell out of that guy and respect him, but...."

He rubbed his hand across his mouth, hissed a breath of air. "Those are some high-powered folks he works for." The lieutenant took off his glasses, tucked his chin into his chest. Several silent moments clicked by and then he finally spoke. "Getting involved in something like this could be career ending you know...for both of us." He leaned forward and narrowed his eyes. "Can you give me one good reason to put our careers on the line?"

"He saved my life. I owe him."

The lieutenant exhaled, nodded and said, "Say no more." He leaned back in his chair, hands clasped behind his head. "After you called, I took the liberty to look up the offending reporter. I needed to know what I was getting myself into. Clean as a whistle — not even a parking ticket. It seems her worst crime is being an opinionated reporter with a big mouth." He scratched his head. "Tough occupation when you're not popular with the powers that be in the middle of an election year."

"Yeah, tell me about it," Detective Sullivan said. "My friend explained she was quietly standing in a corner, minding her own business and having a drink. And then, for no obvious reason, the president's campaign manager asked her to leave. When she refused, four grown men started dragging her out of the room, but not before she loudly exercised her constitutional right of free speech. The problem was she was making some very outrageous, public accusations against the president." He raised an eyebrow. "Unfortunately, this wasn't the first time she's spoken out about this controversial presidential candidate."

"Damn," the lieutenant said. "This could get tricky."

"How do you suggest we handle?" Detective Sullivan asked.

The lieutenant looked at his watch. "Feds are probably on their way to take her into custody. When they get here, I'll try and convince them not to go State with this," he said. "It won't be the first time I've argued jurisdictional territory with these guys."

"I don't envy you," Marty said. "This is a tall order, particularly under these circumstances." He leaned forward, elbows on knees. "How will the summons read?"

The lieutenant thought a moment, and then said, "Disorderly conduct tagged with criminal trespassing. The RS 14:63 probably won't stick because she actually *did* have an official press pass. "If I can get the Feds to agree, we'll do the processing. As soon as she signs the summons, she's out the door."

The lieutenant folded his hands on the desk, looked Marty in the eye. "This is about the best we can hope for. Any federal fallout will be up to your friend."

"Thanks, lieutenant," Marty said. He passed his hand across his mouth and down his neck. He glanced up at his boss. "One more favor..."

Lieutenant Jackson rolled his eyes and glared at Marty. "You're pushing your luck."

Marty stood pumping his hands as he backed toward the door, "I know, I know. But this is the easy part. Don't release the reporter until I've left the building. She can't know anyone has intervened for her. I promise, the last thing I *want* to do is press my luck, but this was the crucial part of my friend's special request.

The lieutenant shook his head. "Get out of here, Sullivan, before I have your ass arrested for taking advantage of my good nature."

CHAPTER 10

PEPPER signed for her personal belongings, gathered them up and stepped out of the police station in the middle of the French Quarter, only a few short blocks from the scene of her crime. She glanced around, curious to see if anyone would willingly step from the shadows and acknowledge they paid her bail or at the very least intervened on her behalf. *Unlikely*, she thought. Hands down, she must be the last person on the planet anyone in their right mind wanted to be connected with. Having a guardian angel roaming the streets of New Orleans was totally unexpected. *But, what a relief*, she thought suppressing an ironic laugh.

As she walked through the 8th District's ornate wrought iron gate, she closed her eyes for a moment and allowed freedom to wash over her. *This felt much better than being hauled off to the Orleans Parish Prison on Tulane and Broad Street*, she thought. Spending the night jailed with the ladies of the night, drug addicts, and drunks was not her idea of a fun evening in New Orleans.

Pepper sighed, then glanced left and right trying to decide which way she should start walking. She didn't dare go back to the office. She rolled her eyes and said, "That is if I even have an office." She couldn't call an Uber because her cell phone was dead. And, the last thing she wanted to do was go back into the police station and ask to use their phone. The longer she stood there that pea-size knot that had started forming in her stomach during interrogation had expanded into a full blown monkey-fist knot. She was

68

in trouble, big trouble. How was she going to salvage what little reputation she might have left? Hell, *keep* her job! *Find* a job! The weight of the last couple hours rested heavy on her heart. "Smile," she said. "At least you're not in jail."

Pepper glanced at her watch and forced a weak chuckle. "This must be a new record for me. It's only ten PM and I've already managed to embarrass the president of the United States, get arrested, and successfully flush my journalist career down the toilet for a second time. And, to think I did it all just so I could exercise my right of freedom of speech."

A red Corvette roared up next to the curb. The window whined down. "Congratulations, that was an award-winning performance you gave tonight. Are you proud of yourself, Penelope?"

Pepper did a double take; her mouth dropped open. "Mark? What are you doing here?"

"The better question is what are *you* doing *here*? Mark Saderfield laughed. He reached over and pushed open the passenger door. "I'd get in if I were you. I wouldn't be so sure the streets of New Orleans are the safest place for you right now."

Pepper hesitated, walked around the front of the Corvette, then climbed in and shut the door. "I suppose you expect me to thank you," she said.

Mark revved the Corvette's engine. "A thank you... *from you*? Heaven forbid," he said. "I'm just the getaway car."

Pepper suppressed a smile. "Okay, *Clyde*, take me to the New Orleans Ferry Terminal. We're done with all the capers for the night. *Bonnie* just wants to go home, pour a full glass of Sazerac, chug it, and pray it will numb me from this self-destructive nightmare I've created."

"I've got an idea," he said. Let me *buy* you that drink instead. The Sazerac Bar is the perfect place for you to hide out and relax."

Pepper tucked her chin and frowned. "At the Roosevelt Hotel? Are you seriously trying to get me back to your hotel room?"

Mark cocked his eyebrow and smiled. "I don't sleep with jailbirds. My only purpose is to get you drunk so you'll spill all the details from this brilliant scheme you cooked up. This might be your best work yet!"

All the built-up tension that had gripped every muscle in her body finally eased. Pepper felt relaxed for the first time in hours. She welcomed the smile on her face. "I'd forgotten how easily you make me laugh. Thank you, Mark. Thank you for being here for me."

He turned, placed his arm across the back of her seat. "Seriously, Pepper, I've got to ask. Didn't you learn *anything* over the last four years?"

Pepper shrugged. "Obviously not."

"Come on. Let me buy you that much needed drink."

She opened her mouth to speak, but Mark quickly added, you can talk, or don't talk. That will be up to you. As soon as you're ready, I'll drive you home and not say another word about tonight," he said raising his right hand in promise.

Pepper reached over and touched his arm. "Not tonight, Mark, I honestly just want to go home. I promise I'll buy you dinner before you leave town and try and explain my motives."

"Why ride that rusty 'ol barge across the river when I can drive you home in style?" he asked, sweeping his arm around the Corvette's plush interior."

She shook her head. "Thank you, but another time. A ride on the ferry is what I need. There is nothing more cleansing, more relaxing than that short ride across the Mississippi to Algiers Point."

Mark shrugged, shifted the car into first gear, and drove up Royal Street past exclusive antique stores, the Monteleone Hotel and Mr. B's.

At the traffic light, he turned left onto Canal Street and headed toward the river. The crowds that were jammed earlier on the main drag were either enjoying a meal at one of New Orleans famous Cajun-cuisine restaurants, strolling on Bourbon Street or inside one of the many French Quarter cabarets. He glanced over at Pepper. "Last chance. Are you sure you won't take me up on that drink?" he asked.

Pepper heard Mark talking, but exhaustion had already captured her mind and body; her brain was in a fog and unwilling to focus. "Ah, what? Oh, I'm sorry, Mark. Drop me off here. The ferry entrance is just a block or two away."

"Here? At Harrah's Casino?"

"Yeah, that'd be great," she said.

Mark laughed and pulled over to the curb and shifted into neutral. "You sure you're not dumping me so you can waltz into Harrah's for a quick pull on the slots?"

Pepper shook the fog from her head. "Wha...what? Oh, no, no, I promise. It's the ferry for me." She managed a smile. "Any other time I would jump at the chance to *dump* you for a quick hand of Black Jack. Just not tonight. Home is calling."

She opened the car door, hesitated for a moment, and then quickly leaned over and pecked Mark on the cheek. "Again, thank you. You remind me of a friend I once had a long time ago." She climbed out of the Corvette and, without looking back, hurried across Canal Street toward the ferry terminal.

***

Mark watched the feisty, but adorable reporter cross the street, then over the railroad tracks toward the ferry entrance heading to Algiers Point.

Well, that was pleasantly unexpected, he thought with a smile still planted on his face. Who would have guessed giving Penelope "Pepper" Mills a ride from jail could crack that steel-wall she's built around herself? He threw his head back and laughed. Pepper might not join him at the bar, but he planned to down as many house specials as he could; particularly after a bizarre day like today. He shifted the Corvette into gear, pulled away from the curb, and headed back down Canal toward the Roosevelt Hotel.

As Mark drove along the main drag toward his destination, he couldn't get over how the very fire that kindled the persona of Penelope Mills had literally been snuffed out. At first her little performance tonight amused him to the core, but at the same time both worried and confounded him. She was one of the best investigative reporters he had met in years — maybe *the* best. Sometimes her methods were unorthodox, but the end result usually produced one hell of a story. The reason she had become a rising star in the first place was because her findings were verifiable down to the last dot of the eye. In fact, the only time he'd *ever* noted a small flaw in her story was anything connected with Dylan Randle the III. That man had to be made of Teflon.

The day's events continued to reel through his mind like a 1930's movie on steroids, but no matter how hard he tried to picture something, anything, somewhat similar to what Pepper had dared to yell out in a room full of people escaped him. He tried to piece everything together from the Superdome to the cocktail party, but his brain struggled to picture the president of the United States attempting to shove his wife off a stage in front of thousands. The very suggestion was absurd. No, outright harebrained. Dylan Randle was a lot of things, but he wasn't stupid.

Mark stopped at a red light on Camp Street and drummed his fingertips on the steering wheel. A streetcar rumbled past as his inner thoughts searched for more answers. Everyone in the president's inner circle had become aware that lately POTUS and Céline seemed more at odds than usual with each other, but dismissed those few occasions as campaign trail fatigue. Add the stress of having to take responsibility of running the country *and* a presidential campaign so soon after Michael Carlton's untimely death, must be mind numbing for the first couple.

The stoplight turned green. Mark shifted into first gear and raced across Camp Street, only to slow and stop at the next light.

There was still one blatant question that plagued him: Who *did* bail out Pepper and why did they choose him, better yet, trust him, to pick up the very reporter that embarrassed POTUS at the cocktail party? It was shocking enough that she would *ever* see the light of day after the stunt she pulled tonight, much less avoid serious jail time. The Dylan Randle he had come to know would not just throw away the key, but do everything in his power to make sure that *this* time the poor woman's credibility and career disappeared permanently.

The only thing he knew for sure was someone had slipped an envelope into his coat pocket as he was leaving the Riverview Ballroom. The message inside promised if he'd picked up Miss Mills in front of the 8th District Police Station, his name would be dropped in the president's ear as a possible replacement for the next White House press secretary.

When he'd first read the note he'd thought it was a joke and remembered laughing out loud. He'd been in this business way too long to take whatever came from *any* White House flunky as a done deal; not to mention whoever was making this request was obviously no friend of the president. After he read the note a second time, he had to admit, for a brief moment, the offer was intriguing.

As Mark revved the Corvette's engine and willed the light to turn green, random thoughts continued to spin in his head. Giving serious thought of becoming White House press secretary was a fool's journey, he reasoned. After working in close proximity to Randle's Administration recently, he should have learned by now how to separate a real promise from a hollow promise. Not to mention Randle was hard to read. His unpredictability alone was a flashing red light. Even if he seriously considered the opportunity, more than likely, he'd just burned that bridge permanently.

Mark rolled his eyes, hissed a breath through his lips. If POTUS even for one second suspected he'd been a co-conspirator in any way springing Penelope "Pepper" Mills from jail, the man would personally jam his head on a spike next to the growing number of his political adversaries — and, that's with Randle being president for only a few weeks.

Deep in thought Mark missed the light turning green and was jolted by the blaring horns behind him. As the light turned yellow, Mark extending his middle finger out the window and turned left onto Baronne Street, only to be caught in more traffic stuck behind a catering truck.

He fiddled with the radio trying to get his mind off Penelope, but once again his thoughts were trapped. There was just something about her that just wouldn't let go. He was nuts getting involved with her again, but obviously he couldn't help himself. He liked her spunk. *She's a bit self-destructive*, he chuckled under his breath, *but had other qualities that challenged him in ways like no one else could — man or woman*. Their conversations were always lively and left him wanting more. He couldn't count the times he'd almost asked her on a real date, but the opportunity, the moment, never seemed right. Maybe, the real reason neither of them pursued the other was because they both enjoyed their casual friendship more than an attempted dive into an unpredictable romantic relationship.

Mark rounded the corner onto Roosevelt Way and stopped in front of The Roosevelt Hotel. He revved the engine one last time, got out of the car and handed his keys to the valet. As he circled around the revolving door to enter the hotel, he laughed. "Ha, who, am I kidding? The real reason I picked up Mills tonight was because she laughs at my cheesy jokes."

He took the few steps in front of him two at a time and strolled down the long hotel hallway. When Mark reached the Sazerac Bar, he stepped through the ornate carved entry into a timeless sophistication and elegance from a time gone by. Soft Jazz music mixed in with the hum of muted conversations. Four bartenders busied themselves behind the curved African walnut bar; the immense Paul

Ninas murals framed on the walls, all but dwarfed the small elongated room. The antique gold camelback sofas with small cocktail tables and adjoining chairs were filled to capacity with chattering guests.

When Mark didn't see anyone he recognized, he nabbed a barstool for a front row seat to watch a bartender shaking two cocktail shakers like maracas in rhythm to a fast-paced Salsa dance. Beads of sweat rolled gently off the bartender's brow.

"What's you makin' there?" Mark asked.

The bartender strained his creation into four Collins' glasses, watched with care as the frothy white liquid rose to the top like a soufflé. "Ramos Gin Fizz," the bartender answered.

"How 'bout making me a couple of those," Mark asked.

The bartender dabbed his brow with a bar towel, leaned in and said, "Do you mind giving me a second? My arms need a minute to recuperate. The longer you shake that drink, the better it is." He winked.

"Take your time," Mark said. "Give me a beer until you're ready. I'm not going anywhere until I try your Gin Fizz."

The bartender drew a cold beer from the tap and handed it to Mark. "This is on the house."

Mark took a long draw from the frosted glass, leaned back in the barstool and shut his eyes. He willed the tension in his shoulder muscles to relax. The harder he tried to unwind, the faster the events of the day jumbled and collided into one pool of confusion. He shook his head trying to urge the twisted thoughts to fall into some kind of reasonable explanation, but he was only left with more questions. Who paid Pepper's bail? Why did she foolishly blurt out such an outrageous accusation against the president? Was she following a credible lead, or was it an over-zealous imagination out of control? Maybe it was a cry for attention?

He rotated the barstool around and eyed the room for anyone he might know, or would like to know, but his focus remained centered on Pepper and the night's events. Whatever the reasons for all of it, two questions still haunted... hooked him like a gaffed fish. If POTUS did in fact intimidate the first lady in some way and in front of thousands, why...? More importantly, had one hardnosed, determined reporter, hell-bent on bringing Dylan Randle the III to his knees finally succeed? Mark shrugged and finished his beer. *Guess time will only tell.*

The bartender slowly strained the Ramos Gin Fizz into a Collins glass, set the drink in front of Mark. "Enjoy," he said.

Mark lifted the glass. "Here's to life's puzzles and putting all the pieces together," he said.

CHAPTER 11

HARSH words and threats echoed from the main hall. Harley suppressed the urge to rescue Dylan from the scolding he was receiving from Burt Harrison, but he didn't dare intervene. He personally, on so many levels, was the root cause for their dispute. But it was Dylan who had tied a big red bow on a whole new list of fires for the campaign to nip in the bud only weeks before the election. Instead, Harley poured two crystal tumblers with Johnny Walker Blue and waited for his dear friend to join him with tail between his legs and threatening to fire his campaign manager.

"Can you believe the impertinence of that weasel speaking to *me* like that?" Dylan barked as he stormed into the den. "If the election wasn't around the corner, I'd fire his ass."

Harley grinned and handed Dylan a tumbler of scotch. "You should have invited him to join us for a drink," he said with tongue in cheek. "Maybe I could've soothed his ruffled feathers."

Dylan jabbed a finger toward Harley. "You, you, my friend, are the spark that started this fire. Penelope Mills? Why her? Why now? Has the booze finally pickled your brain? She could ruin everything for both of us."

Harley pulled a Cuban from a humidor, snipped off the end. "Dylan, relax. This election is in the bag. We both know that there isn't anyone or anything that is going to keep you from being elected president." He picked up the

Waterford lighter and lit the cigar. "If you ask me, you have a bigger problem."

"Oh yeah, what would that be," Dylan asked.

"Your wife. Where's Céline? Shouldn't she be sitting here with us having a drink and laughing about how ridiculous Burt looked jumping around the ballroom tonight like a court jester? You've gotta admit that was a brilliant diversion he pulled off. He's a genius and you should be thanking him instead of getting rid of him."

Dylan nodded and then plopped down on the cushy leather chair. "I don't know *what's* come over Céline over the last several weeks...first Chicago, then Dallas and now New Orleans. She's turned from my loving, supportive, obedient wife to some shrew I don't recognize. I haven't been laid in months. If I didn't know better, I'd swear she and her twin sister have traded places.

Harley inhaled a deep draw from his cigar and slowly released the pungent smoke. "How is that cunt Claréne?"

"Who the hell knows or cares," Dylan said. "I don't keep up with her comings and goings. I assume she's off somewhere on the other side of the world taking her little photographs. All I know is I don't want or need her anywhere near me or my wife — particularly until the election is over."

Harley topped off both of their tumblers; he glanced toward the ceiling. "Have both Burt and Céline turned in for the night?"

"Yeah, Burt stormed upstairs after our 'discussion'."

"Ah, that was the door I heard slam. Or was it your wife's?"

Dylan sighed, swallowed a half glass of scotch. "My darling wife once again is avoiding my bed and informed me when we left the Marriott she'd be staying with her beloved nanny Mama Bea for the duration of this little stopover."

"This has been one hellava night," Harley said. "You hit the trifecta when it comes to bitches, brother — your wife, that pussy campaign manager, and that blonde, razor-wire of a reporter, who showed up and almost ruined your little cocktail party tonight."

"Tell me about it," Dylan agreed.

"What you need is a little..." he paused, "...extracurricular activity away from all this election shit." Harley grinned. "How about it? Might take the..." his eyes sparkled with mischief, "the edge off."

Dylan cocked an eyebrow and frowned.

"No wait, hear me out," Harley said. "Your wife is in Algiers Point, Burt should be sound asleep on the third floor, and the Secret Service detail is sworn to secrecy. What do you say we have our own little Mardi Gras party right here away from prying eyes." He winked, "Just tonight for old time's sake."

Dylan furrowed his brow; opened his mouth to speak.

Harley held up a finger, slid to the edge of the chair. "I own this town and half the state," he said. "I have the ways and the means to make things happen without a word spoken or Paparazzi in sight. You'd just need to trust me."

"You're delusional. The Secret Service would never allow anyone near me without first being vetted," Dylan said with a shake of his head.

"What makes you so sure?" Harley leaned his elbows on his knees. "I'm telling you, buddy. I have connections. You of all people should know that by now. I'm the guy who has watched your back and protected you for over thirty-years and still know how to do it."

Dylan shrugged.

"I know all your skeletons, how to conceal them. Hell, I helped create some of them."

"That's what I'm afraid of," Dylan said with a hesitant grin. "But, what the hell. I'm tired...I'm horny and for at least one day, I want to forget I'm president of the United States.

Harley slapped his knee with his hand. "Hot damn, there's my boy Dylan, my D-Rod. Welcome back, buddy. I've missed the real you." He pulled out his cell phone and held it up. "What's on the menu tonight — blonde, brunette or redhead? Black, brown, yellow or porcelain white? Better yet, you wanna try something different for a change? I've heard transvestites or not only exotic, but know and do some real kinky stuff.

Dylan chugged the rest of his Scotch, went over to the bar and poured another tumbler of Johnny Walker Blue. "You choose. I'm done making decisions for at least the next few hours."

CHAPTER 12

THE REFLECTION of the waxing moon mirrored the path of the murky Mississippi River's current. Errant logs and debris rushed past the ferry as it traversed the river for the final evening's round-trip from Algiers Point to New Orleans.

Céline rested her elbows on the windowsill of the ferry's pilot house, cupped her hands under her chin, and stared out the grimy, convex window. An aura of light sketched the skyline of New Orleans. She only had minutes before she had to make a decision — a decision that made her physically ill.

Today had been the best day she had had in weeks. Riding the ferry back and forth across the Mississippi with her Uncle Beau helped release the inner turmoil that had been tugging at her soul lately. He'd even trusted her to take the helm and navigate the treacherous current of the river on the short trips. She hadn't felt this free, this relaxed since before Dylan became the presidential candidate and slowly morphed into a creature she didn't recognize or want to be around.

How lucky she was to have a clone of herself who always rescued and protected her whenever she reached her lowest point. God bless Clarène for giving her another reprieve from her controlling husband; from those mind-numbing political rallies and press conferences Dylan forced her to attend. Even now she found it difficult to believe she'd actually agreed to her sister's and André's outrageous, cunning, but genius plan — trading places. So far luck had been on their side, but for how long?

A day didn't go by that she didn't marvel how she and Clarène, when put side by side, were identical in every way — every way except their personalities. Unlike her, Clarène had nerves of steel. There couldn't possibly be another living soul who would have had the guts to step in and pretend to be the first lady of the United States — and do it under the scrutiny of so many prying eyes. Why should she be surprised? Her sister had been the captain of her college debate team, could hold her own in any conversation and in any setting. She traveled to exotic and dangerous places with only a camera as a companion. Cèline smiled. Perhaps her sister's most endearing and enviable quality was how she stood her ground and refused to take any crap from anyone.

Cèline sighed. On the other hand, her happy place was a quiet corner reading a book or wandering aimlessly through the halls of the world's famous museums and art galleries. When it came to social situations and the required small talk, she always felt like an animal caught in a trap. It's no wonder she'd earned the reputation as a good listener.

Countless times she'd wished she could be a little more like Clarène, but God gave her sister the outgoing personality, the gift of gab, and the backbone to stand up for what she believed. She on the other hand, preferred to walk a hundred miles out of the way to avoid uncomfortable situations and controversy. Maybe Dylan had married the wrong Fontenot sister. Maybe *she* was the real reason she and her husband were drifting apart.

"We're about to dock in New Orleans, *Chéri*," Uncle Beau said.

Cèline cocked her head and looked up at her uncle, her eyes pleaded. "Can't you just make one more round trip tonight? For me?"

Beau stroked the five day old stubble on his chin. "You've been hiding on my boat all day. Don't you think your sister deserves a break?" His crystal blue eyes dripped with sympathy, but his voice echoed reality. "You are the first lady of these United States and have an obligation to not only your husband, but also your country."

Guilt wrapped around her heart and squeezed until she thought it would stop beating. "I know...I know, but... but...."

Uncle Beau wrapped a burly arm around her shoulder. "Give your husband a break, *Chéri*. He's under a lot of pressure. Without warning he was thrust into the most powerful position in our country. He's barely had time to realize the importance of all his new responsibilities, not to mention running for president of the United States on such short notice."

Cèline leaned against the large man's chest, burrowed deep within his comforting embrace reeking from an honest day's work on the river.

Uncle Beau took her chin in his hand. "Living in the world of politics is not easy, but if anyone can do it, you can. You grew up in Louisiana, home of Huey Long." Beau smiled, turned around and took the helm from the first mate. "Your husband is a pussycat compared to all the politicians Louisianan's have had to tolerate over the years," he said.

Cèline crossed her arms against her chest. "I know you're right," she said. "But the very thought of being in the same house with Dylan *and* Harley!"

The ferry's engine rumbled, vibrated beneath the deck; the boat jerked, shifted and bumped against the pilings as Uncle Beau maneuvered the large commuter barge next to the New Orleans' terminal.

Cèline grabbed the railing and steadied herself as the ferry bumped against the dock and posts. The debate of what to do still battled inside her head. Dylan could be difficult to live with at times, but whenever Harley Durham was around, he was impossible. The frat-boy literally crawled out of her husband; his personality switched from dignified to downright obnoxious — at least toward her. What was even more preposterous was how that snake, Harley Durham, latched onto her husband like a pup to its mom's tit the closer Election Day rolled around.

Céline watched aimlessly as the crew ran through the motions of securing the ferry to the dock, her thoughts remained focused on her husband and his best friend. She was still baffled why Dylan asked Harley to introduce him at tonight's rally at the Superdome instead of the Governor. It was not only ridiculous, but potential political suicide. The unsolvable mystery was *why* their bond had survived for so many years. Their background, their interests, their entire worlds were polar opposites. The dots just didn't connect.

A wave of melancholy swept through Céline. She had to admit that Harley wasn't the catalyst of their problems, just the enabler. She had sensed for months that the man she married was slowly slipping away. Where was that charismatic, flirtatious, sappy romantic she'd fallen in love with the moment she saw him across the room at that Mardi Gras party so many years ago?

She could still visualize the evening she'd first laid eyes on Dylan. All night she'd catch him looking at her from across the room, smiling, then look away and join another group of love-struck women. Every fiber inside goaded her to walk over and introduce herself, but it wasn't in her nature. She was just a silly girl, a freshman at Tulane. He was worldly, mature and the most handsome man she'd laid eyes. If Claréne had been there, her sister would have marched her over and made it happen.

Then her bubble burst. A woman, she discovered was his fiancé, waltzed over to Dylan and his small harem, grabbed his arm and created an embarrassing scene. Moments later Dylan and the shrew fled the house still spouting obscenities at one another.

After that night she never gave Dylan Randle the III another thought. Strangely every Mardi Gras on Fat Tuesday for five straight years a dozen purple, a dozen gold, and a dozen green roses all bundled together were delivered to her with a card that just said *"An Admirer."* Not once did she ever dream they were from Dylan.

On her 25th birthday while attending a Tulane Alumni party she ran into Dylan again. He didn't flirt from across the room this time. He marched right up to her and introduced himself. They left the party immediately and went to the Carousel Bar at the Monteleone Hotel. As they sipped Lemon Kiss Martinis, they tuned the world out. She and she alone had his undivided attention. He reached over took her hand, kissed her fingertips and confessed he was the one who had been sending her the roses. The next thing she knew they were upstairs in each other's arms. Tears welled in her eyes and rolled down her cheek.

Beau touched her shoulder and snapped Céline from her deep reflections. "The ferry's about to head back to Algiers," he said. "What's it gonna be, a night with your husband or Mama Bea's?"

Céline brushed away a tear. "Algiers and Mama Bea's," she said.

Uncle Beau pinched his brows together. "If you're sure...."

The words *I'm sure* stuck in her throat. She nodded instead. Céline hugged her uncle, opened the door of the pilot house and started down the stairs. As the ferry backed away from the dock and headed back to Algiers Point, she stopped a brief moment on the metal stairwell. She closed her eyes and welcomed the tremble, the rumble from the ferry's engines penetrating the soles of her shoes. Ever since she was a little girl she'd loved the tickle on the bottom of her feet. But tonight the energy from the vibrating engines renewed her strength and made her feel free, made her feel powerful.

As Céline pushed through the door, she raised the hood on her black jacket, and then quickly scanned the main deck. There were very few people headed back to Algiers Point. It was only eleven P.M and the party was just beginning in New Orleans. By now the wail of jazz instruments seeped from the numerous cabarets along both Bourbon and Frenchmen Streets and beckoned tipsy revelers to come in for one more drink.

With so few people on board and feeling confident no one would recognize or bother her, Céline walked to the bow of the ferry. She pulled down the hood of her jacket and allowed the breeze to whip, swirl her long black hair. She imagined herself as the prow of the boat, waging war against the murky, treacherous current; she listened for music drifting from the city; but most of all, she tried to forget she was the first lady of the United States of America.

The burner phone tucked snugly in the pocket of Céline's black-hoodie vibrated. She knew who it was and what it was about, but everything in her resisted. She had no choice. She needed to check her messages. She owed both Claréne and André her deepest gratitude. But once she stepped back into reality, the freedom, the peace she had enjoyed all day would vanish faster than a shooting star swallowed into the depths of a far off galaxy.

Before she answered, she whispered into the breeze, "My poor heroic Claréne. Please forgive me. I've been so selfish and don't deserve you as my sister."

Céline entered her personal ID. The burner phone flashed on and listed the many messages awaiting her attention. She scrolled down. There it was — a copy of a tape recording of the night's events glaring up at her and two messages from Claréne. Did she dare listen? Or, should she wait until she was off the ferry and away from prying eyes and ears.

Deep in her conscience she knew that the ill-advised twin switcharoo she and Claréne had been playing was a dangerous game. Yes, they had pulled off the ruse in Chicago and Dallas with the help of André. Attempting it a third time may well have been pushing their luck to the limit, particularly in her hometown. Whatever the messages revealed, every inch of her body screamed it wasn't going to be pleasant.

Céline slipped the phone back into her pocket. She looked up into the black void and prayed she hadn't put Claréne, André, or anyone else, for that matter, in harm's way.

CHAPTER 13

THE INSTANT the crew opened the ferry's boarding gate Pepper skirted to the far side of the stern, ducking past the few passengers who boarded before her. The last thing she needed was some nut job getting into her face. By now her ill-conceived theatrics had been unleashed into the streets of New Orleans and were being circulated like a California wild fire in every bar and restaurant bulging with Dylan Randle the III supporters.

Pepper leaned her shoulder against a support beam and gazed off in the distance toward the West Bank, willing this homeward bound ferry crossing to get underway. A wave of melancholy swept through her like an unwelcome gust of arctic wind. Why was she in such a hurry? There was only a tumbler of rye, a dubious future and a cold, empty bed waiting at home. The way things had been going tonight she'd be lucky if there was enough Sazerac in the bottle to purge this baptism into hell she'd created.

Finally, the engines engaged and nudged the ferryboat from the New Orleans Terminal and out into the open water. Across the short distance to Algiers Point, the lights of Jackson Square penetrated the darkness. Rhythmic beats of a distant jazz band drifted on the cool October breeze, and then out of the blue was swallowed into oblivion.

No matter how hard she tried to absorb the surrounding ambiance and soft splashes emitted by the boat's wake, question after question collided in her brain and provoked a relentless throb pounding against her temple.

A heavy metal door slammed. Pepper jumped, quickly turned and saw a statuesque woman in a black hoodie exit the ferry's pilothouse and walk toward the bow of the boat. At that same moment, out of the corner of her eye, she spotted a man wearing a baseball cap pulled low over his eyes, baggy jeans and a New Orleans Saints jersey sporting the number nine. He lit a cigarette, tossed the match into the river, looked her way and nodded. If it wasn't so dark, she would have sworn he smiled at her, but the smile somehow had a double meaning.

Alarm bells clamored inside her head; sent a chill rippling up and down her spine. *What's wrong with me? Get a grip.* The man was just being friendly and enjoying a smoke. Why did she always make such a big deal out of everything? The universe didn't just revolve around her. Pepper turned away from the man, but could still feel his penetrating eyes.

The more she rationalized, the more her instincts urged her to move away from the isolated spot from where she was standing and find a group, or anyone she might engage in conversation. She pressed her Gucci bag close to her side and as casual as possible, strolled to the front of the boat.

The statuesque woman she had noticed earlier leaving the pilothouse had dropped the hood from her head and allowed the wind to whip her long, shiny black hair. The way the exquisite woman carried herself made Pepper imagine a wild sable stallion racing across a Montana plain toward freedom with its graceful mane flapping in the breeze — there was purpose, enviable self-assurance; she was in control. And yet, there was something else. Even though her features were veiled by the darkness, the woman looked familiar.

As the ferry glided across the Mississippi, Pepper forced her eyes away from the woman and tried to concentrate on the swishing sound the boat made as it cut through the rivers current. She hoped the lady hadn't noticed her staring like an imbecile, but she couldn't help herself. The resemblance was uncanny.

Not able to contain herself, Pepper stepped up to the prow next to the woman. "Excuse me," she said, "has anyone ever told you how much you look like the first Lady?"

The woman quickly pulled the hood back over her head and turned to walk away.

"No wait, please don't go," Pepper pleaded. "There's a man at the rear of the ferry watching me. I don't want him to think I'm alone."

The woman glimpsed over her opposite shoulder toward the stern of the boat. "If you're uncomfortable," she said, "tell one of the crewmen. They'll make sure no one bothers you."

"Thank you," Pepper said. The hum of the ferry's engines, the splash of the river's wake and the cool breeze blowing against her face did nothing to calm her rising curiosity. There was absolutely no doubt in her mind she knew this stranger from somewhere. She never forgot a face.

Her mind looped, sifted, spun like a whirligig attempting to dust the cobwebs from her memory banks. No matter how deep she dug, she couldn't shake the feeling she knew this person from somewhere.

"Are you from New Orleans...?" Pepper rambled on hoping to engage the woman in conversation. "I live in

Algiers Point. Maybe we live in the same neighborhood or stood in line for coffee at Tout de Suite's." Pepper glanced over at the woman hoping for some reaction. Nothing. She continued talking anyway. "Of course, there's a good chance we've shared other rides on this ferry. I'm on this rusty 'ol barge twice a day almost every day."

Realizing she should stop this intrusive behavior, Pepper sat down on a nearby bench. The woman clearly didn't know who the hell *she* was, but something inside of Pepper just wouldn't let go. In the first place, it was ridiculous she thought the woman was the first lady. If this *had been* Céline Randle, Secret Service would be hovering and she wouldn't have gotten within two feet of the woman. Then, the light bulb flickered. The first lady had a twin sister; a famous photographer.

Pepper bounded off the bench. "I know where I've seen you. LSU...you were in my photography class umpteen years ago." She said with a laugh. "You're that renowned photographer often mentioned in the LSU Alumni newsletter."

The woman pulled her hoodie closer to her profile, tucked her chin into her chest and started to walk toward the pilothouse.

"Please stay," Pepper pleaded. "I know I tend to come on too strong. A bad habit I definitely need to work on. It's just...well, I've had one hellava day and just babbling to a stranger seems to calm my urge to jump into the river."

For a brief second Pepper detected a flash of empathy from the woman's body language. She gambled and continued talking, but chose her words carefully.

"I miss the good 'ol days at LSU, don't you?" Still no reaction. "Do you remember Professor Stanley, our photography professor? What a geek. I'll never forget the day he carted his collection of antique cameras into class for us to see. That's a day *I'll* never forget."

Pepper hesitated for a moment hoping for a spark of recognition. The woman continued to ignore her. Refusing to give up, Pepper continued chatting like they were old friends.

"He told us we could come up and take a closer look, but to be very careful when we examined them. Well, klutz that I am chose the old 1912 Speed Graphic Press. I've always been curious about that accordion-like attachment it was so famous for."

Pepper laughed. "Determined to see how it worked, I kept pulling and tugging on that pleat, but it was stuck. That just made me yank and pull even harder. The next thing I knew, the damn thing slipped out of my hands."

"The professor screamed. I started juggling the camera with my arms flailing, feet tap-dancing, while at the same time, trying to catch the camera. The class laughed like they were watching Charlie Chaplin on speed pills."

She glanced over and hoped the woman would react with at least a glimmer of recollection — at the very least give her a smile. Nothing. She continued her monologue.

"Luckily one of our classmates caught the antique just before it shattered on the floor. He got an A plus in that class; I got a C minus."

Pepper shrugged, and then rolled her eyes and chuckled. "Guess the professor thought I had no business around cameras."

The ferry engines rumbled, the barge shuddered, and glided steadily toward the shoreline. Crewmembers unfurled massive hawsers and prepared to toss the ropes to dockworkers on shore to secure the mooring lines. The dozen passengers that were scattered around the deck moved toward the exit.

"Looks like the end of our journey," Pepper said. "I'm sorry if I talked your ear off. Obviously, I've mistaken you for someone else," she said hoping the woman would turn around and say something. "Maybe we'll run into each other again someday when we both are having a better day. Good night."

Pepper headed for the exit convinced she knew the woman and the woman knew her. Why else had she gone to such extremes to protect the sanctity of her anonymity? Pepper glanced over her shoulder one last time. The woman was still standing at the prow of the boat. *The one thing I do know*, Pepper thought as she wheeled her bike off the ferry, *that woman's cloak-and-dagger act just kicked my reporter's instincts into overdrive.*

CHAPTER 14

CÉLINE was trapped. Her heart empathized with the chatty young woman who was obviously lonely, troubled and feeling vulnerable. If she walked away, she was being rude and uncaring. If she stayed and acknowledged her, she'd risked revealing her true identity. And, that was not an option. It was bad enough the woman already thought she was her twin sister from their LSU days. Yes, she probably could have pulled off being Claréne, but she would have been taking a big risk. A person can only play with fire so many times before...

The ferry bounced against pilings; metal clanged. The crew shouted and scurried to batten down the hatches for the night. Céline chanced a quick look behind her, exhaled a sigh of relief. The talkative blonde had disappeared with the other passengers preparing to exit. All would soon fan-out to bars and restaurants in Algiers Point for a bedtime nightcap, a midnight snack, or head directly back to their shotgun houses painted every color of the rainbow.

As the last passengers exited the ferry and the crew completed their chores, Céline climbed the stairs to the pilothouse, gave her Uncle Beau a good night hug, and thanked him for her wonderful day on the river.

"*Chéri*, it's late. I'll drop you off at Mama Bea's after I've finish up here," Uncle Beau said.

Céline squeezed his hand, "No thanks," she said. "I've got Mama Bea's bike."

"No problem," he said. "We'll just toss that 'ol rusty contraption into the truck bed...."

"No really, Uncle Beau," she interrupted. "A ride along the Mississippi River Trail is just what I need to clear my head."

"We can stop at the Old Point Bar for a beer," he said. "A talented new saxophonist is featured tonight." He tucked his chin; his eyes pleaded.

Céline opened the pilothouse door and stepped onto the first step. "Another time." She smiled. "I promise."

"You're gonna get yourself mugged," he called after her as the heavy door slammed shut.

She stepped off the ferry and sauntered the short distance up the metal ramp flanking the Algiers Point Terminal building. With each step, the steel-plated gangway beneath her feet banged, rattled, echoed into the late evening hour. As she rounded the corner, she prayed Mama Bea's rusted Schwinn Stardust bike was still secured to the rack outside the ferry terminal. Each time she borrowed Bea's precious treasure, she feared the bike would get stolen like so many bicycles left unattended in this city — whether they were secured or not.

Céline beamed when she caught sight of the floral trimmed shopping basket, the high handlebars and the banana seat that had been patched and re-patched with duct tape. She rummaged in her tight fitting jeans and retrieved the key to unlock the *Kryptonite* U-Lock she had purchased two Christmas' ago for her beloved nanny. She smiled. *Thank God. If something had happened to that bike, she wouldn't have been able to face her Mama Bea ever again — and that wasn't an option.*

The last members of the ferryboat crew, with empty lunch pails in hand, scurried off the ferry for the night and waved at Céline as they passed. And then, as if a timer dinged, Uncle Beau blasted three long low-pitched bawls from the horn – his signature move that his day was done.

Comforted by her childhood memories and Uncle Beau's predictable consistency, Céline rolled the bike from the rack and headed toward the river trail with its paved and lit asphalt path. As she walked past the ferry terminal, she was still immersed in deep thoughts of days gone by. She couldn't imagine a life without Mama Bea and André. Those two were the reason she and Claréne had survived their childhood. Beatrice Bélair had been more of a maternal figure than her own mother to both she and her sister. André, too, was a permanent fixture in her life, first as a childhood playmate, and now was her protector as first lady of the United States.

For as long as she could remember, she and Claréne would wake up in the morning with a hug that smelled like warm, fried beignets coated with powdered sugar and go to bed at night kissed by the scent of the spicy aroma of Mama Bea's signature gumbo or jambalaya. A warm cuddle from Mama Bea was like being swallowed into a deep cushion of love. God had truly smiled on both she and Claréne when He blessed them with such a doting nanny. They certainly didn't get that kind of love from Miss Lily Mae Lafitte Fontenot.

Their birth mother was too busy with her elite friends, Mardi Gras Balls, and so-called tea parties — more like Mint Julep soirées — to remember she even had two children. Céline rolled her eyes. *Excuse me. More like inconveniences waiting at home.*

Céline tried to swallow the bitter taste fouling her mouth, but the childhood demons were now unleashed. Her mother had been such a fool believing her fair-weather friends actually bought into that ridiculous story she was a direct descendant of the famous pirate Jean Lafitte by both birth and marriage. She even tried to spread the laughable rumor that the reason the Fontenot and Lafitte families controlled the ferry business up and down the Mississippi was because it was the legacy left by the famous pirate. Both her father and Uncle Beau allowed Lily Mae to live in her fantasy world — she wasn't doing any harm and it was good for business. The sad part of the story was Lily Mae became a source of amusement and all because she'd married her second cousin and drank more than her share of Mint Juleps on any given day.

Céline leaned her head back, drew in a deep breath, and slowly released the air hoping to clear the unpleasant memories of her mother. She climbed aboard the bike's banana seat, crossed herself and began to pedal with her knees rising to her chest with each rotation.

As she traversed the levee along the river trail, the brilliant lights outlining the New Orleans skyline in the distance progressively dimmed and gave way to the intermittent bright security lights from the many wharfs that lined the levee's edge on the other side of the river. On occasion the darkness was interrupted by the whoosh of a wake and sporadic beacon of a passing barge. She pedaled passed the historic Algiers Point courthouse, rounded the corner and followed the path up Patterson Street.

From a nearby house, she heard the cry of a baby who obviously resisted falling asleep. Céline smiled. She'd never forget the day when she and her sister were five and Mama Bea brought home a cuddly new baby boy. He was so adorable — like having a living, breathing doll to play with. She laughed. Poor, poor André. He never had a chance growing up; always the object of the twin's imagination; their personal toy. If they weren't dressing him up in pink baby doll dresses or princess gowns and crowned with a jeweled tiara, they were serving him tea under the old Magnolia tree behind the plantation house. The most fun they had was when André was older. He became their brave African prince saving them from river pirates.

Céline smiled; from gallant African prince to bodyguard in real life.

When Dylan was elected vice president and both were required personal protection, André was her first choice to serve as her protector. At first her husband strongly objected, maybe even a little jealous of how close André and she were. Which was absolutely ludicrous – André was like her brother. Finally, after his unrelenting stubbornness, Dylan admitted her childhood playmate and loyal friend was the ideal choice to head her security detail. How could he refuse? André was a former Navy SEAL and once served on the NOPD task force roving the streets of the 6th District — not to mention he aced both the Secret Service exam and interview.

The mournful wail from a saxophone solo drifted through the late October air. Céline had reached the Old Point Bar — a popular dive that had been in existence since the early 19th century. The aging building remained the same. The only change was the clientele that had shifted from turn of the century railroad workers and shipbuilders to local Algiers Point residents and a few savvy tourists.

As the melody drifted from the bar below, Céline climbed off the bike and engaged the kickstand. She sat on a nearby park bench that had been bolted to the levee. The forlorn musical style forced Céline back to reality. With reluctance, she pulled her burner phone from her jacket pocket and wedged the ear buds into place. She opened the phone and tapped the message from Claréne:

Urgent! Must listen to tape. May have screwed the pooch. Sorry! Me and "A" on way to MB's. Will fill in blanks.

Céline's hand trembled; her body felt like a million needles were pricking her skin and every instinct within her screamed run, escape while you can. All she needed to do was race across the path, down the cement revetment into the menacing, murky, roiling river only a few feet away — in minutes it'd be all over.

She flexed her fist again and again. Inhaled, exhaled. Took another breathe and then slowly exhaled again. Céline pressed play on the recording. As the tape rolled, she could hear, feel Dylan's voice laced with venom as he spoke in hushed tones to Burt Harrison and the press secretary. Only the cadence of *"Hail to the Chief"* interrupted his rebuke. At the sound of the music, she could actually visualize her husband's angry face balloon into that classic bogus smile of his. She could see him puff out his chest, tighten his grip on her arm and pull her into the room with him.

As the contents of the tape rolled, she was spellbound by the erupting verbal altercation between a woman and Burt Harrison, and what must have been other law enforcement. It sounded like the person was being dragged from the room, screaming accusations. Céline stopped and rewound the tape hoping to make sense of what the woman was yelling. The moment the assertion was clear she hit the pause button and tried to wrap her brain around the inconceivable scene. She replayed the same part of the tape over and over again until the heart of the message hit home. "Oh, my god, Claréne, what did I get you into?"

The doleful call of a foghorn in the distance deepened Céline's despair. She should play the tape all the way to the end, but how could she knowing the potential consequences barreling down on Claréne and André? Her sister mentioned that both of them were on their way home. What she needed to do right now was climb on the bike and get to Mama Bea's as quickly as possible to speak with her sister and André personally. Assembling the detailed facts from today's events, committing the endless names and the gist of key conversations from her sister's taping would have to wait until later. All she wanted to do was hug her sister and make sure she was truly safe and unharmed.

CHAPTER 15

THE BAND switched from the warm and mellow tenor of the saxophone soloist to a lively, foot tapping Cajun beat. Pepper leaned against the clapboard wall of the Old Point Bar and nursed a NOLA Blonde from an ice cold mug. She tried to focus on the infectious music, but her undivided attention was centered totally on the woman from the ferry now sitting less than a hundred yards away on a levee park bench. The longer she studied the subject of her latest obsession, the brighter the aura of mystery burned.

It was understandable that a woman all alone might be reluctant to talk with strangers on a short ferry ride, she reasoned. Maybe she was shy. Unlikely, Pepper muttered under her breath. Before she even tried to engage the woman in a conversation, she noticed her graceful movements, her in control, confident body language. A person like that would've just told her to buzz off instead of conspicuously trying to conceal her identity.

A couple sitting at a nearby outside table, stood, kissed one another on both cheeks and headed off in opposite directions. Pepper slid onto one of the empty chairs.

"Another NOLA Blonde?" A waiter asked as he removed a couple of plates and glasses from the table, and then swiped a damp cloth across the surface.

Pepper glanced at the beer left in the mug. "Not yet. Still working on this one," she said not taking her eyes off the occupant sitting on the levee's park bench.

Was it instinct or the devil provoking her to once again pry into someone's business without an invitation? She wondered. The answer to that question was yet to be determined. All she knew was when she'd reached the turn off to head home she'd caught a glimpse of the mystery woman riding along the Mississippi Trail on a child's bicycle. Once again she was seduced by curiosity. Without hesitation she steered her own bike along Patterson Drive at the foot of the levee and kept the "ferry-boat" lady in sight the best she could.

Now here we both were, Pepper thought with amusement, *me drinking a cold beer when I'd rather be drowning in a tumbler of Sazerac. The ferry-boat lady, with ear buds plugged in her ears, was engrossed with something on her phone instead of enjoying some of the best music New Orleans had to offer.*

What a bizarre night this has turned out to be, she thought as she sipped her beer. What possessed her to morph from professional journalist into raving maniac and a midnight stalker? In reality that poor woman was probably the doppelganger of someone she'd been acquainted with over the years. After all, there were lots of people who have others who share an uncanny resemblance. Pepper shook her head. Just because she'd screwed up her career and spent a couple hours in jail, what gave her the right to shadow someone because of a crazy-ass hunch? Maybe it was time to put her past in the rearview mirror and rein in her over-active imagination — either that or check herself into the closest psych ward.

Just as Pepper was accepting responsibility for her irrational behavior, the woman abruptly yanked out the ear buds, vaulted from the bench and wrestled with her bicycle's kickstand. She hurriedly walked her bike down the grassy revetment and passed within only a few feet from where Pepper was sitting.

Pepper tucked her head into her chest and watched the woman pedal a short distance down Olivier Street. She quickly laid some money on the table, grabbed her bike and followed at a safe distance. In just two short blocks, the chess piece in her game of cat and mouse turned right on Pelican Avenue, passed Mount Olivet Episcopal Church and three shotgun houses. When the woman reached her destination, she climbed off her bike. Three people greeted and escorted her through the gate of a wrought iron fence. It was too dark to distinguish identities. She would sort out those details after a good night's sleep. Pepper waited for a brief moment longer until the small group of people went inside, and then pedaled past the house and made a mental note of the address.

She rolled by a couple more shotgun houses, and then turned left on Verret. As she passed the Gothic style Catholic Church, a dark sedan coasted past her at a slow speed and turned left at the next block. She couldn't catch a glimpse at the driver because the windows were tinted, but the hackles on the back of her neck signaled a caution that made her pedal faster. Before reaching Eliza Avenue, the same car breezed by a second time. Her heart went from a steady beat to full-blown pounding equal to the speed of Hummingbird wings. Her imagination might be working overtime, but her gut feeling sensed it was the same man from the ferry.

Pepper ducked down Eliza Street, made a quick turn onto Belleview, over to Evelina and then up Elmira. She chanced one last glance over her shoulder. No headlights. No car. *Thank God for one way streets.* She breathed a sigh of relief. *That should keep that bastard confused*, Pepper thought still feeling unsure of her safety.

When she reached her house still pedaling at full speed, she flew up the driveway, jumped off her bike, and let it skid across the sidewalk, back wheel still spinning. Her Gucci bag, contents and all, sailed through the air and scattered across the small manicured lawn. Not wasting a moment, she snatched up keys, cell phone and the ROCKZ external battery pack she'd forgotten was in the bottom of her purse. Without giving the rest of her personal belongings a second thought, she rushed into the house, latched the two locks, and then leaned against the door. Pepper closed her eyes, pressed a hand over her overactive heart and tried to catch her breath.

She chanced a quick peek through the gauze curtains covering the French-window and checked to see if the black sedan had followed. The street was deserted, as it should be at midnight. Hands shaking, she plugged her iPhone into the charger and prayed her phone retained or would soak up enough power to call the police. She quickly pressed the personal ID button and held the phone close to her mouth. "Siri, call the cops."

"I don't know how to respond to that," the monotone female voice responded.

"911...call 911," Pepper screamed into her phone wanting to throw it across the room; instead she punched in the numbers.

"911...how can we help?"

"A man...in a black car," she screamed into the phone.

"Ma'am, ma'am," the dispatcher said. "Take a breath, I'm not going anywhere".

Pepper heaved several deep breaths, exhaled until the tension in her voice eased. "I'm sorry," she said. "It's just that...."

"That's fine, ma'am," the soothing voice on the other end of the phone said. "Just take your time. Tell me how we can help."

"I was heading back from the late ferry on my bike and a car kept circling the block. I know it was following me because the identical car drove past me three times."

"Do you know what kind of car it was?"

"A black sedan. I'm not sure what model."

"How 'bout the license plate?"

Pepper furrowed her brow, "No, no, I... I didn't look. I was too busy pedaling for my life. The license number was the last thing on my mind."

"Did you get a good look at anyone in the car?"

"Not really," she said. "The windows were tinted. But I think it was the same man who was on the ferry with me tonight."

"Excuse me," the dispatcher said. "I thought you were riding your bike."

"I was," Pepper said exasperated. "That's the point. He followed me home. I just know it."

"Are you in imminent danger?" The dispatcher asked.

Pepper peeked through the curtains again. "No I don't think so."

A moment of silence followed before the dispatcher spoke again. "Are all your doors locked?"

"Yes, yes," Pepper said.

"Okay, good," the calm voice answered. "Did you perhaps get a good look at the man on the ferry?"

"Somewhat," Pepper said. "He wore a baseball cap, pulled low down over his eyes and was wearing baggy jeans and a New Orleans Saints black football jersey with the number nine."

Another long moment of silence rolled by until the dispatcher spoke. "Do you have any other details? There are a lot of men living in the State of Louisiana who wear baseball caps and football jerseys with the number nine."

"I know...I know. I'm sorry," Pepper said. "It's just...."

"That's alright, ma'am. Take your time. I know you're upset. Let's continue. Was this man Caucasian, black, Hispanic, maybe oriental?" The dispatcher's voice was beginning to show a slight frustration. "How about short, tall, fat, or skinny?"

"I don't know," tears welled in Pepper's eyes. "He looked Cajun," she said.

"Cajun?" The dispatcher released a muffled chuckle. "And what exactly does Cajun look like?"

A flush worked its way to Pepper's cheeks. "Are you going to help me or not?" she asked.

"I apologize, miss. It's been a crazy night with POTUS's campaign rally and every LSU and Alabama fan from the Tri-state area in for the big game. Give me your address and we'll send a cruiser to canvas your neighborhood."

"Thank you, sir, that's all I ask," Pepper said, and then placed her phone still attached to the battery pack onto the coffee table. She hustled over to the brightly painted Indian motif cupboard where she stored her liquor. She snatched the half-empty bottle of Sazerac along with her favorite jelly-jar glass and poured two fingers. Without hesitation she swallowed the liquid fire in one gulp and poured another.

With drink in hand, Pepper returned to the French-window, glanced across the street, and then stretched to see as far down Elmira as possible without going outside. She wracked her brain trying to recall the type of automobiles her neighbors owned. Headlights moved slowly up the street toward the house. Her heart seized in her chest — dark sedan or police cruiser?

CHAPTER 16

BURT bolted upright jarred awake by the same recurring nightmares he had been experiencing for weeks. Those same haunted dreams had begun to exhibit signs of reality. He rolled his legs over the edge of the bed, held his head in his hands. Maybe a Benadryl would help him sleep, he thought. Taking one this late would make him feel groggy in the morning, but what was new? He hadn't had a decent night's sleep since Michael Carlton's death, and after he reluctantly gave into Dylan's pleas to continue as the campaign manager.

Burt slid out of bed and retrieved his Dopp Kit from his suitcase. *In what universe did he believe becoming Dylan Randle's campaign manager was a positive move?* He reflected, as he rummaged through the kit in search of the elusive pink pill. Trying to constantly keep Dylan focused was proving to be more of a challenge than he was willing or able to handle – not to mention he didn't need the added stress. Four years ago when he worked for Michael Carlton's presidential campaign, he ended up in the hospital, not once, but twice with angina. Both times the doctors warned that if he didn't slow down....

He plopped down on the edge of the bed, held the now empty Dopp Kit in his hand. His stomach burned as the acid fermented with each troubled thought. What he wouldn't give for a large bottle of Pepto Bismol right now. Up to now everything had been running relatively smooth until...

Burt sneered. Until Harley Durham stuck his nose into the campaign and convinced the Randles to deviate from the original schedule. How in the hell was Harley able to convince Dylan that New Orleans would be the perfect setting to reel in a victory for a second term? Bile bubbled up his throat. Louisiana and the Crescent City were already in the bag, a waste of precious time with Allison Benson breathing down their necks. "Who was the campaign manager, anyway?" He snarled. "Me or Harley Durham?"

Burt pressed the heel of his hand against his belly and tried to calm the growing ulcer waging war inside of him. He would never comprehend why Dylan held Harley Durham in such high regard. How does a smart, savvy, influential man like Dylan Randle with a beautiful wife and all the money in the world get mixed up with a swamp rat like Durham?

The only plausible explanation was that scumbag held the key to a hell of a lot of dark secrets, Burt reasoned. It *was* common knowledge those two became friends a long time ago while playing football together at Tulane University. But their social backgrounds, hell their DNA, was about as mismatched as opera is to zydeco Cajun music. If it hadn't been for Dylan and his dad bankrolling Harley's first business venture, that degenerate would probably be conducting alligator tours in one of the nearby swamps instead of living a posh life in a Garden District mansion on St. Charles Avenue.

Burt turned the Dopp Kit upside down one more time and shook it over the bed. He dug a fingertip into the crevices hoping to free the stray Benadryl, but nothing materialized. Burt scoffed. His luck evaporated the moment Harley Durham muscled his way into the campaign. Alarm bells went off the first time he'd met

Durham and to this very day nothing had changed his mind. Every instinct in his body screamed disastrous move stopping in New Orleans. Dylan was already under a microscope, and the last thing his campaign needed was some buried secret crawling out of the swamp.

Burt shook his head. More than once he wondered how Durham had managed to turn a small business into an empire. Regardless of how that man accumulated his fortune, there wasn't a person alive who could convince him Harley Durham had come by it honestly. The last thing he needed was *his* smut contaminating the campaign — particularly so near to the finish line.

"God-damn it," Burt growled. "Where's my Fuah...frigging Benadryl?" He tossed his shaving kit across the floor, grabbed the cheap terry bathrobe Harley provided guests, and stormed out of the bedroom looking for the backstairs to the kitchen.

Burt weaved his way from the third to the first floor. He stepped onto the terrazzo tile, reached for the switch and flipped on a light. He navigated the massive kitchen island, opened the double-wide, dual-door refrigerator and took out a gallon of milk. He rummaged through several cabinets until he found a small saucepan, and then poured some liquid into the pan and switched on the stove.

While he waited for the milk to warm, he sat down at a cozy table tucked in a corner overlooking a lighted garden. The ivy-draped stone-wall bordering the back of the house was reinforced by aged-old, gnarled moss-draped trees that were wrapped with white lights. Scattered around the back were large decorative urns and small hanging pots spilling with red, gold, purple and orange fall flowers. Loud Cajun music and laughter drifted from another part of the house. Burt bit his tongue and resisted the urge to scream,

"Hey frat boys, turn off the damn music and go to bed. People are trying to sleep." He furrowed his brow, a wave of empathy wrapped around his heart. *No wonder the first lady bolted and headed for a more wholesome atmosphere.*

Burt sighed. *He shouldn't blame Céline for bailing on the president when he needed her most*, he thought. *Dylan had given them all plenty of reasons lately to disappear.* Anyone who recognized the "Dark Dylan" avoided him if and when they could.

Burt snorted under his breath. "You knew what you were getting into before you accepted the job, dumb ass." *So true, so true*, he unwillingly gave in. The problem was nothing was getting any easier working with a man who turned a deaf ear to his counsel — not to mention the escalating verbal abuse. If the Party, Céline, and the Senate Majority Leader had not convinced him, begged him to stay to the bitter end, he would have bailed long ago.

He placed his elbows on the table with his fists against his cheeks. He wrestled with his thoughts. It was Céline he was concerned about. Lately the first lady was making his job even more difficult than usual. The closer Election Day rolled around the more she jumped at an opportunity to distance herself from her husband. The last thing a man running for president of the United States needed was a disengaged wife who isolated herself. Why couldn't both Dylan and Céline understand that this campaign needed her? She was the rock, the glue that held everything and everybody together; she was the most capable of keeping Dylan focused with his eyes on the prize.

The timer dinged. Burt got up and poured steaming milk into a stoneware mug. If only Céline would hang in there a little longer, he agonized. *But no, what does the first lady do the first chance she gets...?* He slammed the sauce pan back onto the stovetop; milk sloshed out and sizzled against the hot flat surface... *she escapes to the comforting arms of her childhood nanny.*

Burt pressed his eyes tight and tried to stall the ambush of pain tapping at his temple. Why a Rhodes Scholar, Valedictorian of her college class insisted on returning to her roots on the banks of the Mississippi River every chance she got was beyond him. She was beautiful, shy, unpretentious, and radiated a charm that drew crowds like honeybees drawn to flowers in the springtime. Didn't she realize that with little to no effort she could have the entire world eating out of the palm of her hands?

"Céline...Céline...Céline," he exhaled a deep long breath. "How am I to convince you how important you are to Dylan's campaign?"

Still captured in his thoughts, Burt leaned against the kitchen island and blew the steam off the hot milk. Dylan was no help. POTUS's ego hated sharing the spotlight which probably made Céline the perfect choice for his wife – he got all the attention and she was able to roam the great museums of the world with as little press coverage as possible. Burt sipped his milk. Yep, his job would be a hellava lot easier if only both the first lady *and* Dylan would realize it was Céline who was the president's anchor, the guiding force that kept her husband focused.

Burt sat back down at the table and stared aimlessly into the garden still trapped within his train of thought. Maybe he was being too hard on Céline asking her to shoulder more than her share of the responsibility. He couldn't put his finger on the moment he noticed the spark in her beautiful and spirited eyes flame out, or exactly when she became more edgy and less patient with Dylan. All *he* knew was he had lost the shining star of the campaign when he needed her the most. Hopefully, once Céline spent some time with her beloved Mama Bea, she would become reenergized and ready to help carry Dylan across the finish line.

He got up from the table, went back to the stove and topped off his cup with the last of the milk from the still warm pot. With mug in hand, Burt switched off the kitchen light, snatched a near-empty bottle of brandy off the counter and headed upstairs. "As far as I'm concerned," he muttered, "it won't be too soon for this campaign to be over." All he needed to do was hang on a few more weeks and pray for large rallies equal to the Superdome for the remaining campaign stops.

Burt nudged the partially closed bedroom door with his foot. He took a big sip of his warm milk, and then poured some of the Brandy into the cup. He placed them both on the bedside table, kicked off his slippers, slipped out of the robe and climbed into bed. *The real challenge ahead of him*, he thought, *was to successfully navigate any more shit-storms lurking in the shadows like tonight and do it while hanging onto his dignity.*

Propped against a couple pillows, Burt took another sip from the liquor-laced milk and willed the brew to tranquilize the tension gripping every muscle in his body. Before turning off the bedside lamp, he topped the cup with more brandy and whispered one last despondent sigh. "Swamp rats, troublesome reporters, and an aging frat boy running for president, will be the death of me yet."

CHAPTER 17

HARLEY flipped on the kitchen light, and then glanced at the digital clock on the oven – 2:45 A.M. He opened the over-sized refrigerator and rummaged for leftovers. Not seeing anything remotely appealing, he slid out the deli-drawer and picked up a package of Cracker Barrel cheese slices and caught a glimpse of the nearby Summer Sausage. A burp laced with beer and scotch slipped through his lips. "Forget that," he mumbled and slammed the deli drawer shut. The last thing he needed was indigestion mixed in with whatever else planned to jeopardize the last few hours of sleep he had left.

He snatched a bottle of Kona Nigari Water, searched the cabinets for an Advil or Aspirin, anything to delay the onslaught of self-induced misery waiting for him in the morning. He chuckled. "Tonight was worth every bad choice he made." Harley opened the bottle of Advil, dumped three green Liqui-Gel capsules into his palm. He tossed the pills into his mouth, and then gulped several swigs of the Kona. *When was the last time D-Rod and he had shared a night of debauchery?* He wondered.

As he sipped the artisan water Harley gazed into the lighted garden. It must have been eons ago since they had a night like tonight, but some things never change, he thought with a respectful smile. Even after a deep dive into his little black book, several discreet calls and shelling out a wad of cash thicker than the back of his hand, that rat bastard still managed to wind up with the best broad.

He furrowed his brow, shook his head. What man in their right mind could resist that sumptuous blond he found for his friend — particularly a Marilyn Monroe look-a-like. For the last thirty plus years all D-Rod bragged about was how he used to get off as a kid staring at the pages of Marilyn's nude photo in his father's prized First Edition of *Play Boy Magazine*. At the very least his 'ol buddy could've appreciated the irony, but oh, no, he had to pick *my* black beauty; the one I specifically chose for myself. He scratched his paunch belly and yawned. He'd never understand why Dylan in his darkest moments always fixated on black women. *After that unfortunate incident years ago, you'd think he'd learned his lesson...*

Harley rolled his eyes, and then reached for the bottle of bedtime Brandy that Miss Ruby Jo always left for him in the same place every night. "What the hell?" he muttered, eyes sweeping around the horseshoe countertop. "Who swiped my damn sleep aid?"

He slapped off the kitchen light. "If one of those damn Secret Service guys snatched my bottle, I'll have his job," he grumbled and stomped down the hall toward his personal suite.

When Harley slid open the pocket-door leading into his bedroom, a broad smile and deep affection for his longtime housekeeper melted his earlier irritation. A warm fire glowed in the convex-shaped fireplace; the calming scent of lavender wafted through the room. His favorite hunter green silk pajamas were positioned at the foot of the king sized canopy bed. The lamps sitting on the tables next to each side of the bed highlighted two choices — a glass of water with a new box of Alka Seltzer tablets, and on the other nightstand, two cans of Dos Equis beer iced in a champagne bucket. *Miss Ruby Jo sure does take good care of me*, he thought with a glow of affection. *Better than those three witches he married and who continue to suck the very life out of his blood.*

Harley undressed, took a steaming hot shower and then slipped on his pajamas. He climbed into the already turned down bed and clapped his hands; the lamps switched off. He curled beneath the black satin sheets, nuzzled deep into his feather pillow and willed sleep to snatch him away to dreamland.

Seconds turned into minutes, and then into an hour. Harley tossed and turned; flipped and flopped, but the excitement from the Superdome, the cocktail party, Dylan and those two beauties from last night looped through his mind like an out-of-control roller-coaster.

Harley rolled his legs over the edge of the bed, squeezed his eyes tight and tried to tame the throb tapping against the back of his head. Musical notes from the clock on the mantle chimed the hour. "Christ all Mighty," he cursed. He and Dylan needed to be up and out of the house no later than five for the fishing trip with the Governor. If he had known what fun he was going to have last night, he would've never agreed to go.

He reached over and took one of the iced Dos Equis from the champagne bucket and held the cold can against his head. The last place he and his stomach needed to be was see-sawing on the choppy waters of the Gulf of Mexico and smelling dead fish. Harley inhaled a deep breath and then exhaled. He picked up his watch and double checked the time — an hour before he needed to get dressed.

Harley climbed out of bed, popped open the beer, and walked over to a bookcase displaying his prized Civil War chess set. He loved the miniature cannons, rebel and union soldiers, but most of all, Ulysses S. Grant and Robert E. Lee facing off. He reached over and gently rotated Bobby Lee until the tiny figure's back was to Grant. "Screw you, Ulysses," Harley laughed as a secret door slid open next to the bookcase.

Multiple television monitors lined the wall. The room hummed as activity from every room in the house, the garden, swimming pool area and every outdoor entrance was being recorded. Harley pulled up a chair and switched on the screen to Dylan's bedroom. "Well damn-it," he whispered, his voice laced with disappointment. The black beauty he'd wanted so badly for himself had already left. Dylan was curled around a pillow; soft snores escaped his lips.

Harley switched to another screen and opened the file. A flash of jealousy swallowed him as he watched a recording in full color on a 22-inch screen. *His* intended date was screwing the president of the United States instead of him.

As desire stirred within, a moment of envy seethed inside. *That should be me entwined with Desiree, lost in the fruits of passion, not that bastard Randle. It isn't fair he again walks off with the prize.*

Harley quickly switched to another screen knowing that picking at old scabs from years of kowtowing to Mr. Dylan Randle the III would do neither of them any good. His day would come — just not today. Harley tapped the screen as he watched his friend sleep. "Tread lightly, Mr. President." Harley's mouth twitched with a sneer. "A body can only take so many hits before it revolts. And, I've taken more than my share of blows in the name of the almighty Randle name. With everything I know *you're* the one sitting in the palm of *my* hand. I can protect you, or squish you like a bug."

Harley glanced at his Rolex, jumped out of the chair and raced to his walk-in closet. He threw on his fishing gear and ran out of his bedroom suite yelling, "Dylan, get your ass out of bed. We've got a boat to catch."

CHAPTER 18

DAY TWO

AS SHADOWS faded, a welcome chorus of birds began to serenade the new day's rising sun. Mama Bea stretched her lower back and then leaned forward in an attempt to touch her toes. "Gall darn lumbago," she grumbled. She poured a steaming cup of Chicory, limped through the kitchen door out to the screened porch behind the Creole cottage.

The sweet vanilla scent of clematis lingered on the crisp October air. She set her coffee on a small side table and then snuggled deep into her cushioned rocking chair – the once bright, paisley print was now worn down to the last threads. *How many years had it been since all three of her children had been under her roof, and at the same time?* She wondered. *It seemed time rushed by faster than that 'ol Man River only a few blocks away.*

Mama Bea slowly rocked back and forth, wrapped in the comfort of having her family, finally all together again, sleeping soundly only a few rooms away. *Miss Lily Mae may've birthed those beautiful twin babies, but their heart and soul belonged to her.*

She leaned her head on the back rest; a warm smile rested on her face. For the last couple years André and Céline would drop by now and then when her husband was off traveling somewhere on the other side of the world or doing heaven only knows what else. "That Dylan Randle will never be good enough for my sweet Céline," Bea huffed under her breath. She deserved a kinder, humble man who could appreciate her gentle soul. How those two ever coupled up was beyond her. Cèline was like a lamb put in the arms of the prince of darkness.

Now, when it came to her carefree little charge, Claréne, the oldest of the twins by seventeen minutes, she was the strong one. My little angel travels the world photographing all them po' little children hidin' from them bombs in Afghanistan and wherever else. She goes to Africa and takes pictures of starvin' and sick folks; even took pictures of those gorillas in the rainforest. That little fireball must be made of Pennsylvania steel. Afraid of nothin', and don't take no guff off nobody. Lordy me, heaven save the soul who would dare bully her baby sister, Céline.

"What's you doin', Mama?" André asked.

Bea jerked her head around; her hand flew to her chest. "Oh my, child, you startled me."

"Sorry, Mama, but you promised homemade beignets and flapjacks. And, I don't smell 'em cookin'," André teased.

"Child, you be the death of me yet," she said struggling to get out of her chair. "Ya can't even give an old woman a moment to enjoy day's first light before you put 'er to work."

"The twins have lined up all the ingredients and utensils. The oil is heating on the stove," he said offering his Mama a hand.

"Go on now," Mama Bea said flipping her fingers toward him. "I'll be there in a minute."

The moment she walked into the kitchen both girls jumped up from where they were sitting, wrapped their arms around Mama Bea and gave her one of those lingering hugs she loved so much.

"Now, what's all the fuss about? You gonna get what's promised. Just give me a minute to strap on my apron," she said.

Céline and Claréne gave Mama Bea a quick kiss on each cheek and joined André at the kitchen table already flipping through pages from old photo albums when they were kids. Mama Bea smiled; her heart filled with love as they laughed and joked like when they were no bigger than a doodlebug.

Bea dropped hot batter into the hot oil, watched as the bubbles surrounded the perfect squares and the dough puff up.

"Mama, tell me again who this woman is," André asked raising the album up for her to see.

"What's that?" she asked as she flipped the browning beignets.

André carried the book over to his mother and pointed to a slender black woman light of skin.

Without looking, Mama Bea said, "That be Gabrielle."

"Who was she to us?" he asked. "I know you told me when I was a kid, but I forgot."

A wave of guilt coiled in Bea's stomach. "She was my younger sister...died many years ago."

"Oh, yeah, that's right," André said. "You never talked about her much."

Mama Bea quickly sprinkled powdered sugar on the warm beignets and placed the plate on the table. "Now hush up and eat while their warm," she said.

Bea wiped her hands on the apron and pulled out the griddle for the flapjacks she'd promised. *Someday*, Mama Bea thought, *she needed to sit the boy down and tell him all about his kinfolk. The only family he really knew, for goodness' sake, was her, the twins and their Uncle Beau. All* families' roots run deep and harbor hidden secrets. Too often and without warning, tragedy and heartbreak strike when one least expects. André deserved to know *all* the truths she'd been keeping from him before the good Lord saw fit to take her home.

As she beat the batter for the flapjacks, she noted the kids good-natured conversations had turned to hushed tones. "Now don't you kids be talking around my back," she said. "I taught you better than that."

"Sorry, Mama," André said. "It's just..."

"Just what," Bea said.

"I'm not sure you'd want to know..."

Mama Bea dropped the bowl of batter on the table, they jumped.

"Since when you hol' back from me? You talk to me and you talk to me now."

"It's nothing, really," Claréne tittered. "Céline and I have just been up to our old tricks...."

Mama Bea furrowed her brow. "Aren't you a little old to be playing tricks? What kind of tricks?" she asked.

The twins looked at one another and back at André, all three jaws locked open, but not a word was offered.

Bea looked from one to the other, and then took Céline's chin in her hand. "Chile, you know *you* can't lie to me. You tell your Mama Bea everything and start from the beginning."

Céline poured out her heart sparing no detail; tears streamed down her face.

"You should hear the way Mr. Randle talks and acts toward Céline in private," André said. "Several times I almost kicked in the door and flattened the man. I don't care who he thinks he is or might become."

"Last night the bastard threatened me," Claréne added. "He's dangerous, Mama Bea. What else could we do?"

Bea pulled out a chair and sat down, her eyes narrowed a bit. "You sure you kiddos not exaggeratin' just a little?"

"No, ma'am," all three said in unison.

"How you gonna get yourselves out of this mess?" Mama Bea asked. "The man is the president of these United States."

Claréne glanced at both Céline and André. "Well, we don't have a plan. At least not yet, but we're working on it," she said. "André and I thought it best we try and get a good night's sleep before we did a deep dive into all the disturbing details."

Céline furrowed her brow and said, "Disturbing details? Was there *more* than what was on those urgent phone recordings you sent? What could possibly make things worse than they already are?"

"Well, no, but yes..." Claréne struggled to find the right words. "The recording revealed the verbal contents. It was what you didn't see."

Mama Bea mopped her face with her apron. "You three have gone and put yourselves in danger. I just know it. You dealing with some powerful people, and I don't like it."

André touched Bea's arm. "Mama, you're right, they are powerful. But powerful people who have done some bad things over the years. Their past may have finally caught up with them."

Céline finally spoke. "Is this about that woman who was asked to leave the campaign cocktail party?"

Claréne nodded. "Yes," she said. "But she wasn't just any woman." She took a breath and continued. "Remember that reporter who accused Dylan of rape four years ago and almost ended his career before it got started?"

"Pen...Penelope Mills?" Céline stuttered.

"The same," Clarène said. "The poor woman was just standing in a far corner enjoying a drink. She probably wouldn't have caused a scene if that crazy-ass husband of yours hadn't gone ballistic just because he saw her there."

Céline frowned. "Are you sure Penelope didn't pull one of her big-mouth routines? She asked. "That woman is famous for being quite the trouble-maker; actually shunned out of Washington D.C. because of her antics."

"Come on, Céline," Clarène said. "Think about it. What person in their right mind would make the same mistake twice? Tangling with Dylan Randle the III isn't exactly healthy for anyone.

Trust me. I was there in the room. Without provocation that tiny five-foot two woman was literally accosted by not one man, but three strong men and forcefully extracted from a room full of people. What else could she do? The only way she knew how to fight back was with words. I'm telling you it was like watching karma exposing Dylan's dark side in full color.

Céline rubbed her brow; frowned. "What happened to her after that?" she asked.

"She was arrested and dragged off to jail," André said.

"Is there anything we can do for her?" Céline asked.

"Already taken care of," André said. "An old friend I went through the New Orleans' Police Academy with did me a favor. Made sure the Feds stayed out of it...at least for right now."

"Good," Céline said. She stood, walked over to the stove and poured a cup of coffee; started to speak, stopped and blew the steam curling from the mug. She looked over at the six pairs of eyes staring at her. "I wasn't going to mention this," she said.

"Lordy, lordy," Mama Bea said. "I don't think my po' heart can handle much more."

André reached over and touched Bea's hand. "Mama, we've got this. You've raised three strong people."

Mama Bea patted his hand. "I know, I know." She looked at Céline. "Go ahead, baby, best to get everything out in the open."

Céline continued. "On the final trip on the ferry last night very few people boarded the return trip to Algiers. I took a chance and went out on deck to get some fresh air. Unfortunately, there was a chatty woman who tried to engage me in conversation."

"Oh no," Claréne said. "You promised you wouldn't leave the pilothouse. Did she recognize you?"

"I don't think so. I kept my face concealed with my hoodie," she said. "Of course, I can't be sure..."

Céline sat back at the table and continued. "There *might* be a slight chance it was Penelope. I really didn't get a good look at her."

"What makes you think it could've been her?" Claréne asked.

"She asked me if I went to LSU; it sounded like she thought maybe I had been one of her classmates. Did you ever have a class with Penelope Mills?"

"Geez, I can't remember. That was years ago," Claréne said. "What exactly did she say?"

Céline pushed away her coffee. "She kept rambling about some 'ol antique camera that belonged to some photography professor."

"I'll be a monkey's uncle," Claréne laughed. "I do remember an incident in class where one of the students almost destroyed a precious antique camera belonging to the Professor. And, it wasn't just any camera. It was a 1912 Speed Graphic."

Céline chuckled and shook her head. "You and your cameras."

"You don't understand. It was a 1912 Speed Graphic!" Claréne exclaimed. "The professor and I *both* almost had a heart attack that day. The irony here is that woman on the ferry thought she remembered *me! She's* the one who almost destroyed a piece of history."

"Did you really know Penelope Mills?" Andrè asked Claréne.

She shrugged. "We might've shared a couple classes our senior year, but I didn't know her personally. We certainly didn't run in the same circles."

He shook his head. "What a small world."

"She seemed quite impressed and with you, my dear sister," Céline cut in.

"Did she say or do anything else?" Claréne asked.

"Nothing. The ferry docked, she got off with the rest of the passengers, and I came here. I'm sure it isn't worth a second thought."

"Enough talk," André said. "Mama, I'm ready for those flapjacks. Got any fresh blueberries for mine?"

CHAPTER 19

AS THE morning sun peeked through the gauze curtains covering the French windows, the clock whistled a bubbling cuckoo... cuckoo... cuckoo. Pepper jolted upright and snatched the dull butcher knife still lying on the coffee table from the night before. Gripping the blade close to her chest, she stood and moved cautiously to the windows — the jitters from last night still fluttered inside her stomach.

She slid back the curtain with her fingertips and prayed there were no unfamiliar cars parked on the street or strange men lurking in the shadows. From what she could see the only anomalies were her bicycle lying on its side and her Gucci bag with most of its content still strewn across the lawn.

Pepper exhaled a long breath and tried to ease the lingering sense of foreboding deep inside her gut. She laid the big knife on the coffee table next to her iPhone charging on the battery pack. She picked up the jelly jar glass still containing two fingers of Sazerac, but then quickly set it back down. As much as she loved inhaling the bouquet of the orange blossom scented rye, this morning the aroma from the sweet nectar only made the nausea fermenting in her stomach worse.

Her iPhone pinged again and again. The dark screen announced nine A.M. along with an endless list of messages. Not ready to justify her actions to her curious friends and an irate boss, she turned on the silent mode and flipped the phone face down. She caught a whiff of the wrinkled blouse she was still wearing after the longest day and night of her life. Body odor, mixed with a hint of liquor and the Italian salami and Camembert cheese she had passed around at the cocktail party ignited the acid already polluting her unhappy stomach. She picked up her shoes lying next to the sofa and headed to the back of the shotgun house for a hot shower and change of clothes.

Pepper surrendered beneath the pulsing stream of water and wished all her troubles would wash down the drain. Knowing that wasn't possible, she lingered one last moment and enjoyed the soothing spray, and then turned off the water and stepped out of the shower. Remnants from the shower's hot steam fogged the small bathroom and frosted the mirror. She swiped her hand across the glass. A sad looking face with deep, dark shadows beneath blue eyes stared back at her. Pepper grabbed a towel and wrapped it around her wet head, snatched the kimono off the foot of the bed and returned to the living room.

She curled up on the sofa, pulled one foot under her butt, and then reached down and unzipped the carrying case for her laptop. Pepper switched on the notebook, drummed her fingers on her knee and waited for the endless buffering to stop. Finally, the familiar desktop icons blinked into view. She immediately keyed in Google Maps and entered the address on Pelican Avenue, Algiers Point, Louisiana.

No name accompanied the search as to who might live there. She zoomed in the satellite view of the small Creole cottage. No car was parked in the driveway and only a few other vehicles lined the street — no license plates were visible. Hope for any easy identification slipped through her fingers even before her search had begun.

Pepper exhaled and clicked on the Safari icon for Algiers Point Property Tax Records. She keyed in the

Pelican address. The name that popped up as "Owner" was Beatrice Bélair purchased in 1985 from a Beauregard Fontenot for the sum of one hundred dollars. Pepper did a double take. "What? That can't be right," she said aloud. "Who would've sold a house for less than a hundred bucks in the twentieth century?"

The name Bélair didn't ring a bell, but Fontenot... Now *that* name, for some odd reason, did sound a bit familiar. She tapped her hand on the side of her thigh hoping to jar loose a memory. *Fontenot... Fontenot... Fontenot... Come on brain, think*! Pepper hissed a sigh and closed her laptop. This was getting her nowhere. It was ironic that no matter which way you looked, someone or some place was tagged with a French or Cajun sounding name.

She glanced up at the cuckoo clock hanging behind the sofa; almost eleven. If she hurried, she might catch Ida Jean at the corner coffee shop before she got too busy with the Tout de Suites lunch crowd. If there was a story to be told about a long time resident, a particular house or historical building in Algiers Point, Ida Jean would have the scoop or knew where to find it.

Pepper hopped on her bike and headed for Pelican Avenue in hopes of getting a better look at the Creole cottage and its occupants during the day. If she was really lucky, someone might be in the yard she could casually engage in conversation. This wasn't the first, and it certainly wouldn't be the last time that her relentless curiosity pushed her to find answers. Admittedly, there was always the possibility her overactive imagination had finally gotten the best of her. But, for some unknown reason, this was one of those special times her compulsive behavior challenged her to keep pulling the thread until the ball of yarn unraveled.

When she passed Mount Olive Episcopal Church on Pelican, she braked and climbed off her bike. On the opposite side of the street from the Creole cottage, Pepper negotiated her bicycle the best she could along the uneven brick sidewalk. The pale yellow house with the cerulean blue shutters and gingerbread trim was even more charming in the sunlight. An elderly black woman with a small bag of groceries opened the ornate wrought iron gate and gingerly climbed the steps and entered the house.

Pepper's shoulders slumped as she watched one piece to the puzzle disappear behind a closed door. She *could* march right up the cottage steps, knock on the door, and explain who she was and what she wanted. *And, what exactly did she want?* Pepper thought recognizing the absurdity. Hadn't she learned anything from her impulsive actions from last night and the years before? Could she really be so desperate for a story that she was willing to pour more gasoline on her already fragmented reputation and once again end up in jail?

All true, but how could she ignore her intrinsic instincts that the mysterious woman on the ferry wasn't just a figment of her imagination? Yes, there *were* more questions than answers, but from the depths of her soul Pepper sensed that the encounter on the ferry was more than a chance meeting. There had to be a reason she felt so compelled to follow her instincts with so little to go on.

After weighing all the pros and cons of her compulsive ideas with no viable conclusions, she straddled her bicycle and headed for Café Tout Suites. As she rounded the corner, her spirits lifted when she sighted the colorful flowers and tropical plants painted on the outside walls of the café. The outdoor metal tables and chairs were empty, and there were no customers lined up waiting to get inside to place their orders. She smiled and breathed a sigh of relief. Her timing was perfect. All she needed now was Ida Jean working today and willing to talk.

Pepper parked and locked her bicycle, and then stepped through the dual red doors of the café into a medium size room. The rustic shiplap walls were cluttered with a variety of unique folk art; wooden café-style tables and chairs were scattered around the shop. Ida Jean was sitting on a barstool in the corner sipping a latte and totally engrossed in a *People Magazine*.

Pepper slid onto the stool next to Ida Jean. "May I buy you a refill?" she asked.

Ida Jean looked up. "Lordy, girlfriend," she said with raised eyebrows. "Aren't you the talk of the town?"

Pepper rolled her eyes. "Geez, the news has already crossed the Mississippi?"

"Honey, it don't take long for the beat of the N'awlin's jungle drums to reach the ears of Ida Jean," she smiled. "I'm not just a branch of the grapevine; I'm the root and soul. Nothin' goes on in Orleans Parish without me knowing first."

"The very reason I need to pick your brain," Pepper said.

Ida Jean, a large part of her spilling over the seat of the barstool, swiveled around and faced the journalist. "You tryin' to dig up dirt on somebody else so people will stop talking about you?" she asked with an impish grin; her coal, big black eyes danced with delight.

Pepper laughed. "You know me too well. And, you *are* right. I *do* need a favor.

Ida Jean raised an eyebrow, but said nothing.

"There's a distinct possibility I'm unemployed," Pepper said. "Freelance work may be the only way I'm going to be able to put food on my table. You know everything there is to know about Old Algiers, New Orleans's, the history, and the landmarks. I can't think of anyone who knows more about the historic homes, the people — especially the people than you." Pepper hesitated a moment. "I was hoping maybe you'd consider becoming my source of inspiration until I can land something more permanent. I'd definitely quote you and give Touts as much advertising as possible."

Ida Jean pursed her lips. "Depends on who you might be talking about," she said. "I don't need *my* big mouth getting' me into trouble."

Pepper held up a hand. "No, no. Of course not," she said. "I'm not looking for anything slanderous, only subjects that would be of interest to readers in general. For instance, on the way over to Tout's this morning I passed so many interesting old homes and mom and pop shops. There was one really cute Creole Cottage on Pelican Avenue that caught my eye and captured my curiosity about its history and who might live there."

"Which house you talkin' about?" Ida Jean asked.

"The yellow house with the blue shutters, a garden filled with autumn Clematis and surrounded by an ornate wrought iron fence...the one down the street from Mount Olive Episcopal Church."

"Let me think," Ida Jean said, and then slipped off the barstool walked around the bar and prepared another latte. "Would you like something?" She offered.

"An Americano would be great and that last gooey Cinnamon roll in the glass case," Pepper said.

Ida Jean busied herself with the order. As she placed the Cinnamon roll in front of Pepper, a moment of clarity lit her face with a smile. "Oh my, I haven't thought about

Mama Bea in years," Ida Jean said. "If I'm correct, she's been in that old house pushing close to fifty years now. It seems the past gets fuzzier the older you get."

"Do you know anything of interest about her or the history of the house," Pepper asked.

"I really don't know much," Ida Jean said. "Just know she's been a fixture in the New Orleans area all her life. She used to work for some rich family taking care of kids. Not sure who they all were."

Ida sipped her coffee. "The reason I know the little I know is Mama Bea used to wash dishes for us about ten years ago. But, now that you mentioned her, I *have* seen her walking to the market or riding that silly 'ol bike of hers. I can't help but worry she's going to fall off and break a hip."

Pepper's mind spun like a roulette wheel trying to soak in as much information as she could and looked for the opportunity to interrupt Ida Mae and ask more questions.

Ida stopped talking for a moment and sipped her latte as if her mind was doing a deep dive into her treasure trove of information. She raised an eyebrow. "I do remember this one bizarre quirk of Bea's," she said. "She wouldn't take a step or make an important decision without talking to some psychic. I'm telling you for a fact a week didn't go by without Mama Bea hopping on that ferry to New Orleans."

Ida Jean pursed her lips. "What *was* that spiritualist's name? Everyone who was into that kinda stuff went to this one particular woman. The name escapes me at the moment."

Ida Jean shook her head. "She went to that same crystal gazer like clockwork once a week...Roux...Madam

Dominque Roux. Some place over by Saint Louis Cemetery No. 1 near the French Quarter."

Pepper hopped off the barstool and gave Ida Jean a hug. "Thank you," she said. "You've given me a treasure chest full of ideas to get me started." Pepper reached into her purse and pulled out her billfold to pay for her coffee and roll.

Ida Jean waved off the money with a smile. "Save your pennies, baby. If you ain't got no job, you're going to need every last cent down to the loose change in the bottom of your oversized purse."

CHAPTER 20

BURT finished shaving, tore a corner from the toilet tissue, and placed it on the small nick on his chin. *First time in a long time I've drawn blood*, he mused. *Who would've thought a little bit of brandy in warm milk could knock a man out cold and leave him feeling this sluggish and out of sorts.* Burt splashed cold water on his face trying to wakeup. It was almost noon, and he still needed to go over the guest list and finalize plans for the $25,000 a plate donor dinner to be held at The Eiffel in a couple days.

He slipped on a light blue dress shirt and grabbed a red tie from his suitcase. Dylan's speech for the dinner still needed tweaking to be ready for his approval. Burt's hands instinctively moved through the motions tying a perfect knot in the tie. He picked up the satchel that stored his laptop with one hand and his briefcase with the other and headed down the backstairs to the kitchen.

As Burt descended the stairs, the aromatic scent of fresh brewed coffee welcomed him into the kitchen. Ruby Jo was humming the gospel song "Oh, Happy Day".

"Lovely, Miss Ruby," Burt said. "May I talk you out of a cup of that coffee?"

"Well, mornin', Mr. Harrison. You just coming in or going out?"

Burt laughed and set down his briefcase as she handed him a large mug of steaming coffee. "That big 'ol bed I was snuggled in was just too comfy to crawl out of."

Ruby Jo nodded her head. "Yes suh, I knows what you mean. Some days the body just needs a little longer before kickin' into high gear...may I fix you some breakfast?" She glanced up at the clock. "Or, would you rather have one of Ruby Jo's famous Po' Boy Sandwiches. I'd fry you up some catfish, but Mr. Harley said he was bringing home fresh catch for dinner tonight."

Burt smiled. "Thank you, just coffee for now. I've got a ton of work to take care of."

"You go on out in the garden," she said. "It's a beautiful day, not much humidity...which is a treat here in N'awlin's," she said, opening the door for him. "I'll bring your other briefcase in a minute and maybe some fresh squeezed orange juice."

Burt did as he was told and headed for an over-stuffed cushioned chair shaded by a gnarled-oak tree draped with moss and near an arbor tangled with lingering blossoms of yellow Jasmine. After he sat, he pulled a small table around in front of him and opened his laptop. As the notebook warmed, he placed his cell phone nearby. Burt picked up his cup of coffee with two hands, snuggled deep in the chair, and then closed his eyes and allowed the cool October breeze and the sharp, sweet scent of the Jasmine prepare his mind for the challenging tasks awaiting his attention.

Ruby brought out his briefcase and a tray with a thermal carafe of coffee and basket of biscuits. "Sorry, but we all out of orange juice," she said. "Top of my grocery list today. Mr. Harley can't start his morning without his OJ." She handed Burt a warm biscuit oozing with honey. "Now you let me know if there's anything else I can do for you. I'll be cleaning the downstairs for that big fish fry Mr. Harley is having for all those 'ol cronies that he and Mr.

Dylan run with back in the day." Ruby topped off hot coffee into Burt's cup. "You comin' to the fry tonight, Mr. Burt?"

Burt shook his head. "Afraid not," he said. "This unscheduled stop in New Orleans has added to my workload. If I'm going to get anything done, I think it best I check into a hotel." Burt glanced up at Ruby with a conspiratorial smile, "Harley and his friends are a bit much for me."

Ruby chuckled under her breath. "Yes, suh, yes suh, I knows what you mean."

"Thanks, Ruby Jo, you're a real gem. Is there any way I could talk you into moving to Colorado? I sure could use someone like you to keep me on the straight and narrow."

Ruby smiled. "You could use some fattening up, but Mr. Harley would have nothin' to do with that, for sure," she said, heading back into the house.

As soon as the icons blinked into position on the laptop, Burt set down his coffee cup and immediately checked Dylan's poll numbers. He winced. Allison Benson's numbers had jumped three points over night. Burt slammed the small table with his fist. His laptop and coffee mug danced across the surface. Dylan's little performance last night certainly didn't help the situation, he grumbled. Fortunately, they still had some breathing room. A seven point lead over Allison Benson was nothing to sneeze at. With only a few short weeks left before the election, she had a lot of ground to cover before she became a serious threat.

Burt scrolled through the campaign files on his laptop searching for the two lists he needed to finalize — one was for the updated list of attendees for the $25,000 a plate fund raiser, and the other for potential campaign contributors to add to the invitation list.

There was still a shortfall in the campaign budget, and they needed to tap as many resources as possible. Even though he'd been totally against extending the campaign stay in New Orleans, the Eiffel Dinner *should* help significantly with much needed funds... but, only if they filled the room to capacity. The major pitfall, in this eleventh hour plan, was that the event was only a couple days away, and he promised The Eiffel he'd give them a final headcount today.

Damn, he hoped Harley sent his finalized guest list to campaign headquarters because he certainly didn't give them to him. Burt began to feel the blooming ulcer in his stomach start to burn. *This extended stop was Durham's bright idea.* He grumbled. *The least he could do is complete the one small task he'd asked of him.*

He quickly scanned for an email titled "*Eiffel Dinner Updates*". As soon as he spied the subject, he clicked the message. One sentence bolded, capitalized and highlighted in yellow grabbed his attention: *No updates on donor dinner...still waiting for Mr. Durham's list.*

Burt kicked the leg of the small metal table and knocked over his empty coffee mug. The cup rolled off the edge and shattered onto the brick-paved patio. He slammed the top of his laptop and pushed the table out of his way. With long strides, he crunched across broken pieces of pottery toward the kitchen calling for Ruby Jo. His last ditch hope was Harley had left those important papers with her, or at the very least she would know where to find them.

Ruby Jo wasn't in the kitchen. Burt hustled to the living and dining room areas of the large house hoping he'd find her still cleaning. The downstairs was empty. He yelled up the stairs, but there was no answer.

Burt marched down the hall toward Harley Durham's bedroom suite hoping by some small chance he'd locate Ruby Jo cleaning there. He tapped on the door, called her name; but no luck.

Just when he was ready to give up, he remembered Ruby Jo had mentioned she needed to go to the store to buy groceries for tonight's fish fry. He released an exasperated sigh, started back down the hall and then stopped. He brushed a hand through thinning hair, and then reached down and massaged his eyelids.

Where could those lists be? He could try and call Harley, but who the hell knows if his phone was even on; much less if there'd be a signal out in the middle of the Gulf of Mexico. "I've got to have that list!" Burt growled under his breath. He turned around and headed back to Harley's bedroom.

Before entering he hesitated for a moment. A guest going into someone's personal space without an invitation was not done. His Mama had taught him better than that. But, for Christ's sake he needed that information. Maybe Harley had been in a hurry and left the list on a desk in his rush to meet the Governor's fishing party.

A brief intrusion into another's privacy for such an important matter would be excusable. Right? Harley did want Dylan to win this election as much as the rest of them, he reasoned.

Burt tapped twice with his knuckle, and then slid back the pocket-door. Immediately to his right was an antique roll top desk. Burt rushed over, raised the top and rummaged through a stack of papers until he found the list he was looking for. There were a lot of handwritten notes and scratched out names, but he didn't care. There was enough information to at least get him started.

Burt turned to leave, but stopped. "What the hell?"

A humming noise and a small beam of light peeked through a wide crack in the wall. With the files clasped in his hand he took several hesitant steps toward what appeared to be a concealed room. Burt softly called out. "Harley...? Ruby...Ruby Jo are you in there?" he asked guardedly. Only a low hum and an occasional flicker of light answered back through the crack.

Burt burned with curiosity. He tried to rationalize the light was coming from a closet, but the actual closet door was open and on the other end of the room. He wanted to check it out, but he couldn't make his feet move forward.

There was no doubt in his mind that Harley Durham was capable of just about anything. Hidden secrets behind a wall fit his profile perfectly. A flashback of women's laughter at two in the morning, once again, activated the ulcer already festering in his stomach. Dylan and Harley had been friends for a long time, and he was willing to bet there was plenty of sordid history between those two.

Burt closed the top of the roll top desk and started to leave, but something inside challenged him to stay. His mind spun with a range of possibilities. Behind that wall there could be a mother lode of smoking guns. He cringed. The type of smoke that could not only damage Dylan and this campaign, but maybe other important people who wished to keep secrets hidden from the public's eye. Calculated blackmail against powerful people would be one way to accumulate great wealth and secure a steady income for your golden years.

The longer Burt stared at the steady glow of light seeping through the crack in the wall, the more he was compelled to investigate. But he still wrestled with his conscience. Didn't he have the right to snoop? Wasn't it his duty as campaign manager to protect the president from any nefarious information that might fall into the wrong hands and destroy his candidate's changes for reelection?

Burt flexed his fists over and over again; his heart thumped against his chest. Allison Benson's rising poll numbers ping ponged through his mind and collided with his mother's inner voice reminding him to respect people's personal space.

The steady glow of light peeking through the small crack summoned Burt like the siren's song. All he needed to do was slide the hidden door back, just a little, and take a quick look inside. Only a few feet away were possibly the answers to a lot of unanswered questions that had been nagging him since the beginning of this campaign.

He walked over to the small crack and wrapped his fingers around the narrow opening, but stopped.

What if Harley and Dylan had been blackmailing people together over the years and that was the reason they both had gotten away with so much for so long?

Oh God, what am I doing to myself? This election will be the death of me.

CHAPTER 21

PEPPER gazed at the top of her desk now void of her old-fashioned Rolodex, the Marquetery pencil holder she picked up on her last trip to Spain, and her coveted bobble-head of Drew Brees that he had given to her as a joke. Three years of her life now easily fit into her oversized Gucci bag. She looked across the low partitions separating the staff in the newsroom and hoped to catch sight of her boss. He, along with most everyone else, were either avoiding her, on their afternoon coffee break, or chasing down newsworthy stories.

She heaved the strap of the now over-weight purse onto her shoulder and glanced one last time at the giant mural painted on the wall. The images depicted photos and newspaper pages of historic New Orleans. For a brief moment she was overcome with a bitter sweet nostalgia. As much as she had complained, her time spent here was never as bad as she made it. New Orleans and *The Advocate* had welcomed her with open arms; had offered her refuge from another dark moment in her life. Sadly, once again, she'd managed to burn another bridge. *Would her self-destructive path never end*?

Pepper tucked her head and walked down the ultra modern spiral staircase and pushed open the glass and metal door. For a brief moment she stood outside not knowing which way to turn. She was tempted to go into PJ'S Coffee Shop and try to find her boss to say goodbye and thank him for the opportunity he'd offered. Mostly she wanted to try and explain her bizarre behavior. Instead, she pulled her cell phone out of her pocket and called an Uber. Hopefully, by the time the car arrived, she will have made her mind where she was going. For now, she should probably just take the ferry home, hole up in her cute little house on Elmira praying opportunity would knock on her door.

The Uber pulled up in front of *The Advocate* building. As she opened the door, the driver asked, "Are you Penelope?" Pepper nodded and climbed in.

A short ride later, the driver dropped her off in front of the Westin Hotel on Canal. Pepper glanced across the street to Harrah's Casino. The seductive call from the black jack tables beckoned her to come inside and to drown her sorrows in a game of chance. As tempting as it was, good sense forced her to turn her back on her number one vice and head for the ferry terminal.

When the traffic light turned green, Pepper hurried across the street and over the railroad tracks toward the entrance to the ferry. The steel plates beneath the passageway banged beneath her feet and echoed against the walls. There was already a hodgepodge of characters patiently lined up waiting for the return trip to Algiers Point.

The incoming ferry docked and the passengers disembarked and headed into the city. Out of the corner of her eye, Pepper caught a glimpse of a woman exiting the ferry. That very same person held an uncanny resemblance to the elderly black lady she suspected lived in that cute cottage on Pelican Avenue. Pepper's pulse raced as if she'd been injected with an overdose of adrenaline.

Every instinct in her body screamed — *here comes one of the key links to unraveling the events surrounding most everything she saw last night.*

Pepper tried to fight the nagging obsession, but it wouldn't let go. All she knew was that from the moment she first laid eyes on the familiar statuesque lady on last night's ferry, she was unable to ignore her gut instincts. There was a story — a story that needed to be told.

Holding firm to her oversized Gucci bag and to the ire of the passengers trying to move toward the ferry's entrance, Pepper pushed against the embarking crowd like a salmon swimming upstream. No one, or anything, was going to stop her from keeping the elderly black woman within sight. This may be her last chance to seize the opportunity to speak with her.

CHAPTER 22

MAMA BEA reached up and struggled to pull herself up the streetcar steps.

"Here, let me help you," said a cute little blonde with a purse almost as big as she was.

"God bless you child," Mama Bea said. "Seems my old joints are stiffer than usual today."

Bea scanned her streetcar pass and walked to the rear of the tram. She sat with a group of familiar faces all heading to the same place and at the same time every Monday afternoon.

"Afternoon, Miss Bea. Thought you were about to miss you're ride," one of the passengers said. "Who's that young woman who be helpin' you?"

Bea looked up. "No idea. Just glad she took the time to give this old woman a hand. Why you ask?"

"She just keep on staring at you like she know you, that's all."

"Mind yo' own business now, Mavis. She got nothin' to do with me."

The streetcar rattled its way down Canal Street for several blocks, and then turned right, following the tracks away from Canal, and headed East on Rampart. When the digital reader announced Conti Street, Mama Bea pulled the cord letting the operator know this was her stop. She and several other passengers exited the streetcar and all headed in the same direction. She crossed the divided lanes of Basin Street, passed the Statue of Benito Juarez, and then walked along the battered, but enduring brick wall that had surrounded St. Louis Cemetery since 1789.

The late afternoon shadows had started their slow crawl; the temperature dropped from overly warm to pleasantly cool as if the air conditioner had finally kicked on after being off all day. Along with a small group of people, Mama Bea leaned patiently against the cemetery wall and waited for the tourists to slowly but surely file through St. Louis No. 1's narrow passageway to the outside.

"It already fifteen past four and my po' back is about to give out," Bea grumbled. "Seems the tourists stay later and later befoe' we folks with special passes get our turn to pay our respects to the dead."

Those standing nearby nodded in agreement.

As soon as the final tour group exited the St. Louis Cemetery, Mama Bea presented her pass to the gatekeeper. After she entered, Bea walked past a bank of vaults stacked one on top of the other. Some of the graves located on the ground were partially visible, while many others were hidden beneath the earth offering evidence that New Orleans was, in fact, gradually sinking.

Bea continued to weave her way through the maze of tombs until she reached Plot 347 where the Laveau-Glapion family crypt was located. As she set her shopping bag on the ground, she caught a glimpse of a folding chair leaning against the tomb.

"Lordy, Madam Laveau, the cemetery caretaker must be either a disciple of yours, or my guardian angel. You two must've sensed there's a lot weighing on my heart today and needed to sit a spell. It be true. I do have a lot on my mind." A soft breeze brushed against her cheek. Mama Bea touched her face and smiled.

"Well, I'm not sure where to begin," she said unfolding the chair and sitting down. "Madam Roux always tol' me when nothin' seemed to ease my mind, I should talk to a true healer. There's no one like that around here no more," she said, "justa bunch of charlatans and wannabes. If you willin' to listen, I'm gonna take my chances with the one true queen and speak the truth about what's nagging my heart."

Mama Bea reached into her shopping bag and pulled out a photo. She laid the picture on the ground in front of the tomb. "This here's my baby sister, Gabrielle. She's been bedeviling my dreams lately more than usual. Maybe 'cause my son, André, startin' to ask mo' and mo' questions about my Gabrielle like he did when he was a youngun'.

Bea bowed her head; she clasped her hands beneath her chin and furrowed her brow. "I...I don't know how to answer him." She released a long soulful sigh. "Figured after all these years it don't matter no mo'. But my conscience be hauntin' me terrible. That's why I come to you with my tormented soul."

Mama Bea stood, touched Marie Laveau's tomb. "I knows you, too, had heartbreak durin' your life. We share a similar tragedy back at Lake Pontchartrain. I hear tell your baby girl, Marie II, one of the few of your fifteen children who lived through the yellow fever plague, so long ago, drowned in that big 'ol lake just like my Gabrielle. There's no doubt'n both those gals could get themselves in a mess of trouble; sometimes they did bad things."

Bea lifted her glasses and wiped tears from her eyes. "I'm afraid my Gabrielle's soul won't rest until she's settled everything back here on earth. Her demons and my conscience are restless and won't let me be. Folks here swear you a true healer; one known to have a caring and benevolent heart; one who has a way with the spirits."

With a piece of chalk Mama Bea scratched three X's on Marie Laveau's crypt, turned in a circle three times, and then knocked on the tomb. She cleared her throat and said, "What's Mama Bea to do? Release Gabrielle's tormented spirit from this world, or tear out my André's beating heart with the truth?" Anguished tears poured from Mama Bea until she could cry no more.

Regaining her composure, she reached into her shopping bag for the special offerings she had brought for Marie Laveau in hopes her spirit would grant a favor. Bea discarded dead leaves and wilted buds from one of the stone vases positioned on either side of the tomb's façade and replaced the old with a fresh bundle of sage.

In the second vase she put three white roses. "I hope this offering brings both Andrè and me peace and lets the good energy flow," Mama Bea said. She kissed her fingertips and touched the three X's she'd marked on the tomb.

Just as the sun slipped deeper behind the tall buildings of New Orleans, Bea gathered Gabrielle's photo and the other leftover belongings she had brought. She folded the chair, leaned it against the tomb, and headed for the exit and home.

***

Pepper leaned against the backside of Our Lady of Guadalupe Church across the street from St. Louis Cemetery and waited. More and more cars and busses whizzed past as Monday's workday came to an end. She checked her wristwatch not believing an entire hour had passed. Strange place for a psychic, she mused. How much advice can you get from a dead spiritualist? She rolled her eyes and focused on the cemetery's main entrance.

"Damn gate Nazi," she grumbled. She wouldn't be hanging around like some stalker or street vagrant if that gate guard would have let her step inside the cemetery for just a moment. All she wanted to do was make sure she hadn't followed the wrong woman. But, oh no, she *didn't* have a "Special Pass", wasn't family. The guy wouldn't even accept her measly bribe — money she could no longer spare. Who did he think he was? Saint Peter guarding heaven's pearly gates?

Pepper checked her watch again. There was a good chance she follow the wrong person. With the way her luck had been running lately, she probably had. Right now, her common sense told her to give up this fruitless folly, but how could she after the old man with the keys finally admitted there *was* a woman inside that *did* match the description of Beatrice Bélair. He even went as far to say she had been coming to Saint Louis off and on for years and always to visit Marie Laveau's gravesite.

Pepper stifled a chuckle. A Voodoo Queen! What kinda business would someone have with a spooky woman who had been dead for over one hundred and thirty-years? Pepper rolled her eyes. There were some things about New Orleans she'd never be able to wrap her mind around.

She shifted from one foot to the other. *It was way past time to let go of this dead-end*, she reasoned. Besides, even if she had had the opportunity to speak with Ms. Bélair what would she have said; have asked?

The last twenty-four hours have really knocked me off my game, Pepper thought. The one thing she prided herself for was being properly prepared before interviewing any possible leads. Not this time. This time she'd turned into some nut-job racing around trying to make something out of nothing. When had she become a tabloid journalist?

"Not me. Not today," Pepper said as she hoisted her bag over her shoulder. She needed to go home and do her homework — and that meant some serious time on the computer. If she was good at anything, research, compiling details, and fitting all the pieces together were her best asset.

If she'd learned one thing as she matured as a successful reporter over the years, proper prep work was the key to success. Pepper smiled and said, "And a hellava lot of luck." Today she might have hit a roadblock, but tomorrow was another day. She knew deep down in her gut, one way or the other, she *would* piece together this budding mystery.

CHAPTER 23

"RUUUBY JOOOOOOO"..." Harley yelled at the top of his lungs.

"I'm comin'...I'm coming, Mr. Harley, as fast as my tired 'ol feet can move," Ruby Jo called out as she hustled down the long hallway wiping her hands on a dishtowel.

"Who's been in my Golden Parachute Room?" Harley growled the moment she entered the bedroom suite.

"Mr. Harley, you buck-naked! You know I'm not one of those girls. Too old and not interested." She frowned.

"Hush up, Ruby, and tell me who's been in the house today."

"Well, let me think," she said. "Only Mr. Burt and he been busy all day talkin' on the phone and working on that big event for Mr. Dylan. He hardly left the garden to even go to the bathroom.

"Are you sure he never came back to this room?"

"Well, a body can never be too sure," she said. "But he don't seem like a man go snoopin' around where he don't belong. A real gentleman, if you ask me."

"I didn't ask. You know how important my privacy is. That's why I pay you the big bucks."

"Yes, suh, yes suh, I knows. Are you sure you didn't forget to shut that panel door this mornin' before you went fishin' with Mr. Dylan and the other boys?" she asked, eyes still cast downward and away from the nude Harley. "It's not the first time that door get stuck open like that, ya know."

Harley narrowed his eyes. "What are you talking about?"

Ruby Jo scratched her cheek, looked toward the ceiling. "Couple weeks ago when I come in here to clean, that door be wide open. Don't you remember I tol' you about that? Said maybe you'd needed a handyman to fix it."

Harley grabbed Ruby by the shoulders. "No, Ruby...you *didn't* tell me about that," he said through a clenched jaw.

Ruby Jo tried to pull away. "Now, Mr. Harley, you stop accusin' me of stuff. I've been loyal to you for now on twenty years. You just forgettin' a lot lately."

Harley released Ruby Jo. He walked over to the bed and slipped on his robe. "What do you mean forgetting things?" he asked. "You tell me one important thing I've forgotten."

"You forget about poor Miss Peezee locked up in that crazy house. She calls you again and again to come get her, but you just leave her be. Shame on you, Mr. Harley. Nobody should treat their kin like that. Yo poor sister done suffer enough in her life."

"Don't you have hush puppies and dirty rice to make?" Harley growled. "We've got fifty people headin' our way in about two hours."

"I been tryin' to tell ya I be too busy for this nonsense," Ruby Jo said, as she turned and headed back to the kitchen. She stopped and yelled back. "There's two cold ones iced for ya by the tub."

Harley pulled the pocket door to his suite closed. He dropped the robe to the floor, popped open one of the ice cold beers and climbed into the steaming hot tub of water laced with the aroma of lavender. He turned on the jets and allowed the forced bubbles to massage and soothe his aching back and joints. Maybe he shouldn't have been so hard on Ruby Jo, he thought. She's the only person in the world he trusted with his life and his secrets. That wise bulk of a woman knew him better than he knew himself. He winced. She also knew how to lay on the guilt when he got too hard on her. He downed the last of the first beer and popped open the next.

Harley leaned back on the tub pillow. When he closed his eyes, thoughts of his baby sister drifted into his mind.

Peezee, Peezee my dear crazy-loon of a sister, he reflected. No matter what Ruby Jo thought, Sherri Dee was the last person on earth that should be roaming free. Besides being meaner and more unhinged than a hog-tied twenty-foot alligator, she had too many secrets locked inside that scrambled brain of hers. As far as he was concerned, his sister should to be kept on mind-numbing drugs until she took her last breath. Thank goodness he was the one with the power of attorney — at least for right now.

He ran more hot water into the tub; his mind continued to wander. The one flaw in his plan to keep his sister caged indefinitely was Roland Ongerón, her scheming, drug dealing common-law husband. That bastard was as crazy as his sister... if not more. Fortunately, that loony tune was still upstate in prison — at least he hoped he was.

Harley slid deep into the tub, ducked his head under the water, held his breath for a moment and then resurfaced. He swiped the water from his face. If and when Roland *was* released from prison, that was going to open an entirely new can of worms.

Harley stepped out of the tub and wrapped a towel around his waist. It might be time for him to make a call to his friend the warden. He made a mental note to double check Roland's proposed release date from Angola.

***

Ruby Jo beat the eggs until the yellow was as pale as fresh squeezed lemon juice. "Whooooheee!" She exhaled and wiped her brow with the skirt of her apron. "If Mr. Harley ever find out that Miss Peezee was let loose while he was away on business and I let her sleep here in this house, he gonna feed me to the 'gators," she said as she poured the liquid over the dry ingredients.

"What's that you say, Miss Ruby?"

"Mind yo own beeswax, Rufus. You got Mint Julep punch to make for all Mr. Harley's thirsty friends. They gonna be here befoe we both ready."

"Don't ya'll get all huffy with me 'cause Mr. Harley call you back to his room and yell," Rufus said. "None of that my fault."

"Get on out of my kitchen befoe...."

"I'm goin'...I'm goin'," the bartender said. "Don't know why Mr. Harley keeps you on all these years. You're a mean-spirited woman."

Ruby Jo scraped minced chicken gizzards into bacon fat; the grease crackled and splattered. "Nobody knows half of what goes on under this roof," she huffed under her breath. The things she'd seen and heard. "My, oh my, oh my," she said shaking her head. If she didn't know better, she'd swear that the door to the devil's kingdom was beneath that very house and that Satan and Mr. Harley both be holdin' her soul captive. Ruby mopped her brow with the dishtowel, and then added green and red peppers, the onion, and the rest of the ingredients to the browning gizzards.

Harley walked into the kitchen smelling like a field of lavender in full bloom. He leaned over Ruby Jo's shoulder, plucked a chicken gizzard out of the frying pan. "Smells like dirty rice." He kissed her cheek. "Sorry about earlier. If I can't trust you, I can't trust anybody."

***

The musical doorbell chimed over and over again. Harley cursed under his breath. "Animals. Do they think I'm deaf?" He flung open the front door and planted a phony smile on his face.

"Hey, Durham, 'bout time you answered the damn door. We're thirsty and craving Ruby Jo's hush puppies and dirty rice."

"Yeah," another man said, pushing his way through the door. "You promised fresh grilled Swordfish and all the Mint Juleps we could drink."

"Get your butts on in here, you bastards," Harley laughed. "The party's already started."

As if on cue, a zydeco band struck up the *Mag Hop*.

"Hot damn, Harley. You even hired the best Cajun band straight from the Bayou. You one hellava friend."

Harley laughed, grabbed a Mint Julep off Rufus' tray, chugged it and grabbed a second. His thoughts spun faster than an airboat's propeller. As hard as he tried, he was having a tough time keeping a lid on his resentment toward Dylan. How dare he bail on the party he'd planned especially for him! Dylan was a damn fool, and he'd better hope spending time with his wife was worth losing all the potential money that just walked through his front door? *Well, no skin off my knee.* Harley grumbled to himself. He wasn't the one running for president of the United States and needed money to keep his campaign on track.

Harley grabbed a third Mint Julep and mingled with the crowd. He laughed, joked, and made endless excuses for Dylan's absence. With each passing hour, beneath the fake smiles, his irritation with his friend blossomed into full blown hostility. He was tired of being treated like a low-life Cajun from the backwaters of the Bayou... tired of bowing to Dylan's demands and whims... tired of being his errand boy. Just once he'd like to be given the credit due for all the things he'd done for the Randle family for over thirty years.

A sneer twitched his cheek. Be very careful, my friend. You can only push a fella so far. Best you not forget who knows all your dirty secrets hidden deep within your black soul. *I'm the one who knows where all the bodies are buried.*

As the evening progressed, the lingering die-hard guests sat around tables in the garden, smoked cigars, and rubbed full bellies.

"Hey Harley, time to tap another keg," a guest said. "This one's only pumping foam."

"We don't need any more booze," one of the other guests said. "What we need is for Harley to tell us the real reason Dylan's not here."

Harley inhaled a mouthful of his sweet Cuban cigar and puffed smoke rings above his head. "He's in the middle of Lake Pontchartrain screwing his wife."

"Are you sure it's his wife?" The men laughed.

"Yeah, Harley. You been pimping for Dylan again while he's been out on the campaign trail and the wife find out?"

Harley smiled, sipped his beer and yielded to the banter among his guests.

"Have a little respect for the first lady of these United States," a man said. "Dylan's a fool for straying. Céline is one fine piece of ass."

"Agreed, but we all know that 'ol dog's pecker is always sniffin' the air for new meat. No way could one woman satisfy him.

"If I remember correctly, D-Rod loved his meat dark."

"Nah, I heard he gave those up years ago," a man swimming in the pool said. "Remember when he was engaged to Peezee? She said she'd cut off his pecker if she ever caught him with another one."

Laughter rolled through the group of intoxicated men.

"Speaking of Peezee, Harley, your sister still at one of those funny farms?"

"Shut up, Palazzo," Harley snapped. "It's none of your damn business. Enough of this tea party gossip. Want me to call some broads?"

Just as Harley reached for his phone, large rats with orange teeth and webbed feet scrambled across the ivy-laden wall and raced through the remaining guests. The creatures jumped onto tables, into the pool. The guests screamed like little girls; knocked over chairs. Glassware shattered on brick pavers as the grown men pushed and shoved their way into the house.

As the last guest escaped into the house, Harley slammed the door to the garden. He pressed his hand against the glass pane and glared into his backyard that was swarming with twenty-pound nutria.

Harley turned away from the door. "Party's over," he said as he ushered his guests to the front door. "Sorry about that pesky vermin invasion. Obviously, it's someone's sick idea of a practical joke."

When the last man climbed into his chauffeured car, Harley shut the front door and leaned against the etched glass frame. A bitter taste polluted his mouth; he narrowed his eyes. There was only one person who would dare try to pull such a vicious joke on him and think they could get away with it — and that was one giant rat with dyed, fire-engine red hair. And, she was supposed to be locked away.

Thoughts, answers, questions all swirled in his head at once. Harley grabbed the nearest chair and sat down. How in the hell could his crazy-ass sister pull this off? He paid a bundle of money to that psychiatric institution to keep Sherri Dee under wraps. Not to mention her confinement came with a guarantee she would never see the light of day until *he* flipped the switch. She was clever, but not as smart as him.

Rage mixed with revenge collided like two freight trains on the same track. *Sherri Dee had a lot of nerve using one of his old tricks against him to get attention*, Harley thought with a snarl. *The nuthouse may no longer be good enough for his sister.*

A sinister grin twitched the corners of his mouth. Peezee, Peezee, who always aimed to pleazee. Not this time, my dear sibling, he thought. *You may have finally outlived your usefulness.*

Harley pulled his iPhone out of his shirt pocket and pressed the ID button, "Siri, call a twenty-four hour animal exterminator." As he waited to be connected to the service, he raced down the long hallway to his bedroom suite. He slid back the pocket door to his bedroom and with phone still to his ear, he charged over to the bookcase displaying the Civil War chess set. In his haste he knocked over the pewter replica of Grant along with several soldiers. Harley gave Bobby Lee a one-eighty turn and watched as the secret door slide open with ease; the auto-light flashed on.

As Harley stepped into the small hidden room his hands shook; a breath-denying pressure pressed against his chest as he pulled the lockbox from its hiding place. He fumbled for the magnetic box tucked beneath the desk and retrieved the key. Harley inhaled a deep breath and tried to calm the out-of-control tremble that had seized his hand. He exhaled, turned the key and unlocked the box — empty.

"Peezeeeeeee," Harley howled. "I'm coming for you."

CHAPTER 24

THE VOICES of Diana Ross and Lionel Ritchie crooning "Endless Love" carried across the secluded cove in Lake Pontchartrain; candles flickered as a soft October breeze rocked the anchored forty-foot sailboat. Dylan reached across the table and covered Céline's hand with his. "Thank you for agreeing to see me tonight," he said, oozing as much sincerity he could muster.

Céline gently slipped her hand away and picked up her wine glass. "The purple, gold, and green rose pedals strewn across the deck were a nice touch," she smiled. "Maybe there's still a little of that loveable, romantic I fell in love with so many years ago inside you."

Dylan topped off his drink, leaned forward in his chair. "I want to show you that man again..." He hesitated; his eyes pleaded, "if only you'll let me. I've made a lot of mistakes in my life, my darling, but you are not one of them."

Céline slid her chair away from the table, stood and walked to the stern of the boat. "You couldn't have chosen a more perfect night to be out on the lake," she said. "Away from the city there are a million stars. And the moon...the moon, I can almost reach up and touch the radiant edges and feel a warmth from the glow.

Dylan joined her, placed his arm around her waist, and gently pulled her close. "And, you said *I* was the romantic." He tried to kiss her.

Céline pushed away. "No, Dylan, stop. I didn't agree to come so you could sweep me off my feet."

He grabbed her wrist. "Then, why *did* you come?"

She held up her hand clinched in his fist. "This! This is why I came." She yanked her arm away. "The days for me being your punching bag are over. And, it's just not me. You do it with anyone that doesn't agree with you. How do you expect yourself to be reelected when you've turned into a monster?"

"Céline, what in the hell are you talking about? Punching bag? I've never hit you. I've *never* hit any woman. I admit at times I get a little impatient with people and maybe my tone can get a bit sharp now and then."

He threw up his hands and walked back toward the table. He turned back around and said, "For God's sake what do you expect? The responsibilities of becoming president of the United States overnight weigh heavy on a man. But calling me violent... that's just crazy talk."

"You've changed, Dylan. Your thirst for power is frightening...you only think about yourself...your image. You have no respect for anyone, particularly me." Tears welled in her eyes.

"Poor little Céline. Did the big bad president hurt your feelings? Hold your hand a little too tight?" His mouth twisted into a sneer.

"See! There. That's what I'm talking about. You're becoming more and more aggressive...more verbally abusive."

"What do you expect from me?" Dylan snapped. "I'm in the middle of the political fight of my life. You know how important being elected is for me. That bitch, Allison Benson, is breathing down my neck. I have to grovel for as many votes as I can get. Don't you understand how much I need you by my side? It doesn't mean I don't care. Sometimes I lose my patience."

"Exactly," Céline said, "and therein lays the problem."

"Alright, alright," Dylan threw up his hands. "I apologize...I'll try to do better. Forgive me for wanting the best for both of us." He picked up the wine bottle. "Come back to the table; sit down. Accept my apology and let's get on with our lives." He topped off her wine glass; held it toward her. "We all better now?" he asked sarcastically.

"No, Dylan. Not this time. I've had enough."

"Enough of what?"

"Your threats."

"My threats? You're delusional."

Céline narrowed her eyes. "Ohhhhhhh, you've threatened plenty of times."

"What? When have I ever threatened you?"

"Two nights ago, you almost shoved Claréne off the stage at the Superdome."

Dylan jerked his head around. "What did you say?"

Céline caught the gasp in her throat. *Stupid, stupid woman*, she chastised herself. "I...I said you danced me to the edge of the stage at the rally, and then threatened to let me fall because I didn't join in your little victory."

"No... No," he said with narrowed eyes. "That *is not* what you said. You said Claréne. Why did you say Claréne?"

Céline fought against the paralyzing anxiety clawing its way through her body inch by inch.

Dylan sneered; filled his wine glass to the brim. He slowly shook his head, a menacing smile rested on his face. "So you and your twin sister, Claréne, switched places today. Very clever. I actually fell for your little ruse. Everyone must have. Not one single person even suggested such an outrageous possibility," he said, and then sat down at the table. He took a sip, and then replaced the wine goblet in front of him. He began to gently circle the glass edge with his fingertips until the crystal sang a high-pitched song.

"How long, Céline, how long have you and your clone been pulling this little stunt?"

"Chicago, Dallas, and now New Orleans," she confessed.

Dylan's head bobbed up and down, he ran a finger across his lips. "So that's why you've been avoiding me physically and stayed out of my bed for two months."

Céline wrapped her arms around her shoulders, attempting to ward off the deep chill seeping into her bones. She had to get off this boat. Dylan's mood and reaction to how she and her sister duped him was making her very nervous. He had become so unpredictable the last couple of years and their relationship had only gotten worse. She casually slipped her hand into her pocket.

"What's the matter, Céline, you look a little nervous," Dylan said. "Relax. I'm starting to warm up to your little game of duplicity. In fact, the more I think about it, the more I may prefer this new arrangement you two cooked up. It certainly could spice up our dead love life."

He topped off his wine glass again, stood, and walked to the opposite side of the boat from Céline; a sly grin rested on his mouth. "Your sister *does* have the passion of a tigress. Now that I think about it, I did see that intense fire, defiance in those eyes as I leaned her over the edge, holding her life and limb in my hands. Ohhhh, that look dared me to release her in front of all those people. It actually turned me on. Unlike you and your mousy personality that leaves a man cold and needing more."

Dylan leaned back against the side of the boat, rested his arm across his body. "Hell, feel free to switch permanently with your wildcat sister. What do you say, Céline? You think your twin sister will go for it? I'm in all the way. Just say the word."

Céline grabbed her iPhone and pulled it out of her pocket.

"Who are you calling," Dylan asked. "We're miles from the Marina. I don't know what you're worried about. I won't touch you tonight or ever again...even if you begged me. Trust me," Dylan grabbed his crotch, "there are plenty of woman who want and appreciate what this power package has to offer."

Céline stepped further away from Dylan, but didn't dare turn her back. She punched in a number, waited a moment willing the other end to answer. When the connection was finally made, her face lit up. "André, pick me up and hurry."

Dylan's laugh echoed across the secluded cove. "I should have known you'd have a backup plan. You always do. I respect that, I really do. Was your bodyguard involved in your little game?"

He tossed down the remaining wine in his glass, walked back to the table, and picked up the now empty bottle. He reached back, grabbed a new Pinot Noir, and uncorked it. "Before you leave me out here in the middle of nowhere without a pilot to get this boat ashore, my dear, sweet, loyal first lady, promise me *you*...not your sister Claréne...*you* will be at both the mayor's lunch tomorrow at Emeril's and the Eiffel Donor Dinner." Dylan pointed a finger at her. "You and your sister help get me elected, and then both of you can go straight to hell as far as I'm concerned."

With the roar of a fast-approaching speedboat, Dylan cupped his hand around a candle, blew out the flickering flame. He picked up the bottle and his glass and headed for the berth below, and then stopped and said without looking back. "Have a pleasant evening, my love. I'll see you at Emeril's for lunch. Wear that sexy red dress that shows off your lovely cleavage — definitely your best asset."

CHAPTER 25

CÈLINE sat on the floor with her head in Mama Bea's lap; her body quaked from uncontrollable tears. André paced; Claréne sat next to her sister and stroked her hair.

"Let it out, let it all out," Mama Bea comforted. "You safe now." She glared up at André. "Why did you leave her alone with that man? Isn't it your job to protect this child?"

André sat on the sofa, stood up, and then sat back down. "Sorry, Mama. It doesn't work like that. I was ordered to stay away from the boat and give the president and first lady their privacy."

"I don't care what those men tell you," she chastised. "Céline like yo' sister. What would you have done if something bad happen to her?"

"You don't understand, Mama. Rules are different for the president of the United States," André pleaded for his mother to understand. "There's protocol."

"Harrumph." Mama scoffed. "This child more important than that man and your protocol. You's knows it and I knows it."

"Mama Bea, André did the best he could," Claréne said. "He took a huge risk just being shouting distance from that boat after he was ordered to stay away. It was Céline's choice to go with Dylan. She needed to try and talk some sense into her husband."

Céline heaved a deep sigh, lifted her head from Mama Bea's lap. "It is my fault." she sniffled. Mama Bea handed her a Kleenex. She blew her nose and said, "The night actually started off very pleasant; even romantic. But the more we talked, the angrier we both got. And then, my big mouth let it slip that Claréne and I have been switching places."

"Why you even agree to meet that man after the way he been treatin' you?" Mama Bea furrowed her brow. "You already tol' me he was unpredictable and had a mean streak."

Céline uncurled her long legs and stood. "Dylan is the most powerful man on earth, and I'm married to him. As first lady it is my duty to stand by his side and support him no matter what."

Mama Bea shook her head back and forth. Um...um...um... just ain't right...just ain't right."

Céline sat on the sofa next to André. "I broke the rules playing a dangerous game. I did it because I'm too weak to stand up to Dylan. It was past time for me to take some responsibility and try to make things right between a husband and wife," she dropped her head into her hand. "I put Claréne in danger. André could lose his job. I'm as selfish as my Dylan." Tears began to flow again. "God only knows how this will end."

Mama Bea stood, brushed the front of her quilted housecoat with her hands. "You 'all go to bed now. Let Mama Bea think a spell."

Céline, Claréne, and Andrea each gave Mama Bea a hug and kissed her on the cheek, and then headed to their respective rooms. Mama Bea followed them part way down the long hallway, then ducked into the kitchen and out to her porch. She sat in the rocker, closed her eyes and rocked back and forth. Bea tried to find comfort in the late night serenade from the crickets and nightingale's song, but all she heard was the squeaks and creaks made by the rocking chair. She was alone and being mocked by a past that refused to stay buried.

Mama Bea stopped rocking, picked up the Bible she kept on the nearby side table. She placed her hand on the book and turned her eyes to the heavens. She whispered into the shadows. "Dear, Lord, I hate to bother you with my petty troubles, but I need you. I need you to please send somebody or something to lift this burdensome storm that's brewing over my family. How am I to help these children if I don't know how to soothe my own troublesome soul? My heart keeps telling me it be time to tell André who his real Mama is. But my, oh my, it seems that'll just be the straw that break that 'ol camel's back everybody always talkin' about.

Bea sat in silence holding the Bible close to heart. She looked up one more time at the star laden sky and nodded. "I hear you, Lord. If that be your will, then so be it."

CHAPTER 26

DAY 3

BEFORE the sun even peeked over the horizon, Mama Bea was on her hands and knees crawling inside the back of the storage closet swiping spider webs and kicking up years of undisturbed dust. "It's here." she grumbled. "I know it's here somewhere." She grabbed the edge of the doorframe and slowly pulled herself upright.

Bea stretched her back, and then fanned the dark space with the flashlight. She shuffled boxes around one more time. On her third try, buried inside a water-damaged corrugated box that was tucked in the deepest corner of the closet, she found what she was looking for — Gabrielle's hatbox suitcase. A rush of sadness flooded Bea's heart. She remembered their Mama and Daddy had given her sister that piece of luggage on her sixteenth birthday. *Poor little gal never did get to take a trip,* Bea sighed. *She died before she was barely seventeen, unwed and pregnant with some stranger's child.*

Mama Bea pulled the luggage out of the box and shut the door to the storage room. She carried the heavy bag to her room and placed the once brightly colored flora case onto her bed. Bea grabbed a nearby towel and swiped away as much of the thirty-five years of dust as possible, but the once lovely piece of luggage was forever scarred with large black spots and smelled of mold.

Mama Bea sat on the edge of the bed. She took off her glasses and wiped them with the skirt of her apron. She rested a hand on top of the suitcase in hopes of channeling the spirit of her deceased sister tucked inside the suitcase — a suitcase filled with Gabrielle's precious childhood treasures and teenage memories.

Curiosity, nostalgia, and a heap of sadness wrestled with Mama Bea's emotions like a classroom full of children vying for their teacher's attention. Maybe she should let sleepin' dogs lie. What good would come if she showed André all these things? He never knew his real Mama, just her. Baby Andrè almost died that same day they dragged Gabrielle out of Lake Pontchartrain. His mama's lungs filled with water; a gash sliced across her head. It was a miracle that boy born at all. Only by the grace of God and some fast thinking paramedics saved that baby's life. Mama Bea furrowed her brow. *They tol' me they ripped that child right out of Gabrielle's belly in the nick of time. Um...um...um... miracles do happen.*

With trepidation Mama Bea tried to unsnap the first latch, but the rusted brass hardware resisted. She wiggled the stubborn clasp until it reluctantly released. A surge of uneasiness made her hand shake; more memories rushed to the surface.

There was nobody left to take care of that poor baby but she, Mama Bea recalled, and she certainly was no prize. She had no husband, no home. Luckily, she lived at the plantation house in Chalmette taking care of Miss Lily Mae's two adorable five-year-old twin girls. The missus had been a widow since those poor babies just two years old. *Life do have a way of dealing its share of tragedy and heartbreak when one sits and ponders awhile*, Bea thought.

Bea was forever thankful that Miss Lily Mae insisted she and the new baby boy both come live with her and the girls. Mama Bea rolled her eyes. To this day she don't know if it was Miss Lily Mae's generous heart or a means to give her mo' time to spend in N'awlin's' with her highfaluting friends. *No matter to me*, Bea thought. *Miss Lilly Mae gave her a family and a home to love.*

A beam of sunshine slipped through the closed blinds and rested across the suitcase. Mama Bea clasped her hands together in her lap, stared down at the once bright pink and yellow flowers. A far away voice whispered in her ear. "It must be done." She unsnapped the last latch and revealed the hidden past.

***

"Mama...Mama? Are you okay?" André asked tapping on Bea's bedroom door. Muffled and mournful sobs answered back from the other side of the wall. André burst through the door fearing the worse. His heart split in two the moment he witnessed his mother, her hands grasping a hot pink book covered with hand-drawn hearts held close to her chest. His mother rocked back and forth; tears streamed down her face; her body shook out of control.

A suitcase he didn't recognize was lying on the bed wide open. Photographs, a small trophy, Mardi Gras beads, old report cards, framed certificates, even a couple blue and red award ribbons were strewn across the bed; some items were on the floor; some were in Mama Bea's lap. André rushed over, pulled his mother off the bed, and held her close until he could feel her body relax. He took her by the shoulders. "Mama, what's wrong?" he asked. She wouldn't look at him; tears once again streamed down her face. He took her chin in his hand. "You're scaring me. Talk to me...please talk to me," he pleaded.

Mama Bea backed away from André shaking her head, knelt on the floor, and gathered printed programs, a red ribbon, and several photos. She heaved herself up and dropped the items into the opened case. One photo fluttered to the floor. André picked it up. He looked at the picture and then back at his mother. "This is Gabrielle, isn't it?" he asked. "The sister you never talk about."

Mama Bea nodded, released a forlorn sigh, and sat on the edge of the bed.

"Where did you find all this stuff?" he asked. "A better question, is why did you dig it out if this upsets you this much?"

Bea chanced a quick shallow breath, but still said nothing.

"Is this my fault because I brought up your sister again the other day?" André asked. "Did you dig up all this old stuff so I'd stop asking questions?"

Bea furrowed her brow and tried to answer, but instead slowly nodded her head.

André gathered the loose items and placed them back in the case. "We're going to put all these sad memories back where they belong," he said, "and then I'm going to burn it. I can't bear to see you this way." He picked up a handful of small items and gently laid them in the case. "I'll never forgive myself for making you dredge up..." His arms made a wide sweep around the room, "... this...this heartbreak," he said as he shut the top of the hatbox.

Mama Bea reached over and touched André's arm. "No, no son. It's time you know the truth...all the truth. Your mama has been keeping too many secrets locked away in her heart and from you way too long. She handed André the book she'd been holding close to her chest. "You need to read this," she said, her voice just above a whisper; deep black circles beneath her eyes were growing darker by the minute. "Gabrielle's small diary will explain a lot, but not before I confess somethin' to you first."

André sat next to his mother; she cupped both his hands around hers. Mama Bea shuddered with a sigh; hesitated for a moment. She forced her eyes to meet André's. With guarded words she revealed the dark secrets hidden in her heart.

CHAPTER 27

"MR. PRESIDENT, we'll be touching down at Mr. Davidson's Plantation in ten minutes."

"Thank you," Major," Dylan said. He continued to gaze through the window of Marine One as it followed a path along the winding Mississippi River. The early morning sun glistened off the water; an occasional barge, pushed by a tugboat, maneuvered the cargo toward the Port of New Orleans. *Sometimes I wish my life was as simple as those lucky bastards who are floating down the river without a care in the world*, Dylan thought with an edge of envy. If they only knew the burdens the leader of the free world shouldered...

He checked his watch and then reread Burt Harrison's latest email message of gloom — another day and down *another* two points in the polls. What in the hell was happening to his campaign? Allison Benson was inching closer and closer to stealing this election from him. He may have only been in the job for a few weeks, but long enough to know that there was no way in hell he planned on losing the presidency. It was his turn. Heat flushed his face; he clenched his teeth. *Burt had better get his act together and do it fast.* Dylan seethed inside. *I'm just minutes from canning his ass.*

Dylan shifted in the passenger seat and tried to once again focus on the Louisiana landscape below, but for the first time in years he felt his control slipping away. Thanks to that delusional reporter, his campaign manager's incompetence and his *darling*, rebellious wife and her twin sister, his campaign was taking a nose dive straight into the crapper.

Bitter resentment butted against his already foul mood. If he could get rid of Céline's bodyguard, André, without too much blowback, he'd bury him into the deepest hellhole he could find. How dare that bastard conspire with those two bitches to dupe him? At the very least his actions must be treasonous.

A slow burn of anger and revenge mushroomed deep inside Dylan's core; a sneer played at the corner of his mouth. When the time was right, he'd make sure that black punk would never resurface into the civilized world again.

Chatter through the helicopter headphones interrupted his train of thought. He took a sip of now cold coffee and searched for a pleasant thought, anything to lighten his mood before they landed. A smile twitched his cheek. Those rats breaking up Harley's redneck shindig last night *was* pretty funny — thank God he was sleeping in the middle of Lake Pontchartrain overnight and missed that horror movie. If Céline and Burt were right about one thing, he had no business being at Harley's party in the first place, much less staying in his home during such a pivotal time in the campaign.

Dylan furrowed his brow. *What in the hell was Durham thinking inviting all those former swamp rats?* Many of them were friends back in college; and, yes, some were actually very rich and quite successful businessmen. They definitely could help bolster the coffers of the campaign, but...

Didn't his old friend understand political campaigns needed the big buck contributions, understand that he needed to be in the company of distinguished captains of industry — like Mr. Samuel Davidson — and, not frat boys from their heyday?

The more he thought about his association with Mr. Harley Durham, he realized how toxic their relationship was. It was time to cut ties with his old friend. Despite what that alligator-wrestler might think, and the secrets he claimed he owned he had no power over him. Who would people believe? Harley Durham, a low-life who crawled out of the swamps, or him, Dylan Randle the III, President of the United States and soon to be reelected?

Thank God, Cèline arranged for him to stay at the Davidson's plantation tonight, particularly after that fiasco with that unhinged reporter, and then the craziness at Harley's, so called, campaign party. He needed a break from New Orleans — even if it was for only one night.

Dylan checked his seatbelt as the helicopter hovered and began its descent onto the heliport. Ancient oaks dripping with moss whipped and bent as if they were in the path of an EF-0 tornado. As Marine One touched ground, Dylan caught a glimpse of a stately gentleman in a white suit. The old gent, with one hand on a cane and the other fighting to keep his white cowboy hat from blowing away, stood at a safe distance. If he didn't know any better, he'd swear that Colonel Sanders was alive, well, and still peddling fried chicken. Standing next to Mr. Davidson was a handsome, robust woman unbothered by the swirling winds. If he had to guess, she probably held the purse strings in that marriage.

As the helicopter engines whined down, a crewmember helped Dylan down the steps. The president, along with a secret service agent, crouched down beneath the still turning rotors. With a hurried pace, they both joined Mr. Davidson and his wife.

"Welcome, Mr. President," Mrs. Davidson said, reaching out her hand. "It's a shame the first lady couldn't join us. I was so looking forward to becoming reacquainted with my distant cousin. The last time I saw Céline, we were playing dolls beneath these same old trees while our mothers sipped Mint Juleps on the veranda."

Dylan brushed his fingers through his wind-blown hair. "Family, you know," he said forcing a smile.

The woman pursed her lips. "I thought most of Mrs. Randle's family was deceased."

"A long story," Dylan offered with a titter in his voice.

"Pay no attention to my wife," Mr. Davidson said with a wink. "She's just jealous that I'll have you all to myself for the day. She'd like nothing better than to show you off to all those 'ol biddies in her Mahjong circle."

"I'm sorry I'll miss that," Dylan smiled and winked at Mr. Davidson.

"Nonsense," Martha said. "We're both honored you chose our home, even for a one night stay. I'm sure I'll have another opportunity to spend time with the first lady," she added.

"Absolutely," Dylan said. "As a matter of fact, I contacted my campaign manager this morning before I left New Orleans and instructed him to seat you and your husband next to the first lady and me at tomorrow night's dinner at the Eiffel."

"Wonderful," Mr. Davidson said clapping his hands together. "We look forward to the festivities. I'll convince Martha to bring her checkbook."

"Samuel, don't be gauche," Martha said.

They left the heliport and walked among a double row of live oaks that gracefully arched across a brick-paved walkway leading to the antebellum mansion.

As the three climbed the steps up to the columned veranda, Martha spoke first. "We have warm beignets and fresh chicory coffee," she offered. "When you're ready, one of the servants will show you to your room. Cocktails are at five; dinner at seven."

"Perfect," Dylan said. "I'm looking forward to a day of leisure with such an old and very distinguished Louisiana family."

CHAPTER 28

PEPPER crawled out of bed, looked at the time on her cell phone, and considered taking a shower. She sighed, "What's the use. I don't need to be anywhere today." She flopped back down on the bed and pulled her knees to her chest. "Life sucks," she mumbled, and then dozed off.

Cuckoo ... cuckoo ... cuckoo... the clock whistled from the living room. Pepper bolted upright and threw a pillow at the bedroom doorway. "Damn cuckoo. You're going in the trash today." She checked the time on her iPhone and discovered she'd fallen back to sleep for another two hours. "This is no way to live," she grumbled. "There's got to be more to life than waiting for the song of that damn cuckoo bird."

Pepper scooted off the edge of the bed and rummaged through laundry piled in the corner of her room and searched for the loosest pair of jogging shorts she owned and her New Orleans Saints number nine jersey. She slipped on the football pullover and then headed toward the kitchen hopping along first sticking one leg and then the other into the soiled loose-fitting shorts. Pepper slammed one cabinet door after another looking for a canister of coffee, or maybe a teabag, but the cupboard was bare. She opened the refrigerator and grabbed an opened, half-empty can of cola, and then strolled into the living room sipping as she walked.

She picked up the remote control, but even before pushing the power button, she remembered the television needed repairing. She shrugged. "Oh well, no Rachael Ray or Turner Classic movie in my future today," she said and then tossed the remote onto the coffee table.

Her eyes roamed the room looking for that book she'd been meaning to finish, but the area was void of any reading material. She peeked out the window to see if her upstairs neighbor's newspaper was still on the porch. Disappointed, Pepper turned around and headed back to her bedroom to take another nap, but stopped. Her computer case and her entire career were sitting in a corner still stuffed in her oversized Gucci bag. The mere thought of unloading her meager belongings from the office just made her sadder. No TV...no coffee...no food...no money...no life. She plopped on the sofa, grabbed a pillow, and hugged it.

The longer she sat staring into space, the stronger the urge to open her laptop. She mustered the energy to get off the sofa and unzip the case. Pepper pulled out the computer and flipped the on-switch. While the notebook buffered its way to life, she checked the cupboards and refrigerator once again for at least a snack to satisfy the gnawing in her stomach. She returned to the living room with a stale Pop Tart and a warm can of Diet Coke.

For several minutes Pepper stared at the icons on the computer's desktop. Was it really worth the time and effort to probe into that poor old woman's background in an attempt to unearth some baseless theory she couldn't let go of? Who was she to judge an elderly woman who enjoyed going to old cemeteries and visiting the tomb of a famous voodoo queen? Even if it turned out she *was* connected to the mystery lady from the ferry, hadn't she caused enough chaos for a lifetime this year? If Ms. Bélair was lucky enough to buy a house for less than a hundred dollars, it certainly wasn't any of her business.

Pepper closed the laptop and leaned her head on the back of the sofa. *When you think about it*, she mused, *nothing Ms. Bélair did was unnatural behavior for New Orleans.* The city's charm *was* its colorful past and suspected ghosts that roamed the streets and houses. To some degree most everyone who lived in the city possessed an enviable free spirit tinged with an aura of zaniness. It was presumptuous of her, a hick from the hill country of Texas, to judge a unique place like the Crescent City. Even she, when she first arrived in NOLA, visited a spiritualist and actually considered returning for additional sessions. Pepper shrugged. *Why didn't I return? I do remember being quite intrigued, and even felt some comfort after that visit.*

She laughed. Even the annual New Orleans Voodoo Fest was one of her favorites. "God, I love this city," Pepper blurted. *There was no place on earth with more charm, more fun-loving people, more...*

A rap on the door startled Pepper; she choked on the gasp caught in her throat. She ducked her head, tried to make out the dark figure muted behind the gauze curtains. Anxiety clawed its way into her stomach. Her mind raced remembering the man and car that had followed her the other night, and then looped back to her arrest. What if more charges had been filed against her and it was the police taking her back to jail? A hundred possibilities jammed her thoughts and paralyzed her in the very spot she sat. Maybe if she remained very still and was quiet, whoever was at the door would go away.

The knocking continued. Pepper's eyes widen; unwanted adrenaline revved up her heartbeat. Whoever was standing on her front porch was certainly persistent, but no way in hell was she going to open that door. For one thing she didn't have a bra on and haven't brushed her hair or teeth for...well, she couldn't even remember how long ago.

"Miss Mills are you home," a male voice called out as he knocked again. "I really would like to talk to you if you have a few moments," he said.

He doesn't sound dangerous, Pepper determined. *I could at least ask who he is and what he wants.* But then again, it's never a good idea to open the door to uninvited strangers.

"My name is André Bélair. My mom lives in Algiers Point."

She dropped her chin to her chest. "Oh crap," she hissed through clenched teeth. That's the son of the woman she'd been stalking for two days. She held her head in her hands. Would she *ever* be able to get this damn monkey called trouble off her back?

"I know a stranger showing up at your door may be alarming," he said, "but I assure you I mean you no harm. If you're interested, I may have some information you might like to take a look at."

Pepper slid the laptop off her lap onto the coffee table and cleared her throat. "What kind of information?"

"Information pertaining to Harley Durham." He paused and then continued. "And, possibly President Dylan Randle."

***

Pepper stood on her front porch with a hot pink book covered with hand-drawn hearts clutched against her chest; her mouth still hung open in disbelief as André climbed on a bicycle and headed down Elmira Street. "Th... thank you," she managed to call out before he was too far away. Without turning around the nice young man gave her a farewell wave over his shoulder.

Still in shock, she sat on the steps of her house and wondered if what just happened was real. Could she still be asleep? Still dreaming that a handsome knight with a buff body, deep golden skin and the whitest teeth she'd ever seen just now ride in and salvaged her career and life? *Funny*, she chuckled under her breath, *just yesterday during her deepest despair she had managed to joke about opportunity knocking on her door.* She shook her head in disbelief. This must be a dream. Her instincts were good, but what was just handed to her may well be manna from heaven. She laughed aloud.

A woman walking by scowled; stared at Pepper as if she was crazy.

"I'm not a lunatic, I promise," Pepper called to the retreating woman. "My life has just been..."

Pepper swatted the air with her hand. "Never mind, you wouldn't understand anyway."

She got up and went into the house leaving the front door open. A cool October breeze rushed in and cleansed the stale air inside. With the diary still held close to her chest, Pepper sat down on the sofa, shut her eyes, and tried to put all the pieces of the puzzle together.

Not only was André Bélair the bodyguard of the first lady of the United States, but he'd been responsible for getting her charges reduced and out of jail — at least for the time being, he warned her.

Beatrice Bélair was his mother and the former nanny of Céline and Claréne Fontenot — both women famous in their own right. She had even been correct that she had recognized the mystery woman on the ferry — just mistaken that it actually *was* the first lady instead of her twin sister, the photographer. The revelations he had just shared were reassuring that she had been correct on so many levels. The question that still remained, was what did this old diary, Harley Durham and maybe the president of the United States have in common?

Pepper shrugged, unsnapped the lock on the diary, and began to skim the damaged, yellowed pages:

> *August 15th, 1979 — Dear Diary: Today is my thirteenth birthday. Yea! I'm finally a teenager.*
>
> *September 9th — summer is officially over and is the first day of school. I wonder what 8th grade will be like. Will the boys think I'm pretty?*

Pepper furrowed her brow as she flipped through the pages of the mundane scribbling of a budding teenage girl.

She turned toward the back and read some more.

> *March 6, 1984 – Dear Diary: Mardi Gras Fat Tuesday. I fell in love for the first time today. I met two very handsome Tulane students. They want to get together this weekend...*

"Was this some kind of joke?" She grumbled. "Why did she care about Gabrielle Bélair's teenage years and first love?" Do you suppose she was being baited and the visit from the handsome black gent was only a subterfuge to redirect her attention away from the first family?

Maybe she was being punished because of her overzealous imagination and had picked the wrong people to mess with. It wouldn't be the first time. Pepper smiled as the irony sunk in. What better way to keep a nosey reporter busy chasing rainbows until the president and first lady left town? After all, her credibility, right now, had about as much value as the money in her savings account — zero. Her stomach grumbled.

Pepper marked her place with the attached gold ribbon, set the book aside and ordered a pizza and molten lava cake for dessert. While she waited for her order, she headed for the shower.

As Pepper shampooed her hair, more questions sprang to the surface. *Maybe she was being too skeptical*, she thought. After all, the bodyguard of the first lady of the United States *had* just been standing at her front door and handed her a presumed "gift". Why would he willingly surrender a personal item belonging to his family, and what did it have to do with the president and Mr. Durham? The very fact that the secret service agent may have jeopardized his career getting her released from jail, defied all logic. To add more twists to the plot, why would the Fontenot twins switch places during an important campaign stop?

Nothing made sense. There had to be a plausible explanation, but if there was, the answers escaped her. One illogical thought after another began to clog her brain.

Pepper lifted her head and let the shower's warm, steady flow rinse the shampoo from her hair. *If* Mr. Bélair's "gift" held any useful tidbits, those juicy morsels had to be deeply imbedded within the pages of the diary. From what she had read so far, it would take a cryptologist to decipher any useful information.

She turned off the shower, grabbed a towel and wrapped it around her torso. She swiped the fogged bathroom mirror with her hand. "My unexpected visitor was certainly a man of few words," she said to the image staring back at her. "He obviously was well-trained by the guarded answers he gave, and was visibly reluctant to share too many of the pieces of this very large puzzle."

Pepper brushed her fingertips across her lips. Agent Bélair emphasized the real story was in the diary. He insisted that she quit looking into the first lady, her sister and his mother. He, also, warned that if she chose to pursue the story, she could possibly become a player in a very dangerous game.

No kidding, Pepper thought. She couldn't even imagine what Dylan Randle would actually say or do when he found out about the twins' deception; found out his wife's personal bodyguard was the one who bailed her out of jail, and now may have handed her possible damaging information about him and Mr. Harley Durham's tainted past. The bigger question was how far would President Randle go to keep any knowledge of his past out of her hands — the very hands that would do about anything to bring him down?"

As she was drying her hair, she once again heard a knock at her front door. "Ah, my pizza," she said and grabbed a fresh pair of jogging shorts, slipped on a tank top, and hurried into the living room. "About time, I'm starving," she said as she opened the door. Pepper's mouth dropped open. "Ma...Mark? What are you doing here?"

Mark Saderfield grinned from ear to ear and handed Pepper a bottle of Sazerac and a dozen yellow roses. "You promised me dinner before I left town. After all, I did drive the getaway car when you made your escape from jail," he laughed. "Time to pay up, lady."

Realizing she'd forgotten to put on a bra Pepper crossed her arms across her chest. "You should have called," she said. "I'm not prepared to entertain."

"You look pretty damn sexy, if you ask me," he said with a cocked eyebrow and impish grin.

"Aren't you going to ask me in? I drove all the way across the Crescent City Bridge in snarled traffic just to see you. You could at least offer me one drink from that bottle of rye."

"It's only noon," she said. "A little early to be hitting the hard stuff, isn't it?"

"This is New Orleans. Isn't it always five o'clock here?"

"Oh, alright," she said with furrowed brow, "come in, but only for one drink. I'm busy."

"Busy, huh?" Mark asked. "Rumor is you're temporarily unemployed... again," he teased.

"Very funny," she said. "I can still do freelance work. If you must know, I have a possible lead for a story. Old Algiers Point is full of ghosts about the past waiting to be told," she said, and then headed for the back of the house with the bottle of Sazerac and the roses.

***

Mark's eyes roamed around the sparsely decorated room. Most of the art hanging on the wall was colorful folk-art depicting New Orleans-style shotgun houses, Jackson Square, and a dog with soulful eyes. "Are you a collector?" Mark shouted toward the back of the house.

"What?" She asked peeking from her bedroom door.

"The art on your wall...are you a collector?"

Pepper said something, but he didn't hear. Mark sat down and picked up a hot pink book lying on the coffee table. He scanned the pages of what looked like the ramblings of a teenage girl; most of the entries were dated in the 1980's. Just as he was about to close the book a name jumped off a page — Harley.

"Put that down," Pepper scolded standing in front of him with two tumblers of Sazerac. "You have no right going through my personal belongings."

"I'm sorry," he said, tossing the book onto the table. "I just got a little bored waiting for you to bring me that drink."

Pepper set both glasses on the coffee table and picked up the diary. "I think you should go," she said. "This isn't a good idea."

"Come on," Mark said. "I'm truly sorry. You're all dressed. Let me take you out for an early dinner. You can show me the 'real' New Orleans as only a resident can."

Pepper opened the front door. "Like you said, I'm 'temporarily unemployed'. I want to focus on some... some information that recently came to my attention. I need to make a living, Mark. I don't have time to give tours of the city."

Mark stood, chugged his tumbler of rye. "Well, thanks for the drink. I hope you find what you're looking for."

He stepped onto the front porch, turned and looked at her. "Pepper, be careful," he said, and then hopped down the four steps. He glanced at her one last time. "Whatever you plan to write, be sure it isn't the final nail that completely buries you and your career."

CHAPTER 29

MARK sat in his rented red Corvette outside the Garden District Mansion; traffic whizzed down St. Charles Avenue. He gazed up at Mardi Gras beads dangling and glistening in the branches of age-old trees that lined the street. The longer he sat there, the angrier he got. How did he get here? Was it worth destroying other people's lives to get ahead? The questions weighed heavily on his conscience.

For the last four years the news media throughout the fifty states envied his status as Dylan Randle's golden boy. The buzz within the journalistic world indicated he was at the top of the list to win a Peabody, and possibly an Emmy for the third year in a row. Was his precious career as a newscast anchor for the number one Network news station really worth selling his soul to the devil?

An exterminator truck backed out of Harley Durham's driveway. Mark climbed out of the Corvette, opened the wrought iron gate, and headed up the stone sidewalk. He climbed the few steps and rang the doorbell.

A woman dressed in a crisp white uniform and shiny black shoes answered the door. "Yes suh," what can I do for you?" she asked.

"Is Mr. Durham home?"

"He's not seeing visitors right now," she said. "We had a little problem last night, and he busy takin' care of it."

"Ruby Jo," Harley yelled from the back of the house. "Who is it?"

She turned and yelled back, "Some nice lookin' man askin' for you."

Harley walked to the front door with a bottle of Dos Equis in his hand. "Mark?" he said with a surprised tone. "If you're looking for the president, he's no longer staying with me. Apparently, I'm 'too toxic for his precious campaign'," he said while making the double quote sign with his fingers."

"I... I'm not here to see the president," Mark said.

Harley raised an eyebrow. "Oh, well come on in. I'll get you a beer."

Mark followed Harley to the kitchen and watched as he popped open a beer and hand it to him.

"You here personally or professionally?" Harley asked.

"Let's just say I'm here paying my dues to the devil," Mark answered as he sat down at the breakfast table.

Harley joined Mark and stretched both arms across the back of the breakfast nook booth. He smiled. "I'm surprised you're not with the Randles today having lunch at Emeril's with the Mayor and the *more refined* citizens of this fine city." He leaned forward on his forearms and cocked his head. "Tell me, old friend. What could possibly make you unhinge your lips long enough from Dylan's butt to come and see *me* — the man who got you the job in the first place?"

Mark tried to look away, but Harley's glare had locked onto him like an armed torpedo; for a moment he felt his vocal cords wedge in his throat. He never dreamed the day would come he would stand toe to toe with pure evil, but here he was with no escape.

"Well," Harley said. "You gonna just sit there and waste my time or tell me what's on your mind?"

Mark picked at the label on the bottle and tried to find the right words. He took a sip of beer and then met

Harley's glare with his own. "Is there anything in your soulless past you don't want revealed?"

A grin twitched at Harley's cheek; he leaned back in the booth. "Why do you ask?"

Mark rubbed his thumb across his lips and considered whether he was doing the right thing. He was trapped like a cornered animal. Revealing what he had just discovered at Penelope Mills' had consequences — consequences that could affect the election; repercussions that could very well put a young journalist in danger; backlash that would most definitely destroy his reputation and career no matter how he handled the situation. He had no choice — his loyalties were bought and paid for. Mark glanced toward the ceiling, inhaled a deep breath, and then said, "Does the name Gabrielle mean anything to you?"

Harley straightened up; narrowed his eyes. "Where did you hear that name?"

"I'd rather not divulge my source," Mark said.

"The hell you say," Harley growled. "I own you, Mark Saderfield. You wouldn't be God's gift to cable news without me. Now cough up your source."

Mark heaved a reluctant sigh and said, "Penelope Mills."

Harley did a double take. "Wha...who? You don't mean that trouble-makin' reporter. She's in jail."

Mark rolled the beer bottle between his hands; avoided eye contact once again. "She's out."

"No. No way," Harley banged the top of the table with his fist. "I had a man watching her every move. Made sure she was sent to Tulane and Broad until the Feds officially charged her. You've got it all wrong."

Mark shrugged. "Sorry, but that *'trouble makin' reporter'*, as you call her, was released from jail two nights ago."

"How in the hell would you know that?" Harley raised his voice.

"That's not important," Mark said. "I'm only here because I owe you one. I wanted to give you a heads up in case you need to cover-up some of your illicit footprints from the past."

Harley threw his beer bottle against the wall. "This can't be happening," he said. "I had that base covered. My man was watching her and was supposed to report back to me if anything changed." He stood and began to pace. "I'll have that red-neck's ass," he screamed. "Doesn't anyone know how to follow orders anymore?"

Mark eased his way out of the breakfast nook, pumped both hands in front of him. "If the president is to win this election, he can't afford scandal from you or anywhere else," Mark said. "I happen to believe in Dylan Randle and that is the *only* reason I came here. After today you and I are paid in full. Don't call me again," he said. "I quit."

Harley continued to pace, his thoughts seemingly lost deep in the past. "Yeah, yeah, Mark, I've heard that before. You hear anything more, get back to me."

Mark hurried out of the house, jumped in his car, and shot up St. Charles toward the city. No matter how hard he tried, he couldn't tame the war being waged in his head. He banged the steering wheel with the butt of his hand. *What have you done? You feel better being a tattletale? Was it worth the blood money you're paid to be a snitch?* Bile crawled up his throat. Of all the people to betray, that little lady did not need more grief in her life.

Mark pulled into The Roosevelt Hotel parking lot. He climbed out of the car and handed his keys to the attendant, and then headed for the bar. Somehow, he had to make things right. He didn't know how at the moment, but he was sure a door would open. When it did, he would be there — at least he hoped he would be and prayed in the mean time nothing bad would happen.

*****

"Buck, get your ass over here now...I don't care if this is your *only* day to visit your kids," Harley screamed into the phone. "You had one job...one simple job and you blew it." Harley hurled his cell phone against a cushion curled in the corner of the leather camelback sofa. "Incompetence...I'm surrounded by incompetence."

He paced back and forth, tempted to grab every breakable object d'art he owned and shatter it until he was knee-deep in porcelain, crystal or whatever all this crap was made of. He narrowed his eyes, clinched his fist and growled. "If only I had a baseball bat."

"Mr. Harley, whatcha got your drawers all in a twist about now?" Ruby Jo asked.

He whirled around, pointed his finger. "*You!* You, too. The one person I thought I could trust betrayed me."

Ruby Jo backed away. "What you talkin' about, Mr. Harley. I never betrayed you in over the twenty years I worked for you. You my only family."

He narrowed his eyes. "Where's Peezee? I know you know where she is. You let her sleep under this roof when you knew she was supposed to be locked away, didn't you?"

"Now, Mr. Harley, you makin' somethin' out of nothin'," Ruby said standing her ground. "I let that po' girl stay here one night until her husband come and pick her up the very next day. She say her doctors done every thin' they could and she be cured from the demons. Seemed like the right thing to do with her just getting' out of the hospital and you out of town and hard to reach."

Harley furrowed his brow. "Husband? You talkin' about Roland Ongerón? Not possible, he's still up state in Angola."

"No suh," she said. "Mr. Roland released from that prison and come get Miss Peezee as fast as he could 'cause both know you don't want nothing to do with either of 'em." Ruby wrung her hands. "I promise, Mr. Harley, it was one night and one night only. She begged me not to tell you. Said I'd get into trouble...trouble just like I'm in right now."

Harley jerked his head around when the doorbell chimed. "What now?" He growled. "Answer the door, Ruby Jo. If that's Buck, send him to the library." He stomped toward the back of the house, and then turned around. "Where's the Pepto Bismol?"

"By your bed, Mr. Harley, where's I leave it every day," she said.

Harley marched back to his room, drank half a bottle of the indigestion medicine, and tried to calm the bile churning in his stomach. This was absolutely the worse time to lose control. His gut burned with anxiety. Despite all his overseas *friends'* technological efforts, Dylan's lead in the presidential race continued to drop faster than New York's crystal ball on New Year's Eve. His not so patient *associates*, were breathing down his neck, and will wrap his balls around his neck if Dylan loses this election.

The more Harley brooded, the angrier he got. This all started with that disruptive blonde bitch with an overactive imagination. Miss Penelope Mills was way too nosey for her own good. He had plans for that tiresome reporter, but not before he got his hands on Buck Broussard. Obviously, that lazy, incompetent swamp rat needed a demonstration what real intimidation looked like; needed to understand the importance of perseverance while following through until a job was completed. With the presidential election on the line, he thought he had made it perfectly clear to that imbecile that both his and the president's lives and reputations depended on keeping Penelope "Pepper" Mills silent.

CHAPTER 30

ANDRÈ fidgeted as he stood in the corner waiting for the luncheon hosted by the mayor of New Orleans to be over. Not once did he take his eyes off the first lady. They were playing a dangerous game and Dylan Randle no longer trusted either of them. By now the president had his own network of spies watching every move he and Céline made.

He adjusted his stance, swept his eyes over the room and tried to enjoy the atmosphere and aromas lingering in Emeril's Wine Room with its warm lighting, convex shiplap ceiling, and walls laden with racks of expensive wines. The mouth-watering scent from Emeril's signature dish of Andouille Crusted Drum smothered with Creole Meunière Sauce was enough to bring a grown man to his knees.

André shifted his focus away from food and back to Céline. She appeared to be listening to Dylan as he entertained the seventy or eighty top business men and women from New Orleans, and other key cities from around the State of Louisiana. He marveled how President Randle could captivate a crowd. Every soul sitting in that room appeared to be hanging onto every line of bullshit he was slinging. If they only knew the kind of man he really was. Right now, he had one responsibility and that was keeping Céline safe and out of harm's way from all outside threats — but mostly from that unscrupulous man standing at the podium selling his political rhetoric.

His thoughts flashed back to the young reporter he had visited that morning and wondered if he had been too eager to hand over a possible bombshell to such an unpredictable person. He couldn't help himself. His heart ached when he thought about Mama Bea and the torment she'd endured for a lifetime holding onto a secret; a secret that could destroy so many lives — his included. Even though it was unlike him to allow his emotions to drive his decision making, this one time he couldn't stop. This was personal. He hoped from the depths of his soul he wouldn't regret his hasty decision, but after reading that diary...

André released a slow breath and tried to refocus his attention back to protecting the first family, but every time he looked at Dylan, heard his voice, his thoughts looped back to Gabrielle's diary and her teenage pregnancy. Did he really need to know who his biological father was? He still hadn't digested the fact that Mama Bea wasn't his actual birth mother. There was never any reason to question that. They not only shared the same last name, but also DNA. It was a little late in life to question why or how Mama Bea had been capable of having her name listed as birth mother instead of Gabrielle's...

Loud applause erupted; the room stood giving their president a standing ovation. People rushed forward vying for an opportunity to shake Dylan's hand, or try to make some memorable impression on the president of the United States. These were the moments that made André and every other secret service agent the most anxious — a converging crowd on a president was the most difficult to control.

With everyone's attention fixated on the president, André caught a glimpse of Céline. A conspiratorial smile slipped across his face as he watched her casually reach over and grab Dylan's luncheon napkin. In her haste she dropped it on the floor. Just as she was about to pick it up, a man rushed over. They both reached down and came up with a corner of the linen together.

André stifled a laugh at the disgusted look on the first lady's face. The man clinging to his portion of the same napkin engaged her in small talk without once taking his licentious eyes off her cleavage.

Just when André was about to intervene, a woman stepped between the man and Céline. She apologized to the first lady, grabbed the man's arm and steered him toward the exit. Céline quickly stuffed the napkin in her purse and with a forced smile, joined Dylan at the podium and nodded in agreement to everything he said.

***

Céline and André watched as the presidential convoy pulled away from the restaurant. As soon as the train of black vehicles was out of sight, he opened the door to the black Explorer and helped the first lady in. "Are you sure you want to do this?" Céline asked.

He didn't answer. He shut the door and walked around to the driver's side and climbed in.

"André, answer me," Céline said as he started the engine. "This is important and there are things you need to understand."

He glanced at Céline, started to say something, but stopped.

"You do realize we only have half the puzzle," she said. "Either way the result might make you want to jump into the Mississippi River at flood stage," she said trying to bring levity to the situation.

"Yes, I'm sure. I *need* to know and the sooner the better," he finally said. "Who is running the test?" he asked, changing the subject.

"Liz, my old biology lab partner from our days at Tulane. She said she would put a rush on the results and keep a lid on the findings. She needs you to understand that with such a small amount of DNA on the napkin it may take longer than if she had an actual blood sample or hair follicle. Céline laughed. "I'd be happy to get one or the other for you."

"You!" He managed a smile. "If I remember correctly, you're the person who'd almost faint whenever Claréne or I skinned our knee, or squashed a bug. Now your sister on the other hand..."

Céline laughed. "You're right, but Claréne would end up draining every ounce of blood from Dylan's body, or scalping him with a dull knife. Bad idea. Let's just stick with the original plan."

André turned off St. Charles onto Nashville and headed for Ferret Street. For the next several blocks they both remained locked in their own personal thoughts. He finally spoke again.

"Are you sure your friend won't get into any trouble using the University's facilities?" André asked?

Céline laughed. "Not only is Liz the head of the Biology Department, she is a force of nature who lives in her own nerdy world. Her nose is totally into her research projects, but most of all she loves a challenge. We just need you to be patient. Finding the results could take a minimum of three to five days, possibly weeks. Most of all, we both want you to be sure you *really* want to know who your biological father is." Céline hesitated for a moment, and then asked again, "*Are* you sure?"

He furrowed his brow. "Honest to God? I don't know...I really don't know. What would you do?"

"Depends on the real reason you're searching for answers," Céline said.

"Well, when you put it that way," André said with a grimace.

"We can turn the car around and head back to the West Bank and just get on with our lives and forget Mama Bea ever mentioned that damn 'ol diary," Céline suggested. "We both know she is your real Mama; the one who raised you and loved you and has always been there for you since the day you were born."

André gripped the steering wheel until his knuckles turned white. "I know...I know, but Gabrielle was raped. Not by one man, but two. From what I could understand from reading the last entry in her diary, she went out on that boat that day to confront both Harley and Dylan to ask at least one of them to help support the baby. And, what did they do? They threw her into the Lake like she was a bag of trash and hoped she'd drown. If it hadn't been for that fisherman scooping her out of the water and rushing her to shore, I would've died, too. No one should get away with that."

Céline reached over and touched his arm. "André, you know I'm on your side. But, you need to consider the reality that the tragedy of this story is you have no concrete proof except a few suggestive ramblings from thirty-five years ago by a love-struck teenage girl; one who put herself in the wrong place at the wrong time not once, but twice. Thirty-five years ago, the authorities ruled her death an accident. The case was closed."

André nodded, "I understand, but...

"You'll be going against two of the most powerful men in the country," Céline interrupted.

André choked back the raw emotions rushing to the surface. He looked at Céline; his eyes burned with anguish and rage. "Drowning wasn't enough. They may have bashed in her head, too." He narrowed his eyes. "If one of those bastards is my father, it will prove they raped and killed Gabrielle. One of them is going to pay."

Céline pulled her phone from her purse and punched in a number. "Liz, hi, it's me your old lab partner. I can't come up to the laboratory, security issues and all that," she said. "Would you mind coming down? I have that package we discussed earlier... Uh huh... Yes, he understands...thank you. We should be there in about five minutes. Look for a black Explorer with government tags."

CHAPTER 31

PEPPER pushed her half glasses to the top of her head, rubbed her tired eyes, and leaned her head back on the headboard. Her mind was literally clogged with bits and pieces from Gabrielle's diary; research results from archived newspaper articles from the 1980's, and a few school records she could find. All the information she'd unearthed, to this point, was tantalizing, but she still lacked the glue to pull it all together — too many missing pieces and too many sources to verify. She had to think. There had to be a better way to connect the dots.

She moved the notebook off her lap onto the floor, picked up the last piece of pizza that had been sitting for the last six hours, and then tossed it back in the box. *Yuck*, she thought. She needed to get out of the house, breathe fresh air, and drink a couple ice-cold beers in a frosty mug. Most of all she needed to clear her head. Spending all day in bed swimming in a quagmire of innuendos, vague facts, and suggestive whispers from an old diary was getting her nowhere.

Pepper quickly changed clothes, gathered all the notes she had jotted down during her research and stuffed them in a backpack along with her phone and phone charger. She locked the front door, climbed onto her bike, and switched on the headlight attached to the handlebars.

For ten minutes she bumped along the uneven street pavement of Algiers Point toward one of her favorite watering holes. When she pulled up in front of the Dry Dock Café with the blue and white striped awnings, the three wrought iron tables, shaded by umbrellas, were already filled to capacity.

She parked and locked her bike next to the "No Parking" sign, and then walked around the corner. She smiled and said hello to a few familiar faces as she stepped inside the cozy building with its L-shaped wooden bar and walls of brick. She climbed onto a bar stool in the corner and hoped no one would engage her in conversation, and then ordered a NOLA Blonde draft. She sipped her beer and allowed the cold brew to soothe and quiet her tired brain. Slowly her mind relaxed, as did the tension that gripped the back of her neck.

"Are you all right, Honey?" the bartender asked.

"I'm getting there," Pepper smiled and picked up her mug. "I just needed this and a place to unwind."

"Let me know when you need another," she said, and then turned her attention to the couple who were sitting nearby.

Pepper leaned her head against the brick wall and allowed her mind to wander.

As much as she loathed Dylan Randle, most all the research she'd uncovered, so far, pointed to Harley Durham. Whether she liked it or not, President Randle, at least on paper, was relatively squeaky clean. He had to be. Presidential candidates were vetted pretty thoroughly.

Pepper sipped her beer. Why would a wealthy kid from Pennsylvania hook up with a guy like Harley Durham in the first place? What could they possibly have in common besides playing football and being college roommates for a year or two? Pepper cocked an eyebrow. Maybe Mr. Durham had something on the president, and that was the reason they remained "friends" years later. What if "Mr. All Powerful" Dylan Randle just thought he was in control and was actually a puppet of Harley Durham's?" She chuckled. It certainly would help explain the president's foul temperament, and that would be a story in itself.

Pepper reached into her backpack for the notes she had jotted down earlier in the day hoping to spark another train of thought. She skimmed the key points she'd written down from the diary:

Mardi Gras, March 6, 1984. G goes to party with H and "D-Rod".

All she knew for sure was Gabrielle was supposedly meeting two boys the evening of Fat Tuesday, March 6th. One was a Harley, but not necessarily Harley Durham. The other was "D-Rod". Who was "D-Rod"? — Obviously a nickname and a good friend of "Harley's". She raised an eyebrow. The "D" could stand for Dylan; but that was stretching it.

Pepper inhaled a deep breath and slowly exhaled. "I've got to stop focusing on Gabrielle and get back to the living," she reasoned and signaled the bartender for another draft.

Harley Durham grew up somewhere in the Louisiana swampland. That was going to take a little more digging, she thought, and maybe a road trip. He'd played football for Tulane for a couple years on scholarship, and then quit school for an undocumented reason. He and Dylan Randle were in the same fraternity and roommates their freshman year.

Pepper closed her eyes and once again pressed her head against the brick wall behind her. She tapped her forehead with a fingertip. *Come on, brain. Think. Work your magic. I need you to piece this puzzle together. Time to dig deep.*

Harley's parents were both dead. He had a sister. What was her name? Sss...She...Sha...Sho...? Whatever the sister's name, she'd need to try and check that out later. *It could be important*, Pepper thought, making a mental note.

It was still unclear how Harley had actually crawled out of the swamp and became such a rich man, especially after quitting or being thrown out of Tulane before he graduated. Why did he leave college? Where did he go? What did he do? He was originally a poor boy living on a houseboat in the swamps. His only way out was being an All American football player in High School — which lead to his scholarship to Tulane.

Pepper took a sip of beer and skimmed her notes one more time. She'd already looked for juvenile arrests, but found nothing – or, maybe the records had been sealed. His grades in high school were barely good enough to graduate. She pinched the bridge of her nose and tried to determine what she was missing. If there was anything to be found, it eluded her. The only logical explanation was either a benevolent alumnus, or the Randles owed Mr. Durham a big favor and set him up with his first business.

Pepper sighed. She needed to get off this dead-end street that she was stuck on and work another angle.

She pulled out her phone, tapped Safari, and typed in relatives of Harley Durham. She scrolled through until she found the Durham she was looking for. And, there it was: Sherri Dee Durham Randle Ongerón. Pepper did a double take. Randle? You don't suppose...nah that would be too coincidental. A sly grin played at the edge of her mouth. But, she thought, even a rudimentary suggestion of such a personal connection between those two men drove this chase into a whole different direction — a direction that may be well worth jumping into the rabbit hole.

She signaled for the bartender. "Will you bring me a bowl of Gumbo?" she asked.

"Anything else?" the bartender asked.

"Maybe a glass of water."

The bartender handed her water and headed back to the kitchen.

Pepper continued her search on Sherri Dee Durham looking for notifications of marriage, divorce, a death certificate, anything that might help find Harley's sister. There wasn't much, if anything, to go on. It was like the woman had disappeared from the earth for the last twenty or thirty years *and* without a death certificate. Pepper keyed in link after link on Safari. Curiosity rolled into frustration.

The longer she searched, the more her instincts screamed Miss Sherri Dee was the one person who could fill in the blanks. Why couldn't she find anything? As a last resort, Pepper reached into her backpack for Gabrielle's diary hoping to find Sherri's name mentioned somewhere within the bounds of the book.

"Oh crap," she said as she rummaged around the inside of the backpack. The one item she meant to bring she'd left on the bed. "Dumb!" she cursed under her breath. Pepper took out the ROCKZ battery pack, attached it to the phone, and continued her search on Sherri Dee.

After a frustrating twenty minutes of drawing a blank, Pepper dropped the Sherri Dee angle and typed in the name Roland Ongerón — last known spouse. If she could find him, perhaps he would know where Sherri was or how to locate her. Moments later Roland's name popped up with a phone number. She took three quick bites of lukewarm Gumbo, laid money on the bar, and went outside.

Pepper punched in the telephone number and waited. She inhaled, exhaled trying to calm the beat of her heart drumming in her ears like a Marine Corp percussion band.

The intermittent buzz on the phone repeated over and over again and seemed to last an eternity. Finally a click...followed by a moment of silence.

"Hello...Hello?" Pepper said. "Anyone there?"

A male voice finally spoke. "Who is this?"

"My name is Penelope Mills. I was wondering if you knew how I could get in touch with Sherri Dee Durham."

More long silence. "Hello?" Pepper tried again.

"Why do you want to speak to her?" a gruff voice asked.

"I'm a journalist," Pepper said, "and have questions about her brother Harley Durham and her ex-husband Dylan Randle."

Pepper could hear a muffled conversation.

"What makes you think Dylan Randle was my ex-husband?" a female voice asked.

"Oh...OH! Hi," Pepper said, fumbling to keep a firm grip on her phone. "Sherri, Sherri Dee."

"I said," the woman barked. "How do you know I was married to Dylan Randle?"

"Fou...found the information archived in Public Records," Pepper answered.

"Not possible," the woman said. "That marriage was annulled, supposedly wiped off all records," she said.

Pepper noted a bit of bitterness in the woman's tone. The beat of her heart revved up. "Is there any way you would consider talking to me?" Pepper asked. "It sounds like you have a story to tell and perhaps no one has listened to you for a very long time?"

Two more minutes of silence passed, but there was no way she was going to break the connection. Pepper said a little prayer and waited. Finally, the man returned to the phone.

"One A.M. at the Stennis Rest Stop off I-10. If you're late, don't call again." The connection broke.

Pepper's hands shook. Anxiety, jubilation, and raw fear rushed through her like a rocket launched into space. She quickly glanced at the time on her iPhone — ten P.M. She had just enough time to get home and hope the battery wasn't dead in the car she hadn't driven in at least a week. If it was, she *would* find a way to get to that Rest Stop. Nothing was going to stop her. She hopped on her bike and pedaled as fast as the rusty contraption would go.

Eight minutes later, Pepper wheeled into her driveway, jumped off her bike and raced up the steps to her porch. The motion detection light flashed on. A scream caught in her throat. Her voice box, along with every muscle in her body, seized. A dead rat, the size of Texas, dangled from the same butcher knife she'd used for protection just two nights ago when she'd feared for her life. The words *"Stay out of my business"* were scrawled in drips of red across the front porch wall.

She whirled around and searched for something, anything for a weapon. Out of the corner of her eye, she caught a glimpse of a car pulling away from the curb. A dark sedan moved slowly passed her house, switched on the headlights, turn the corner and then zoomed up Opelousas Avenue.

Pepper couldn't catch her breath; she fumbled for her door key, all the while trying not to faint. She reached for the knob, but the front door swung open. Her mouth fell open; she gasped. The sofa was turned upside down, ripped, and torn; feathers from throw pillows dusted the floor; paintings were slashed to shreds. She raced into her bedroom. Her heart leaped into her throat. The diary... her laptop... they were missing. She could have sworn she had left them both on the bed.

She threw back the bedspread and found nothing. Pepper dropped to her knees and started tossing dirty clothes from the perpetual pile of dirty laundry. She swept her arms across the floor and under the bed until her hand caught the edge of metal.

She grabbed her laptop; held it close to her chest and tried to make sense of what the hell was going on. "Oh my God," she screamed in agony. "Gabrielle's diary... where was the diary?" Pepper raced into the living room, righted the sofa and coffee table — no diary. She stood in the middle of the floor, turned in circles on the verge of tears. What am I going to do? She moaned and dropped to her knees. Pepper covered her face with her hands and released an anguished wail.

The cuckoo clock whistled 11:00 P.M and snapped Pepper back to reality. She needed to think... she needed to pull herself together and call the police... she needed to get to the Stennis Rest Stop off I-10.

CHAPTER 32

THIS was the third time Burt walked past the Sazerac Bar. Every instinct in his body screamed take a walk... go to your room... take a cold shower... find an AA meeting.

The next thing he knew, he was sitting on a barstool with his back to the entrance holding a double Scotch. Burt closed his eyes and raised the glass to his nose. He inhaled the aroma that had caused two failed marriages, the inability to have a relationship with his two daughters and a life that left him hollow inside.

How long had it been since he was happy... truly happy? The first few years of his marriage to his second wife Charlotte were blissful — he thought he'd truly finally found his soul mate. That woman loved him with a depth he couldn't even understand, and she knew him better than he knew himself. Burt sniffed the Scotch one more time, but sat the tumbler back on the bar. He picked up the water he'd also ordered and took several sips.

He should have listened to his wife when she begged him not to get involved in politics. Charlotte feared the unrelenting pressures of the job would make him fall off the wagon. She warned that the added stress would be the death of him — and it almost was. Four years ago, during Michael Carlton's first presidential campaign he slipped into bad habits and every night when he'd return to his room alone he would empty the hotel mini-bars of every ounce of booze. The cherry on top with only weeks before Election Day, he ended up in the hospital for three touch and go weeks from a stress-related heart attack. Burt nodded in appreciation of his ex-wife's intuitiveness. "I guess Charlotte got the last word on that one."

Burt leaned back on the barstool and stared at the ceiling. Maybe he should call his ex and let her know she'd been right back then, and was even more right now. He was willing to bet his darling ex was keeping a list that would fill a binder as to why he shouldn't have gotten involved with such an unpredictable narcissist like Dylan Randle. If he called Charlotte, maybe she still loved him enough to convince him to get out now before it was too late.

He pushed the tumbler of Scotch a few more inches away. When he thought about it — no, admitted it — his ex-wife was always correct about so many things, on so many levels. She had a sixth sense about people, situations and more often than not predicted the end result. Numerous times she had saved his butt when he was about to say or do something really stupid and couldn't take it back.

Burt shifted his weight on the barstool, reached into his pocket and pulled out a brass key. He held it between his forefinger and thumb. He stared down at the company name stamped on the key — *Diebold, Inc. Canton, Ohio*, and then flipped the key over and looked at the embossed number — *two hundred and ninety-one*.

The irony, the pure irony, he mused. *Two hundred and ninety-one*. The exact number of days he'd been on this campaign, and in addition, it was made in Ohio — the very State that could hold the "key" to getting Dylan elected.

The weight of taking over a campaign on such short notice with a candidate that had no more business being president of the United States than Mickey Mouse lured

Burt to pick up the Scotch glass one more time. He allowed the liquid to dampen his lips.

All the Randles needed to do was follow the schedule he'd prepared and let it take them to the finish line. A wave of anger flushed his cheeks. Dylan's poll numbers were falling faster than a two-ton bomb — which meant one thing and one thing only. Dylan had committed political suicide with his latest two antics. If only his candidate were campaigning in Ohio instead of New Orleans, maybe...

Who was he kidding? The choice was never his. The moment the campaign deviated from the original schedule and entered this God forsaken city, the success of Dylan's campaign was set for failure. Why hadn't he been more forceful with the president? Make him understand, recognize, he jeopardized the campaign the moment he insisted on the last minute change.

Burt gave his head a nod; he sneered. "I sensed how wrong the change of schedule was *then*. And, I *know* it now."

His mood slipped from melancholy to full-blown depression. All the long days and sleepless nights, eating fast food or nothing at all were all for naught. He rubbed his thumb over the key and agonized. All the blood and sweat he'd put into this campaign was wasted energy, had jeopardized his health and had cost him his marriage. Was any of it worth it?

Burt gazed with vacant eyes at the Paul Nina's mural at the rear of the Sazerac Bar. He unconsciously swirled the Scotch around the glass and created a tiny whirlpool just like the thoughts circling through his mind. What would Charlotte tell me to do with this key, he wondered — tell Dylan about it... the first lady? Or, would she tell him to lose it and allow the contents of that safety deposit box to be forever forgotten.

Burt's guilt... anxiety and good judgment spiraled out of control, collided and left him more confused and desperate to know what was the right thing to do. He had no business intruding into Harley's hidden room with all those monitors and sickening sex videos. On the other hand, Harley had no business collecting and storing all that potential blackmail material — particularly on a supposed friend who was campaigning for president of the United States. What in the hell did he plan to do with all that information?

Burt dropped his head in his hands. His mother would be so ashamed of him right now if she knew he openly took something that belonged to someone else. She wouldn't care the reason; she'd only remind him he had dishonored the Harrison name. Burt furrowed his brow. Maybe this time she was wrong. Wasn't it his duty as campaign manager to protect his candidate by any means necessary? He'd be doing a great service for Dylan *and* the country by getting rid of potential blackmail material. Of course, he thought with a deep sigh. The worse part of his discovery was that Dylan *was* guilty on so many levels. Was this man even worthy to be president of the United States, or did he belong in jail? A sharp pain stabbed Burt's left arm.

He was getting too old for this. The smart move for him, with everything he suspected was going on, was to climb off the barstool, go upstairs, pack, and get on the first plane to Colorado. His remote cabin tucked in the valley outside Breckenridge with deer and elk grazing in the field, trout jumping in the small cold water lake out back, was the best place for him and his health. He didn't need Dylan... he didn't need his secrets... and, he certainly didn't need any part of Harley Durham and whatever sinister entanglements he is or has been involved with. *The further I stay away from him, the better.*

Burt placed his forearms on the bar; tucked his chin and shook his head. He looked one last time at the brass-headache he held in his hand. Millions of keys like this all over the world; millions of secrets locked away from prying eyes. How in the hell was he going to handle this, he wondered, and then slipped the key back into his pocket.

***

Mark Saderfield sipped his Sloe Gin Fizz and studied Burt Harrison sitting at the other end of the bar. Strange Dylan's campaign manager, a recovering alcoholic, was here, all alone, in a bar *and* in the middle of a presidential campaign.

He cocked an eyebrow. One would think those types of guys would literally stay welded to his candidate until the election was over. It's really kinda sad sitting here watching a recovering alcoholic who is obviously trying to face some sort of demon and battle with his conscience. But, who could blame the man for wanting to drink? There was absolutely nothing normal about this campaign, particularly since Dylan Randle and his entourage arrived in New Orleans.

Mark shook his head in awe. If he didn't know any better, he'd swear this city had a living, breathing soul and that soul smelled bad juju from all these campaign intruders and wanted them gone, or suffer the consequences.

He signaled the bartender to make him another Gin Fizz. He slid off his barstool and headed toward the back of the bar.

"Are you going to drink that Scotch, or is sniffing booze the new rage for recovering alcoholics?" He asked sitting next to Burt.

Burt did a double take. "Mark. I didn't see you," he said pushing the glass of Scotch away.

"You looked like you could use a friend," Mark said. "Why aren't you with Dylan?"

"Are you asking as a reporter, or as a friend?"

"Your choice, but thinking more friend than reporter," Mark smiled.

The bartender placed a fresh Sloe Gin Fizz on the bar and asked Burt if he would like one.

Burt frowned.

"Bring my friend a Club Soda," Mark said, as he handed the bartender the glass of Scotch,

Burt managed a smile. "Thanks," he said. "I almost blew four years of sobriety."

"Glad I could help," he said.

The two men sat in silence, sipped their drinks, and avoided eye contact. Several times the bartender passed by to check on them, but each time they both waved him away.

"If you don't mind me asking," Mark finally asked breaking the silence. "Why *aren't* you with Dylan? I thought you were staying with him at Harley's for the duration of this stop."

Burt grimaced. "How long could *you* spend in the company of Harley Durham?"

Mark laughed. "As little as possible, thank you."

"I've lost total control of this campaign," Burt confessed staring into his glass. "I schedule it...Harley Durham changes it. POTUS tags along behind that red-neck like he had him on a spiked-leash." He took a long swig of his Club Soda. "I no longer know who the campaign manager is."

Burt signaled the bartender for the check. "Mark," he said. "You're a journalist."

"News anchor," Mark corrected.

"Whatever," Burt said. "Do you know how I can get in touch with Penelope Mills?"

"You mean Pepper?"

"Yeah, the little blonde troublemaker."

Mark furrowed his brow. "Seems like a strange request coming from Dylan Randle's campaign manager."

"Do you have the information or not?" Irritation laced Burt's voice.

Mark took a pen out of his suit pocket, grabbed a fresh napkin, and wrote Pepper's address and phone number down. "Not even a little hint as to why you want to reach her?" he asked, handing Burt the napkin.

Burt tucked the note in his pants pocket, and then downed the rest of his club soda. "Thanks for everything," he said and walked out of the bar.

Mark's mouth fell slack. "What the hell just happened?"

***

Burt slid the keycard into the lock of his hotel room. He switched on the light and headed straight for the desk. He opened the drawer took out two envelopes and a sheet of Roosevelt Hotel stationary and began to write:

Dear Miss Mills:

I have information I believe you should have. Wait three days after you receive this letter, and then come to the Roosevelt Hotel and ask for the Manager. He will have an envelope in the hotel safe with your name on it. Bring proper identification with photo ID. I've instructed the manager to give the envelope ONLY to you and ONLY after the designated waiting period.

Anonymous Concerned Citizen

Burt addressed and stamped the first envelope to Penelope Mills and pushed it to one side.

He took the safety deposit key out of his pocket and laid it on the desk. Burt addressed the second envelope to both the Hotel Manager and Penelope Mills. He picked up the key, gave it an affectionate squeeze. "I'm doing this for you, Charlotte, my love," he said. "I honestly believe I finally understand everything you've been trying to tell me about politics and politicians over the years — at least I hope so. Maybe for the first time in our lives I'm doing something that will make you proud of me." Burt smiled as he slipped the brass bombshell into the second envelope and sealed the nail to his coffin.

CHAPTER 33

DAY 4 – 1:00 A.M.

IT WAS fifteen minutes before one A.M when Pepper exited I-10 onto Mississippi State Road 607 and followed the signs to the Hancock County Welcome Center. The deserted parking lot was well lit; the Welcome Center buildings were dark — as was expected. Instead of stopping she chose to wend and weave around the circular parking lot looking for another car, or, hopefully, a couple waiting at a picnic table or hanging out somewhere around the buildings. The jitters she thought she had harnessed after those harrowing events at her home had now returned with a vengeance.

Coming all this way may not have been her brightest idea, she thought. But, after losing Gabrielle's diary, whether she liked it or not, chasing an elusive Sherri Dee Durham might possibly be her last shot to try to unravel this evolving mystery. Obviously, she had poked a hornet's nest and was in too deep to give up now. Did she dare park and look for Roland and Sherri Dee in the shadows? Good sense urged her to keep moving in case she needed to floorboard the gas and make an escape. No need to take unnecessary changes, she reasoned. Particularly when it was evident the man in the black sedan, or someone he worked for meant her harm.

On her third rotation she saw a flame flicker from a cigarette lighter, and then a tall, thin man stepped out of the shadows. Pepper parked, but remained in the car with the engine running. She waited for a moment and then flashed her headlights. Moments later the man she assumed was Roland Ongerón jogged toward her. His head seemed to be on a swivel as he continually checked over his shoulder and behind him in every direction for any interruption of their clandestine meeting.

The closer he got, the more nervous she became. As a precaution, Pepper stepped on the brake, shifted into reverse, and then opened the driver's window.

"Roland?" she called out.

"Yeah," he said still checking the surrounding area as if he expected danger was lurking behind every dark shadow. "Don't get out of the car," he warned. "Follow the Rest Stop road like you were heading back to I-10, but instead of turning left, turn right. Drive a short distance and turn right again onto Discovery Circle. That road will take you to the Infinity Science Center. Peezee is waiting there."

"Who?"

"Peezee... I mean Sherri Dee. Pull into the parking lot turn off your headlights and then switch them back on. Once she sees that signal, she'll come to your car. You'll only have fifteen minutes."

"Fifteen minutes?" Pepper said. "I need more time than that."

"It's too dangerous," Roland said. He looked at his watch. "You now have thirteen minutes," then he turned and jogged toward the woods.

Pepper fumbled for her iPhone; pushed "record":

"Interview with Sherri Dee Durham Randle Ongerón, 1:15 A.M, Tuesday, October 22nd, location, Infinity Science Center at Mississippi Welcome Center, Hancock County," she said into the microphone, and then slipped the phone into

the pocket of her jacket. "This might not be a long conversation," she vowed, "but every word is going to be recorded."

As Pepper pulled away from the well-lit Welcome Center into the unpredictable darkness, she tried to restrain the foreboding that was bullying her. She could not, would not allow the fear of the unknown, the fear of failing, the fear she was making the biggest mistake in her life overpower her instincts. The more she uncovered, the more she was determined to complete this journey of redemption for not only her, but also for all the others who had been caught in Dylan Randle's web of deceit.

The mile long S-shaped Discovery Circle road was tucked deep in the woods; an eerie ground fog amplified the already dark night. As she drove along the deserted street, one question after the other bombarded her mind like a Wyoming hailstorm in July. Why was Roland so jumpy? Why did he race off into the darkness like *he* was in danger? The location he picked couldn't have been more secluded. What could he and Sherri Dee have been so concerned about that they had turned a simple interview into the likes of a Tom Clancy spy novel?

Pepper eased her foot off the gas pedal. Now that she was here and stared reality head on, it *was* strange Roland had chosen a Rest Stop off I-10 in the middle of the night; even stranger that he had picked a location in Mississippi and not Louisiana.

Gut wrenching fear knotted in her stomach as the events of the last couple days scrolled through her thoughts. Why had someone nailed a dead rat on her porch wall; ransacked her home? Who was driving that dark sedan that stalked her in the night?

Her breath caught in her throat. For all she knew, the mystery stalker could be Roland Ongerón, and he lured her away into this secluded place to complete a job he hadn't finished.

The car slowed to a crawl. Roland *was* a criminal, she reminded herself, and only recently released from Angola Prison. She had already forgotten why he'd spent almost twenty years of his life in jail.

What if he was a serial killer and his M.O. was to lure women to isolated areas? Her heart pumped faster. Where had Sherri Dee been for the last several years? Why hadn't she been able to find more information about the elusive woman during her research? What if she...

Pepper hit the brake and shifted the car into park and left the engine still running. She fought back the growing anxiety, the confused dilemma of what she should do. Impulsiveness had not been her friend lately. What was she doing? Why was she really here? Hadn't someone just broken into her home and trashed it just hours ago? Didn't someone scrawl a message in rat-blood across her front porch with the warning *'Stay out of my business*? What made her think this was a wise decision to meet two strangers who may or may not have information she could use for some wild story she hoped to put together."

"Stupid...stupid...stupid," she screamed at the top of her lungs. Pepper dropped her chin to her chest, and covered her face with both hands. *This obsession with Dylan Randle the III and Harley Durham needed to stop and stop now*!

The passenger door swung open. Pepper jumped, her breath caught in her throat as a woman with fire-engine red hair climbed in.

"Roland said to drive to the end of Discovery Circle away from Infinity Science Center," Sherri Dee said. "He's waiting there...doesn't like me out of his sight for too long."

"Not before you prove you're Sherri Dee Durham," Pepper said with her hand on the door handle. "How do I know you didn't lure me here so you could kill me?"

Sherri Dee laughed. "The only person that might be killed is me," she said. "My beloved brother has kept me locked away for over twenty years and would like nothing more than to see me dead."

Pepper shifted into drive and proceeded up the road. She immediately started firing questions at Sherri. "Did you know a Gabrielle Bélair?"

"How could I forget that pretty little thing," Sherri said. "She was so in love with D-Rod."

"D-Rod?" Who was D-Rod?" Pepper asked.

Sherri Dee laughed. "Dylan Randle the III, Mr. President of the United States, my short-time husband who used me, and then discarded me like a piece of trash." Her mood flipped from light-hearted to venomous. "He, along with my brother, locked me away from the world to keep my mouth shut. It wasn't right what those two did to that poor pregnant girl."

A man jumped out of the woods, ran onto the road with arms waving and screaming at the top of his voice. "Peezee, get out of the car, run, run. They're here."

"Stop, stop, the car," Sherri Dee begged.

Before Pepper could completely come to a stop, Sherri Dee jumped out and ran into the woods with Roland.

As the car rolled to a stop, Pepper's hands froze to the steering wheel. "Who, who is coming?" she shouted to the retreating couple. "What do I do?"

Pepper turned off her headlights and continued to follow Discovery Circle past Infinity Science Center to the dead end. She jumped out of her car and ran into the woods.

Gunshots echoed through the forest.

Without looking back, she ran as fast as she could and zigzagged, like she'd seen in the movies, dodging trees, and jumping over logs. Briars snagged her jeans and slowed her progress, but Pepper pushed forward away from the danger she knew was behind her.

Out of breath, she stopped for a moment leaned against a tree, inhaled and exhaled until the heaving in her chest calmed. She took out her cell phone, but there were no bars. Where in the hell was she? What was she going to do? Who was after Sherri Dee and Roland — maybe even her?

The waning moon attempted to break free from a massive storm cloud, but slid back into its hiding place and shrouded the forest with a blanket of darkness until even the shadows were lost. Two more gunshots echoed in the distance. Pepper burst into another full sprint, then tripped and fell, hitting her head against a rock.

CHAPTER 34

PEPPER jerked away from the cold fingers pressed against her neck. She tried to focus, recognize the person that had touched her, but the only thing that her fog-laden brain registered was a deep penetrating throb pounding in her head and garbled words. Instinct pushed her to stand and run, but her legs were numb – whether she was paralyzed, or just cold she couldn't tell.

"Lay still," the voice said. "You're injured."

Pepper finally managed to sit up; the urge to throw up was overwhelming.

"Can you stand?" The same voice asked.

Pepper wanted to answer, but the dizziness only made her want to lie down and go to sleep.

"If you can walk, we need to leave now before they find us. There's a car waiting just on the edge of the woods."

Pepper registered the urgency in the voice and fought to regain her senses. Darkness gave way to diffused light that grew brighter as the sun crawled its way to the horizon. The facial features of the voice were blurred, but there was no mistaking the fire-engine red hair.

"Sher...Sherri Dee?"

"Yes," she said and helped Pepper lean her back against a tree. "You must have tripped and hit your head on a rock. When I found you an hour ago, you were out cold and bleeding. I tried everything to wake you before Harley's men found us, but..."

"Harley?" Pepper managed to say.

"Don't talk," Sherri Dee said. "I need you to try to stand and walk. We've been lucky so far. The woods have been dark and dense, but it is getting light now and we'll be easy to spot. We need to move."

Pepper allowed Sherri to lift her to her feet. "You're bleeding," Pepper said.

"Yeah, no kidding," Sherri replied. "A bullet grazed my shoulder while running away. Roland wasn't that lucky."

"You... you mean..."

"Dead," she said without an ounce of empathy. "Bastards murdered my one and only ticket out of this God forsaken country and away from my brother and his lynch mob."

Without another word, the two women hooked arms and hobbled at a snail's pace forward. The light grew brighter as the sun peeked through the trees; birds twittered; a spooked doe and fawn ran past them.

Pepper stopped; she furrowed her brow. "Where are we going?"

"Don't stop," Sherri Dee said. "Keep going. It's just a little further. Roland stashed my old VW a mile or two away from the Welcome Center. He was afraid something like this might happen."

"He's dead because of me, isn't he?"

"Don't talk," Sherri said. "Save your energy. I'll explain everything later."

Thirty minutes later a flash of red penetrated through the dense woods. Pepper and Sherri Dee quickened their pace until they were standing next to a red VW, almost the exact same color as Sherri Dee's hair.

Sherri reached her hand up the wheel-well, pulled out a magnetic box, took out a key, and unlocked the car.

Before climbing into the VW, Pepper reached into her jacket pocket for her cell phone. Panic seized her heart. "Stop," she yelled. "We've got to go back. My cell phone... I dropped my cell phone. Our interview... it must be taped or no one will believe me."

"If you don't get in the car right now," Sherri warned. "I'm leaving you here."

"No... No, you don't understand," Pepper said. "I need..."

"The only thing we *need* to do is move. You didn't lose your phone," Sherri said. "I took out the Sim card and buried them both before you woke up."

"What? Why," Pepper snapped. "Your story doesn't work if you're not recorded."

"You haven't watched many spy movies, have you," Sherri said with a sly grin. "Your phone would give away our location no matter where we go. I can't afford that luxury." She reached over and patted Pepper's knee. "Besides, what do you need with a recorder? You have a live, breathing witness sitting right next to you. I'm not going anywhere until I have personally destroyed the lives of Harley Durham and Mr. Dylan Randle the III like they have destroyed mine.

Pepper furrowed her brow. "But..."

"Please, shut up," Sherri said. "I need to think...I need a pain pill...most of all I need to slow the bleeding in my shoulder."

After driving for over an hour through the back roads of Mississippi and Louisiana the VW pulled onto the Chalmette ferry and started the ten-minute journey across the Mississippi River to East New Orleans.

Pepper climbed out of the VW and walked to the bow of the car ferry. As she passed the vehicles, she caught people staring at her, and then remembered she still had dried blood in her blonde hair and along her face. She didn't care; she needed to get away from Sherri for a few minutes and think.

She closed her eyes and allowed the soft breeze and the methodical swish of the ferry's wake clear her head. Sporadic moments from the last twenty-four hours flickered in and out of her memory leaving her dumbfounded as to how she ever reached this point. Everything Sherri Dee had shared with her for the last hour was outrageous. Nothing made sense. Even if she had been able to record every word, who would believe the rants and raves of a vindictive, schizophrenic woman who had spent years locked away because of her mental condition?

Pepper fought back tears. A man died because of *my* willfulness. Nothing made sense any longer. Maybe she should ditch Sherri Dee. Beg a ride from one of the other strangers on the ferry... maybe she should get on the next Greyhound Bus for anywhere but New Orleans. She'd never be able to make up for all the damage she'd already done to so many lives in less than a week. Who did she think she was? What gave her the right...?

An arm slipped around her waist. "It's time to get back in the car," Sherri Dee said. "You got me into this mess and you're going to help get me out. This was *all* your idea."

Sherri opened the passenger door and helped Pepper in. "You, my new friend," she said, "after I help you, you are going to help me get out of the country, or we both will die trying."

Twenty minutes later Sherri Dee pulled into a long driveway and followed it all the way back. She parked on the grass behind the shotgun house where her car couldn't be seen from the street.

"Stay here," she said as she climbed out of the VW. "Don't come inside until I signal it's safe. You're in as much danger as I am now. We need each other."

"Where are we," Pepper asked.

"The only place I'm welcome in New Orleans," Sherri Dee said. "Maybe the United States since Dylan became such a Washington bigwig."

Sherri Dee knocked on the backdoor, and waited. She tapped again. When there was no answer, Pepper saw her lift a flowerpot and take out a key. She opened the door and entered the house.

Several minutes later, Sherri returned to the back porch and waved her to come inside.

Pepper hesitated, and then surrendered the impulse to bolt. She had no phone... no money... and an unknown force may wish her dead. She had no choice. As she climbed the steps to the back porch, the dull throb in her head switched to full blown pounding once again. She needed a minimum of three Advil and a gallon of water. Pepper entered the house just as an elderly black woman shuffled down a long hallway pulling on a robe.

"My, oh my, oh my," the woman mumbled. "You be the death of me yet, girl. Why you bringin' that reporter into my house... the same one who interviewed Mr. Harley and be so disrespectful to the president?"

"Don't worry, Ruby Jo," Sherri said. "Harley probably thinks I'm dead right now. If he discovers I'm not, I should still have a couple days before he comes looking for me. That's all the time I need to get out of the country."

"But, why you have to come here, Miss Peezee? You knows how Mr. Harley feels about me keeping stuff from him."

"My dear brother won't even know I was here," Sherri leaned against the countertop, "unless you tell him."

Ruby wiped her glasses with the corner of her robe as she sat in a chair. "You can't keep nothin' from Mr. Harley. He has a third eye. You and I both know he belongs to the devil."

Sherri Dee knelt beside Ruby Jo; her eyes welled with tears. "I wouldn't be here if I didn't need your help." A tear rolled down her cheek. "There wasn't any other place I could go and not be in danger."

Ruby gently wiped the tears off Sherri's cheek. "I know, Chile. Life's been unkind to you, and Mr. Harley partly the blame."

Sherri forced to keep the tone of her voice calm and reassuring. "I need you to get something from Harley's Golden Parachute Room," she said patting the elderly woman's hand. "It's really important to me."

"Oh, no Child, no!" Ruby Jo said. "I can't do that. Mr. Harley already believes somebody done stole something from that room. He got all up in my face just the other day. That be the time he found out you'd slept in his house while he was gone."

"No... NO... NO!" Sherri screamed and then fell back on her haunches. She covered her eyes, and dropped her head in her hands. "This can't be happening. Why didn't I get all that evidence while I was there? What's wrong with me? I should have known better."

Sherri sprung to her feet. "Do you still have that gun Harley bought you for protection?"

"No, Chile. No. Mr. Harley might be an evil man, but his judgment belongs to God, not you."

"How much money do you have in the house, old woman?" Sherri's demeanor had gone from calm to unstable in a flash. She raced through the house, pulling out drawers, screaming at the top of her lungs. "Where is it, old woman...where is it? I know you have a gun...I know you have money."

Ruby Jo jumped out of her chair and began to pace wringing her hands. "My...oh my...oh my," she mumbled.

"I'll kill you, Harley Durham. I'll kill you," Sherri screamed as she ran out of the house like she was on fire.

Ruby Jo sank back in the chair and sobbed. Pepper tried to comfort her, but didn't know what to say, or what to do.

Ruby looked up. "Child, I don't know why you're here, but if I was you, I'd get out of this house as fast as you can. When Miss Peezee get like this, nobody know what she gonna do next... nobody."

CHAPTER 35

BEFORE Detective Sullivan could finish dressing and strap on his service pistol and badge, his phone blew up with messages from his boss, Lieutenant Jackson. As Marty skimmed the text, the blood drained from his face. Penelope Mill's name was plastered across the phone's screen bolded and in all capital letters. He rolled his chin to his chest. You've got to be joking," he moaned. "Harassing the president of the United States wasn't enough, so now she goes to Mississippi and becomes a Person of Interest in a murder and is presumed missing?"

He took one last sip of energy drink and grabbed his keys. Unbelievable, he thought. The sun had only been up for a couple hours and this day had already morphed into a pile of steaming crap. His dear 'ol former friend had a lot of balls getting him and NOPD involved with that crazy-ass reporter in the first place. She was Fed business for God's sake. Now the Lieutenant and the entire NOPD Police Department was going to have *his* neck in a noose before noon — all because he felt obligated to repay a debt to the man who saved his life a long time ago. Marty locked the front door and headed to the car. *One way or the other, Mr. Secret Service agent, you're going to help me fix this.*

Before he started the engine, Detective Sullivan checked for the last known address of André Bélair in Algiers Point. He pulled up the GPS and punched in an address on Pelican Street. Marty backed out of the driveway faster than he should have and headed for Highway 90 East. If he had any luck today maybe law enforcement in Mississippi would locate Miss Mills, and she could become their headache, he thought as he drove cross the Crescent City Bridge toward the West Bank.

Marty's mind continued to reel as he approached the General De Gaulle Exit. It seemed the moment the presidential campaign arrived in New Orleans, the craziness in the city had doubled. *Most likely effects from that damn full moon we're having right now*, he scoffed under his breath. It seemed once a month when that celestial body blossomed into a big old pumpkin all types of chaos exploded on the streets. Every cop, hospital, and EMT tech held their breaths until that moon rotated from full back to a manageable crescent.

Detective Sullivan pulled up in front of a pale yellow cottage with cerulean blue shutters and tapped in a phone number.

"Bélair," the voice on the other end of the phone said.

"What the hell, André? You said there wouldn't be any blowback. You said the reporter wouldn't cause me, or NOPD another minute's trouble. Well, guess again, my dear 'ol friend. Thanks a hellava lot!"

"Who *is* this," André asked.

"It's me," Detective Sullivan said, "your former classmate... the dumbass you dragged out of the Pacific Ocean."

"Sullivan?"

"Yeah, the same, your old BUDS buddy and Police Academy classmate... no longer friend."

André rushed out the front door of the cottage still holding his cell phone. "What's going on?" he asked.

"Your girl... that reporter you asked your old friends in NOPD to go easy on."

"Penelope Mills?"

"Yeah, that one," Marty said. "She's making news again — at least on Police radios and across State Lines."

"Whaaat? Why?" he asked now standing next to the car.

"Get in," Detective Sullivan said. "You're coming with me."

Before André could shut the door, the car began to move down the street.

"Where are we going?" André asked.

"That reporter's house. She lives around here, right?"

"Yeah," André said. "Turn here on Elmira. She's up about four or five blocks. What's going on, Marty?"

"She's missing and the Mississippi State Police need to question her, but not before I get my hands on her first," Detective Sullivan said.

"Come on, Marty," André said. "That poor lady's only crime is having a big mouth and not knowing when to keep it shut."

"Not this time," Detective Sullivan said. "Mississippi wants to question her about a murder at one of their Rest Stops off I-10. She was the last call on the murdered victim's phone," he glanced over and furrowed his brow. "Not to mention her deserted car was parked at the end of a dead-end near the crime scene."

"That doesn't prove anything," André said. "She's a reporter... talks to a lot of people. Writing and reporting the news is all part of a journalist's game."

When they pulled into Pepper's driveway, they froze in their seats; eyes wide; mouth ajar.

"Does that look like a game to you?" Detective Sullivan asked. "When was the last time you saw a giant rat nailed to a wall accompanied with a message *stay out of my business*?"

The two men climbed out of the car with pistols drawn. "Go around back," Detective Sullivan barked as he eased up the front steps. He holstered his weapon long enough to take a picture of the slaughtered animal and the scrawled message written in blood.

André raced to the back of the house, and then quickly returned. "All's secure," he said, as he joined the detective on the front porch.

Marty banged on the front door. "NOPD, are you home Miss Mills," he called out. "We need to speak with you."

Silence. Marty and André glanced at one another, tried the knob, but the entrance was locked. The Detective quickly kicked in the door and split the doorframe. With guns still drawn, they charged into a room that was turned upside down, paintings slashed, and glass broken. Marty immediately pulled out his radio. "This is Detective Martin Sullivan with the 8th. Please send a unit and forensics to Elmira Street in Algiers Point."

CHAPTER 36

STREETCARS rumbled past; cars honked their horns and whizzed by Pepper who was still standing in the middle of the street even after the light turned green. She had wandered aimlessly in a daze for hours, maybe minutes; she didn't know — she had lost all sense of time.

She vaguely remembered people asking if she was okay, or if they could help, but she ignored them as if they were all players in a bad dream and wouldn't hear her even if she answered. She didn't know where she was going, and there were moments she wasn't even sure who she was. No matter how hard she tried, her mind couldn't focus because of the piercing pain and incessant throb camped in her head. The one thing she *could* trust was her feet and she planned to follow them to wherever they planned to take her.

***

Pepper clutched the rail of the high, black wrought iron fence; prayed she would remain upright just a little longer. She wasn't sure where she was, but the ochre colored building was familiar; she knew she had been there before, but didn't know when or why, but every instinct inside verified she had arrived and it was the right place to be. She opened the door and stepped inside. A huge desk that faced directly in front of the entrance wrapped around the room in a half circle. Adorning the façade of the large counter were individual, small framed paintings depicting scenes of Old New Orleans. Elongated wrought iron chandeliers hung from the high ceiling. The lobby was empty except one female police officer on the phone sitting behind a huge desk.

Pepper stepped up to the counter, opened her mouth, but nothing came out. The pretty blonde officer glanced up, jumped to her feet, and raced around the desk.

"Miss," she said, "Are you okay? Who hit you? Have you been in an accident?"

Pepper collapsed in her arms.

CHAPTER 37

STRANGE voices mumbled nearby along with the sound of a rhythmic beep. Pepper tried to open her eyes, but she couldn't. As a cool cloth brush across her face, she caught the scent of antiseptic. *Where in the hell am I*, she wondered. *This must be another bizarre scene from this wild dream I can't seem to wake up from.*

"She's suffered a severe concussion," a female voice said. "Scans indicate there is no bleeding in the brain, and that's very good news."

"When will we be able to talk to her?" a gruff male voice asked.

"You'll need to wait until the sedation has worn off and she is alert before I determine that," the female voice said.

"Is it alright if I sit with her?" another man asked, "Until she wakes?"

"Of course," the woman said. "When she does, please get one of the nurses immediately. We'll want to check her vitals and make sure she is lucid before you interrogate her."

Concussion? Nurses? Am I in a hospital? Interrogate? Oh wow, this is one crazy dream, Pepper thought trying to make sense of the disjointed dialog.

Pepper focused on the nearby rhythmic beep; slipped in and out of consciousness. She was floating on a cloud; birds flew by and serenaded her with a pretty song. They sounded like Taylor Swift who looked like an angel sitting on a passing cloud playing a lyre; she smiled and waved. The soft, fragrant breeze that kissed her cheeks suddenly switched to a turbulent wind, the sky turned black, lightning flashed. She clung to the cloud but inch by inch it dissipated; she was falling, falling into blackness. Pepper screamed and bolted upright.

A crew of medical staff raced into the room.

"Welcome back to the world," a woman in a white coat said. "You had us worried. Do you know your name and where you are?"

Pepper glanced around the room; she furrowed her brow. "How did I get here?" She asked

The woman in the white coat gently took her wrist, smiled as she checked Pepper's pulse. "Paramedics brought you in," she said. "You have a concussion. Can you tell me your name?"

"Penelope...Penelope Anne Mills," Pepper said as a light was flashed across her eyes. "And, it looks like I'm in a hospital."

The woman smiled. "Excellent," she said. "Are you up to answering a few questions from these nice gentlemen?"

Pepper peered around the doctor. There was one man with black wavy hair who looked at her with unsmiling eyes. She didn't recognize him. Another man stepped next to her bed. Pepper's mouth fell ajar; it was the handsome knight in the black hoodie that had come to her house. "Agent ... Agent Bélair?" she asked amazed to be seeing him standing next to her bed.

André smiled. "Hey, Miss Mills, welcome back. You've suffered quite a blow to your head and had us all a bit worried. This is my friend Detective Sullivan. He'd like to ask you a few questions."

"Keep your questions short," the doctor ordered. "By no means agitate my patient. If her blood pressure rises in the least little bit, I'll have you escorted to the waiting area," she warned as she stepped out of the room.

André took Pepper's hand. "You up for this?" he asked.

"I think so," she said. "My memory is still a bit fuzzy, but I'll try."

"Anything you can remember will be helpful?" Detective Sullivan said. "Do you know what you did and where you were last night," he asked. "Try to start from the beginning if you can."

"I was at home working on leads for a story all day," she looked up at André, "from the book you gave me," she said. "I took a break around six and went to the Dry Dock Café for a couple beers, ate a bowl of Gumbo and came ho..." Pepper's mouth fell open, the heart monitor beeped louder.

Both André and Detective Sullivan glanced over their shoulder as if waiting for a barrage of medical staff to shoo them out of the room.

"Are you here because...?" And then, her eyes widen as memories rushed into her head. "My house... someone trashed my house and stole some items."

"Is that where you sustained your injuries?" Sullivan asked.

Pepper squeezed her eyes tight and tried to force the details from her memory. A dull throb inched into her temple. "I'm... I'm sorry. My thoughts are still disjointed... fuzzy," she said. "May I have a sip of water?"

As André held a glass of water with a straw to Pepper's lips, Detective Sullivan's radio blasted an alert:

"*Signal 20... Vehicle Crash Westbound CCC past Tchoupitoulas exit... 3 vehicles... red Volkswagen, silver Camry, white pickup... medium height woman... red hair suspected as a 103M. .. Gun visible.*"

"Sherri Dee!" Pepper screamed. "Stop her. She's the key to everything."

The doctor and a nurse raced into the room. "Get Out! Get out now," she snapped at the two men as a nurse injected Pepper with sedation.

CHAPTER 38

HARLEY stared at the spectacle unfolding right before his eyes in vivid color on the sixty-inch television. News helicopters hovered over the Mississippi River, cameras zoomed in on Sherri Dee tottering on the upper edge of the Crescent City Connection Bridge. One moment she pointed the gun at her head; the next she pointed the weapon at the police — this horror movie had haunted his nightmares for years. If his sister would just go ahead and jump, half of his problems would be solved. How was he going to explain this fiasco to Dylan? He had promised his friend thirty years ago that he would get rid of Peezee permanently; promised she would never again resurface and threaten to reveal their dark secrets to anyone. For over thirty-five years, he had succeeded keeping that promise — until now. After all these years how had his dear sister manage to slither through the cracks from hell?

He picked up his cell phone, punched in five numbers and stopped. What in the hell was he doing? Perspiration beaded on Harley's forehead and rolled down his cheek. Dylan was the last person he should call — he was the very reason they all were staring into the cradle of damnation. *He* was the one who lured that sweet piece of dark meat into his arms, and then insisted they both have their way with her. *He* was the one who nine months later convinced that pregnant teenager he was going to take care of her and the baby forever. Dylan Randle the III, Mr. President of the United States, was the one who left Peezee and me to clean up *his* mess on Lake Pontchartrain.

Years of repressed resentment seized his chest; gasps of breath caught in his throat. *Breathe, Harley, breathe,* his brain screamed. *You* weren't the one who slapped that poor girl around, knocked her out, and left her bleeding on the deck. *You* weren't the one barking orders to toss her body overboard, and then speed off in the opposite direction in the yacht's dingy. If anything, you and Peezee were as much a victim as that young girl.

Harley switched off the television; paced back and forth trying to silence the ancient history clawing its way to the surface — he tried to concentrate on his future. The more he attempted to escape the past, the faster the unwanted demons invaded his thoughts. Harley squeezed his brows together and forced back the negative and searched for the positive. Of course, he was grateful that Dylan's dad set him up in a lucrative business. But, it was his resourcefulness over the last thirty-five plus years that lined his pockets with gold. Harley smiled with a sneer. Admittedly, his dear old friend deserved *some* of the credit for the cash-cow that fed the coffers of his retirement fund. After all, Mr. Dylan Randle the III was the one who introduced him to the art of blackmail.

Harley glanced back at the now dark television screen. A wave of nostalgia mixed with pity inched into his thoughts. Peezee... poor, poor Peezee. The "D-Rod" captured your heart from day one. You would've done anything for him — and you did. That bastard broke your heart more times than your sick little brain could handle.

He shrugged. Who knows? Maybe his baby sister would've still been married to the president of the United States today — that is, if that damn disease had not poisoned her mind. It was Dylan's extracurricular activities and total disregard for their legal marriage that aroused

Sherri's vindictiveness and turned her into a Tasmanian devil on a rampage. Once his sister ramped up the threats to expose Dylan's part from that fateful day and the type of man he actually was, she sealed her destiny.

Actually, Sherri should be thanking him for keeping her locked away all these years. If Dylan had had his way, he would've dumped her into the deepest part of the swamp and let the alligators deal with her.

The scream of a siren snapped Harley back to reality. What was he doing just standing there hashing over what was and what could've been? The clock was ticking. What made him think he was safe after everything that had transpired in just the last 48-hours? That reporter's curiosity and Peezee's little stunt on the bridge has, more than likely, kicked Dylan into survival mode.

This very minute Homeland Security, FBI, NOPD, and God only knows who else, were probably racing down St. Charles Avenue with their sirens wailing, lights flashing with he, Harley Durham, best friend of the president of the United States, as their target. Apprehension mushroomed inside him and played tug-of-war with the last shred of good judgment. Harley tried to calm his out-of-control inner turmoil; he tried to move, but his feet were glued to the floor.

He swiped away a trail of sweat inching down his brow, gathered his determination, and marched toward the back of the house. The only person that mattered right now was him. To hell with Peezee... to hell with Dylan Randle. What more could he have done to try to stop that runaway train wreck of a reporter? It wasn't his fault she kept digging and digging and digging into their past. It wasn't his fault intimidation had no effect on Miss Penelope Mills. This freefall started because that crazy bitch was unwilling to let go of a story. The reality of it all was he had no control over what his dear sister may or may not have spilled from that scrambled brain of hers.

Harley headed for his bedroom suite straight for the bookcase and the Civil War Chess set. He reached over and gave Bobby Lee a twist to open his Golden Parachute Room. After the door slid open, he twirled the combination until the safe clicked open. He pulled out three fake passports and several credit cards with corresponding names. He opened and checked inside a large maroon velvet bag that was filled with several million dollars' worth of diamonds. He ripped out the hard drive of the computer and poured acid into his file cabinet and onto the computer components. Taking one last look around, Harley grabbed his emergency "getaway" suitcase and rushed out of his Garden District mansion.

CHAPTER 39

WITH cell phone clenched in his fist, Dylan stood in front of the television frozen in place, jaw dropped to his chest, his heart pounding. A ghost? Or, was he lost in some sick nightmare he couldn't wake up from? He punched in Harley's telephone number for the third time; listened to the unanswered ringtone again and again; waited for an answer and the barrage of endless excuses.

Why? Why now? He wanted to scream, but fell back onto the edge of the colonial bed instead. Dylan stared out the opened veranda doors across the moss-laden oaks. Any hope of a breeze had been stifled by the late October heat wave. In a matter of minutes, the tuxedo shirt he had just put on plastered against his freshly showered body.

Years ago, he should have listened to his father, and then Céline when they begged him to cut ties with Harley Durham. How many times had they both told him that keeping his old friend in his life was a one-way ticket to a catastrophic end? Little did either of them realize that the last chance for "any ending" occurred before *he* was barely twenty years old? Once he stepped across the wrong line and begged for their help, he no longer had a choice. They both became the only two people in the world he could truly trust; who understood and accepted his demons.

Dylan unhooked the studs and peeled off the sweat soaked shirt. He opened the mini-fridge, took out a bottle of water, and held it next to his hot flesh. He strolled onto the upstairs balcony in his underwear and sat in the Brumby Rocker and willed a breeze to break through the heat. The reality was not even a wintry gust was going to cool the slow burn boiling inside. Harley had assured him Sherri Dee was out of their lives forever. He'd never asked exactly what "forever" meant; he didn't want to know; didn't need to know. He only wanted that crazy bitch out of his life; completely erased from his past. Harley being the creative guy he was, assured him he had taken care of everything. He never doubted his friend's loyalty. Not once in all these years had they spoken about *that* day, or Sherri Dee. The past was the past. Both their hard-earned successes spoke for themselves.

The longer Dylan sat outside, the more uncomfortable he became. *Anxiety or the heat?* He wondered. Whichever it was, he needed to get it under control. In exactly two hours he and the Davidson's' would be on Marine One headed back to New Orleans and the donor dinner at The Eiffel. Somehow, he needed to get word to Harley that under the circumstances, his attendance at the donor dinner would be disruptive. The media would be focusing on the events of the day once they discovered Sherri Dee was his sister. They would start asking questions no one was ready to answer.

Dylan went into the bathroom for a second shower. He stepped out of his underwear and into a mist of cold water. He placed his hands against the wall and allowed the water to refresh his sweat-drenched skin. He stared down at the small whirlpool created by the water encircling the drain, and then disappeared into the dark hole. *If only the sins of his youth were as easily washed away*, he thought. Dylan lifted his face into the spray. What was he worried about? When he was twenty years old, he'd proved capable of concealing a major crisis with both skill and cunning.

Nothing had changed. If anything, he was better equipped than ever to handle a crisis.

Dylan turned off the water. The difference between then and now, he was more powerful. He was the president of the United States of America and leader of the free world. *He* was about to be reelected. No one could touch him. No one would dare question his authority, much less what he said. He couldn't remember the last time his loyal base bought into that load of crap the media and his political enemies tried to sell every day during the news cycles.

He stepped out of the shower, grabbed a towel, and wrapped around his waist. Right now, he had one focus and one focus only and that was to impress the hell out of all those donors at the dinner tonight; convince them *they* needed Dylan Randle the III more than he needed them.

Dylan swiped moisture from the full-length mirror. He narrowed his eyes; determination tightened his jaw. "Nobody better get in my way," he said. "If they do..."

CHAPTER 40

BURT HARRISON'S hands shook as he retied the bowtie for the third time. Why was he so nervous? He'd attended hundreds of these functions over the years. He should be giddy. The first lady called him today, apologized for being AWOL during these final days of the campaign, and promised she was one hundred percent on board. Dylan's poll numbers, even after all the publicity with Harley's sister threatening to jump off the Crescent City Bridge today, had actually bumped up instead of going down for a change. He smiled and winked at the image in the mirror. The best news of all was Harley Durham was no longer welcome on the campaign trail or near the White House *ever* again.

He dabbed a small amount of cologne on his neck, shut his eyes and relished the positive turn the campaign had made in just twenty-four hours. He hadn't felt this good and encouraged since the Party's convention in August. Shame on him for allowing such negativity to influence his almost disastrous behavior last night — he had been so close to sabotaging four years of sobriety because of Harley Durham and his Secret Room. Now that Harley was out of the picture, he needed to relax and get Dylan elected president of the United States.

Burt slipped on his tuxedo jacket, straightened his bowtie. *Thanks to my quick, but not so legal thinking*, he reasoned, Dylan should no longer have blackmail problems from that disgusting swamp rat. *My mother would disagree*, he thought, but still felt a surge of pride. Stealing that box,

249

filled with compromising documents, photos and CD's about the president was perhaps the smartest political move he'd made in his career. Now he was the one who had control over Dylan Randle's destiny, not Harley Durham.

He cocked his head and glanced in the mirror at a man torn between doing what was right, or what was wrong. He frowned. "Come on, Charlotte, get out of my head," he begged, and then shook his head. This wasn't the time to allow her judgmental voice to send him on another one of her guilt trips. Yesterday his heart told him that revealing the truth about Dylan before the election was the honorable one. That's why he originally sent the anonymous note to the reporter in the first place. But after sleeping on it, his gut now insisted the timing to reveal the truth wasn't right. He was paid to do one job and one job only and that was to get Dylan Randle the III elected. The best course of action for him now, was to lose the key to the safety deposit box and not cause a scandal so late in the game.

Burt picked up his cell phone and called to see if his car was ready; he checked his watch. He didn't have time to retrieve the key from the Hotel Manager's safe. No worries. There was no rush. Tomorrow morning was soon enough when he checked out. The note he'd mailed to Penelope Mills wouldn't be delivered to her house for another day or two and only after the campaign party was back in Washington preparing for a victory celebration. When that reporter received the cryptic message and came to the Roosevelt in hopes for the mother lode of all scandals, the hotel won't know what she's talking about; and she certainly won't know who the letter was from. Burt flashed thumbs up at the image in the mirror and said, "You've got this. There's absolutely nothing to worry about."

CHAPTER 41

CÉLINE punched off her phone and released a nervous sigh. She pinched the bridge of her nose and closed her eyes. *Would this nightmare that had become her life ever end?*

"What's wrong?" Claréne asked. "Who was that?"

"Martha... Martha Davidson."

"One of Lily Mae's old cronies?"

"The crony's daughter. She's our fourth cousin," Céline said.

"Why was she calling you?" Claréne asked as she styled her sister's hair. "How do you even know her?"

"Come on, don't you remember. We became reacquainted with Martha years ago at one of the family reunions. We played dolls with her once or twice when we were kids."

Claréne shrugged and completed the finishing touches to the twist set low on the nape of Céline's neck. She pulled a few tendrils of hair from each side with the tail of the comb and curled them with a curling iron. "There, she said, "you look beautiful. I hope Dylan will appreciate this extra effort you're making."

"Dylan wants eye-candy. I'm going to give him eye-candy," Céline said.

"What you're going to do is make him seduce you. Please don't wear that dress. Pick something more conservative."

"Don't start with me," Céline said. "I'm not strong like you. I need to heed Martha's warnings; convince Dylan I care about him and am serious about getting him elected."

"Oh crap," Claréne cursed. "I should have known that phone call would be about Dylan. What has he done now?"

Céline checked her makeup in the mirror, brushed a loose strand of hair from her eyes. "I don't want to get into it right now."

Claréne took her twin's hand and pulled her down on the edge of the bed next to her. "Why not?"

"Martha suggested maybe I was getting in too deep and should be careful," she said.

"What did *you* do?"

"I asked her to bug Dylan's room."

"How is that possible?" Claréne asked. "All his communications would be on his cell phone, plus the Secret Service would sweep the entire house before he even stayed there."

"Have you forgotten, I'm the first lady of the United States and have my ways?"

"Well then, what's the problem?"

"After speaking with Martha, she made me realize I may have gone too far; she suggested I take a look in the mirror and ask myself if I'm part of the problem."

"Ridiculous," Claréne said.

"No, not really. I *have* been a witch lately. The poor man is under a lot of pressure and with all my recent antics I haven't made things any easier for him."

"Where are you going with this?"

Céline hesitated. "I let Harley Durham's influence with Dylan get into my head, and it has all but destroyed our marriage. I accepted a long time ago Dylan wasn't a choirboy, but at least he's always been discreet. The pressure of this campaign has drained me; maybe even tainted my judgment at times. I think I should give Dylan the benefit of the doubt."

"You've got to be kidding me," Claréne said. "How can you even suggest such a thing after everything we've learned these last couple days? You're being ridiculous."

Céline stood. "No, I'm not. I'm the one who ran home to Mama Bea. I'm the one who has been less than enthusiastic during this campaign and have driven both Dylan and Burt insane with my out of character behavior."

"You're being too hard on yourself," Claréne said. "Sounds like an old-fashioned guilt trip to me. Even André agrees you needed to put some distance between yourself and your husband. He's been worried about you."

A tap on the door interrupted the women. "The presidential limousine is ten minutes out," André said. "You almost ready?"

"She'll be there in a minute," Claréne barked. "It won't hurt Mr. Dylan Randle the III to wait a few minutes." She leaned her back against the door. "I'm not letting you leave until you tell me exactly what Martha said that set you off."

Céline stood and straightened the wrinkles in her form-fitted royal blue gown with the deep V-neck and a side-split to the thigh. "I was the one who called Martha first and asked that Dylan come stay with them for at least one night. When Dylan agreed, I was relieved."

"One little act of doing the right thing for a change, doesn't turn the man into a saint overnight."

Céline moved toward the door. "Please let me pass."

"Not before you tell me why all of a sudden you've stepped into the dark side."

"Martha didn't just call to lay a guilt trip on me," Céline said. "She called to warn me things didn't go exactly as planned and to be very careful with what I did and what I say."

"You're scaring me," Claréne said. "What happened?"

"During cocktails before leaving the plantation on Marine One for the donor dinner tonight, a copy of the tape Martha made for me fell out of her small clutch. Dylan gracious picked it up, smiled at her and said, "What an odd item to be carrying in such a small evening purse."

CHAPTER 42

BURT paced back and forth at the entrance of The Eiffel; he checked his watch, and then the time on his cell phone. *Where were they?* The question bit deep into an already anxious moment. What if Marine One had crashed on the way back from the Davidson plantation, or the first lady changed her mind at the last minute and decided to ditch tonight — a night that could very well make or break Dylan's chance to be election. His tuxedo shirt began to stick to his back. He took out a handkerchief and wiped his brow. "It's October, for God's sake, doesn't it ever cool off in this wretched city?" He cursed under his breath.

He hurried up the steps and then up the ramp to The Eiffel and went inside to cool off. Burt scanned the six thousand square foot room. From the teardrop lighting that dangled from the skylight in the high ceiling to the gold-plated place settings on the round tables that encircled the room, everything was perfect. Bartenders double-checked their stock while waiters hustled around making final preparations. *Relax, Burt, your capable staff has this; they always do*, he reminded himself. *Quit micromanaging. Stop fretting.*

***

Police motorcycles and patrol cars, followed by the presidential convoy, sped across the Crescent City Bridge from Algiers Point back to New Orleans. As the motorcade exited the Pontchartrain Expressway onto Camp Street, Dylan reached over and took Céline's hand. "Tonight is a night for new beginnings," he said. "I've ignored your warnings about Harley far too long. Forgive me for that and everything else I've put you through for the last few years."

Céline furrowed her brow. "Dylan, please don't. Not tonight."

As if on cue, a tear perched in the corner of his eye and threatened to roll down his cheek. "Give me one more chance," he said, "I'll make it up to you for the rest of my life," he kissed her fingertips. "I promise."

Céline inhaled a shallow breath, and then gently released the trapped air between closed lips. "Let's just take care of business tonight. After that we'll see where the chips may fall," she said leaving her hand entwined with his.

"I've planned a little surprise for you," his voice was laced with affection. "Something to try and prove my honest devotion to you and you alone," he said.

Céline forced a smile, squeezed his hand, but her eyes remained focused forward; her resolve strong. This was not the time to let her guard down. If Dylan was anything, he was charming, but underneath that charm lurked a degree of deception that was often unpredictable.

The motorcade pulled up in front of The Eiffel — the same Restaurant that once stood atop the Eiffel Tower in Paris until 1981 and was eventually transported in pieces to New Orleans.

The first lady and the president stepped from the limousine onto a red carpet. White string-lights sparkled along the fencing and up the elevated walkway toward the iconic steel structure with its walls of glass. A black gentleman dressed in a white tuxedo and top hat, walked down the ramp and staircase. He bowed and handed Céline two dozen white roses wrapped with a purple, green and gold ribbon. He took a red velvet box from his pocket and gave it to the president.

Dylan took his wife's hand, turned to face the large crowd that had gathered on and around St. Charles Avenue that had been temporarily closed to traffic. "My friends," he said, "this is the last night my beautiful wife and I will spend in your gracious city." He held his head a little higher, cleared his throat and spoke a little louder. "When I return to the Crescent City, I will be your president." The crowd roared.

"As many of you know, the first lady calls New Orleans home," he kissed her hand. "I can't think of a more perfect time or place for me to renew my love vows and heartfelt devotion to Miss Céline Fontenot Randle." He smiled, dropped her hand, and opened the velvet box.

Céline raised her eyebrows, tilted her head and whispered, "Dylan what are you doing?"

The president smiled took out a gold-plated "Love-lock" with their names and wedding date engraved on each heart, and then snapped the lock onto the fence at the entrance of The Eiffel, and handed her the key. "You and you alone now hold the key to our happiness," he said.

"Oh, Dylan," she said as tears rolled down her cheeks. "Paris... just like our honeymoon... on the Pont des Amoureux Bridge."

Dylan lowered his voice and spoke only to her. "I needed to remind you I still believe and hope in that everlasting love I professed to you nineteen years ago in Paris." He took her in his arms and kissed her. Céline melted into his arms.

The crowd erupted with a roar of cheers and hoots.

The first couple, arm in arm, climbed the fan-shaped stairway. When they reached the top they turned and waved at the crowd. Hundreds of cameras flashed; videos rolled and captured their special moment.

***

Burt grinned from ear to ear like a proud Papa. Why had he been so worried? Even if he had tried, he couldn't have scripted a more masterful photo op or scene. He knew his president was capable of pulling it together, but never dreamed Dylan could create *the* perfect setting for their last night in New Orleans. His romantic gesture toward the first lady would, without a doubt, top every news story throughout the world; touch every heart. A warm sense of satisfaction wrapped around Burt's heart and gave it a hug. He'd just witnessed that beacon of hope he had prayed for to get this campaign back on track. *Eat your heart out Allison Benson*, he chuckled under his breath. *The scales just tipped back our way.*

Burt's cell phone vibrated in his pocket. A message flashed on the screen: *Extremely Important!!! Meet me across the street at the Pontchartrain Hotel... now. Matter of life and death.*

He stared at the message, tried to disregard the obvious urgency. What could possibly be more important than being inside with Dylan and Céline and enjoying the fruits of their labor? He had endured enough drama over the last several days to last a lifetime. The *only* place he should be at the moment was inside this little piece of Paris drinking champagne and convincing donors to cough up the big bucks. He slid his phone back into his pocket and snatched a flute of champagne from a tray.

Burt mingled with the crowd, laughing and enjoying how well everything was going. A staff member tapped him on the shoulder and handed him a note. Burt unfolded the message and read the contents. *Who the hell was Buck and what could possibly be so important for this man to insist he meet with him?* He crushed the note into his fist, jammed it into his pocket and continued to work the room. The words *"Life and Death"* continued to nag him. *What if something had happened to one of his daughters, or to Charlotte, his ex-wife?*

Burt quickly signaled for one of his staff members. When she arrived, he gave her several instructions, and then told her he needed to step out for five to ten minutes to run an errand across the street, but he'd be right back.

With a hurried pace, Burt hopped down the stairs of the Eiffel, and walked to the corner. Traffic once again flowed swiftly down St. Charles. He shifted from one foot to the other while he waited for the pedestrian traffic light to turn green. His anxiety eased when he caught a glimpse of agents perched on nearby rooftops and the presence of both the NOLA Police and the Secret Service who were watching diligently for any suspicious activity.

Burt again looked at his watch, and then back at the party inside. *This fool's journey better be worth his time*, he grumbled under his breath. He pulled the note of warning from his pocket, read it once again, and then raced across the street before the light turned green. He hustled past an oncoming streetcar into the path of a speeding car. The last thing he felt was the *"Life or Death"* note still clutched in his fist.

CHAPTER 43

THREE DAYS LATER

AS PEPPER was wheeled out of the hospital, her mouth dropped open; tears welled in her eyes. Mark was standing next to his rented corvette with an assortment of balloons and a single yellow rose. He raced over, handed Pepper the balloons and helped her out of the wheelchair.

"Are you now my brother's keeper?" She asked with a sheepish grin. "First you bail me from jail and now the hospital?"

Mark handed Pepper the single rose. "If anyone needs rescuing on a regular basis, obviously it's you," he said as he opened the car door. "I'm beginning to think this has become my personal cross to bear." He laughed and then shrugged. "Guess you'll have to learn to accept your fate. I have."

Without arguing, Pepper climbed into the low riding car holding her one yellow rose and the cluster of balloons. Confusion and suspicion wrapped with a smidgen of affection laced her thoughts. Why was Mark still in town? The presidential entourage left days ago, and it was not in his nature to be this far away from the political action — particularly so close to the election.

Mark climbed into the car and pushed the ignition button. The corvette roared to life and sped away from Tulane Medical Center. "Before I take you home, will you let me buy you lunch?"

"Mark," Pepper furrowed her brow, "I appreciate the special attention; I really do. But, what is the real reason you're here?" Pepper asked.

He released a heavy sigh. "Why does there always need to be an ulterior motive with you?" he asked. "Can't a guy just try and do something nice for a lady he's grown to respect and care for?"

Pepper started to say something, but was afraid it would be the wrong thing and chose to keep her eyes focused on the road ahead of them. The Corvette zoomed onto the ramp leading up to Highway 90 West and the Crescent City Connection.

As they crossed the bridge, Pepper released the balloons. She cleared her throat and broke the silence. "Does anyone know what happened to Sherri Dee Durham after her wild escapade on this bridge?

Mark nodded. "Really sad," he said. "First they hauled her off to the nearest psych ward. She was there less than twenty-four hours."

Pepper did a double take. "What... why? Aren't psych patients first evaluated, and then held for seventy-two hours before determining their fate?"

Mark shrugged. "Usually, but not in her case," he said. He chanced a quick glance at Pepper. "You're lucky to be alive. That nutcase escaped from the mental institution where she'd lived for over twenty years."

Pepper started to say something, but stopped.

"Since her brother has disappeared and her husband is dead," Mark continued, "there was no one to take responsibility or speak up for her. They've made Ms. Ongerón a permanent ward of the State."

"Do you know exactly where they took Sherri Dee? I still have so many unanswered questions."

Mark frowned. "You never take a break, do you? It's always dig, dig, dig." He turned off 90 West onto the General De Gaulle exit. As he turned right onto L. B. Landry Avenue and headed toward Algiers Point he said, "Sherri Dee is dead."

"What... How... Why?"

"The day after she was readmitted, they found her in the hospital dining hall restroom. She had ripped open her wrist with a fork and bleed to death."

Blood drained from Pepper's face. Sherri may have been mentally ill, but didn't deserve to die the way she did. What an injustice no one would ever hear her story... what a crime that Harley Durham and Dylan Randle wouldn't be held responsible for the way they treated Sherri Dee and poor Gabrielle. Now, there was nothing she or anyone could do to right all the wrongs.

Pepper's stomach knotted with guilt. What was she thinking? What had she done? In her Don Quixote quest to destroy Dylan Randle, two people were now dead — and those were the lives she knew about. If only she had bridled her obsession, swallowed her pride maybe both Roland Ongerón and Sherri Dee would be living happily ever after somewhere on a beach in Mexico.

As Mark turned onto Opelousas Avenue and headed for Elmira, Pepper's breath caught in her throat; she closed her eyes and tried to steady her runaway heart. She reached over and touched Mark's arm. "I... I don't think I'm ready. Take me anywhere but home."

Mark patted her hand. "It's okay," he said as he turned onto Elmira. "Open your eyes and take a closer look."

Pepper hesitated, but finally chanced a quick glance. The front of her house had a fresh coat of paint. A variety of colorful potted plants lined the edge of the porch. She glanced at Mark. Confusion was written all over her face. "How? When?"

Mark climbed out of the car, came around, and opened the door for her. "While you were in the hospital and with the permission of your landlord, I came over and repainted the front porch, cleaned the house and replaced your furniture."

"Why... why would you do that? I haven't been very nice to you since you arrived in New Orleans," she said. She scrunched her nose. "I'm not sure I even like you."

"Yeah, you've made that perfectly clear. So, I thought if I did something nice for you — no strings, you'd go out with me," he laughed. "At the very least let me help you finish that bottle of Sazerac I bought you."

Pepper ran up the steps and opened the front door. She turned around, fought back tears. "Mark, it looks the same. You've replaced everything with duplicates. Th... Thank you... I don't know what else to say."

"Don't say anything. Just pour me a tumbler of rye so we can celebrate you getting out of the hospital in one piece."

Pepper gave him a quick hug and headed for the kitchen.

"Hey," he shouted after her. "I left your mail on the dinette table."

Moments later Pepper walked back into the living room holding an opened letter. She stood there speechless and handed Mark the note:

Dear Miss Mills:

I have information you may like to have. Wait three days after you receive this letter, and then come to the Roosevelt Hotel and ask for the Manager. He will have an envelope in the hotel safe with your name on it. Bring proper identification with photo ID. I've instructed the Hotel Manager to ONLY give the envelope to you and ONLY after the designated waiting period.

Anonymous Concerned Citizen

As Mark read the note, Pepper found her voice. "Did you write this?"

"Me? You're kidding, right? Why would you ask that?"

"You're staying at the Roosevelt. The note is on Roosevelt stationary."

"True, but a lot of people from the campaign stayed there."

Pepper plopped down onto the sofa next to Mark. "What do you think it means?"

"I think we need to get back in my car and go to the Roosevelt Hotel and find out what this is all about."

***

Pepper glanced over at Mark as she replaced her identification back in her billfold. Her stomach felt like a hundred Mexican jumping beans were ricocheting inside it. Moments later the Hotel Manager brought her an envelope with her name on it. She glanced at Mark and back down at the weighted package. "I... I can't do this anymore," she said handing the envelope to Mark. "My snooping into other people's lives has caused too much damage to too many. If I want to save what's left of my greedy soul, I'm done."

"I completely understand," Mark said. "I quit my news anchor job two days ago for similar reasons. People like us try to control power, but in the end, power controls us and we become the losers."

"What are we going to do with this... whatever this is?" Pepper asked.

"I have a good idea who may have entrusted you with the future of our country, but unfortunately he was stricken down by a hit and run driver in front of the Eiffel.

"Are you talking about Burt Harrison, Dylan's campaign manager? That doesn't make sense? He was the one who had me arrested for interfering in the first place."

"Maybe not, but we both know that the moment the presidential campaign entered the city of New Orleans, numerous unexpected and bizarre events transpired. If you trust me, I know exactly who should have whatever is in that Safety Deposit Box," Mark said. "If you agree, I'll make sure she gets it."

CHAPTER 44

ONE WEEK BEFORE
THE PRESIDENTIAL ELECTION

CÈLINE looked at her wedding photo, and then back at the image in the mirror — the likeness was the same, but they were two different people now. One was a woman who fell deeply in love with a man she thought was her soul mate; the other faced humiliating, and possibly, destroying that same man during the most critical and important time in his life.

How did she get here? Was she naïve or was she just a coward unwilling to face reality? The one thing she *was* sure about was today was a day of reckoning for both she and her husband. She needed to be honest with herself that what she was about to do, she was doing for the right reasons. Her heart ached wanting to give Dylan the benefit of the doubt. Her husband truly seemed sincere at the Eiffel Restaurant the other night and made her once again fall back in love with the person he once was. The look in his eyes, the sincerity in his voice convinced her he wanted to change. Until...

Turning the picture away from her, Céline replaced the photo back onto the dressing table. She opened the bottom drawer, rummaged through her collection of feminine products and pulled out a hot pink diary. Whether intentional or not, Dylan had left the journal partially exposed in his unpacked suitcase after their return from New Orleans.

Céline took the book from the drawer and laid it on her lap. It was unlike her husband to be so careless. Dylan was anything but stupid. She sighed. Whether she liked it or not, developments from the last couple of days and the ramblings from the diary of a teenage girl was the smoking gun. After she was given the key to a safety deposit box and its contents, she could no longer ignore the truth. Dylan had gotten away with far too much for far too long. From the depths of her heart, she wished it all was a plot from a B-rated movie. The nausea churning in her stomach and the inner turmoil that surged through her veins told an entirely different story.

For several days she had wrestled with her conscience and finally came to the conclusion it was too late for not only their marriage, but also for Dylan to seek redemption. Too many people had been adversely affected by the lies he'd told, for the unspeakable deeds he'd done over so many years.

After their return to Washington, more revelations from Dylan's past boiled to the surface faster than lava erupting from a volcano. Too many fingers were primed to point at her husband and expose the type of man he really was — too much circumstantial evidence led to one conclusion. Dylan was guilty and needed to be stopped.

With a presidential election just days away, the people in the United States deserved to have the best leadership possible — a man or woman they could trust and believe in for the right reasons. It no longer mattered how much she once loved Dylan and believed in him, she didn't have a choice. There was no easy way to handle this situation, but the least she could do was give him the opportunity to step down as a candidate before a scandal broke and ripped the country apart.

Céline picked up the phone and called her office downstairs. "Have my guests arrived?" She asked. "Good... Give me fifteen minutes, and then send them to the Oval Office.

Her hand shook as she completed the finishing touches on her makeup. She picked up the diary and placed it in a gift bag.

Céline exited the White House presidential apartments and walked down the stairs toward the Oval Office. Today of all days she hoped friendly staffers who wanted to be friendly and chat wouldn't impede her progress to complete her unpleasant mission. The last thing she needed was to lose her nerve. She needed to stay focused.

The first lady entered the outer office where Dylan's personal secretary acted as a buffer for unwanted intruders and coordinated the day to day operations. "Is the president busy?" she asked.

"Good morning, Mrs. Randle," Elizabeth said. "No one is scheduled for another hour, but I warn you he's in a... a mood. He was just given the latest poll numbers and isn't a happy man. If you want to take your chances, don't say I didn't warn you."

Céline shrugged. "Wish I had a choice," she said. "But I'm about to make things even worse for him."

"Good luck," the assistant said.

"Oh, by the way, Elizabeth, in a few minutes I have four guests coming to the Oval Office who'll be joining me. We don't want to be disturbed. Trust me when I say this may well be the toughest day of Dylan's political career, but it needs to be done."

The assistant started to say something, but stopped.

Céline gathered as much confidence and courage as she could, threw back her shoulders, held her head high, and barged into Dylan's office.

Dylan jerked his head around; jumped up from his chair. "What the hell, Céline, I'm busy. Make an appointment if you want to talk to me."

"Just give me fifteen minutes of your time," she pleaded. "Some important matters have come to light that you need to be aware of."

"I don't have time for your trivial prattle. I've got bigger problems to worry about."

The bundle of nerves tied in Céline's stomach unraveled and unleashed a surge of anger that even surprised her. "No, Dylan, you're wrong," she said. "Right now, *you* have problems that not even *you* are capable of sweeping under the rug this time."

Hands on hips, he narrowed his eyes. "You'd better have a good reason for this intrusion," he warned. "There is nothing you have to say that is more important than getting me elected president. Now close the door on your way out and tell Elizabeth, that under no circumstances, do I want to be disturbed again."

Céline sat on the corner of his desk; folded her arms across her chest. She raised her voice an octave higher than usual. "Reason? You want a reason? I have four *very* good reasons you're not going to like, but need to listen to."

"Who in the hell do you think you're talking to?" Dylan glared at his wife. "You of all people know I haven't got time for this kind of nonsense. Have you lost your friggin' mind?"

Céline started to speak, but Dylan held up his hand, shook a finger toward her. "Wait, wait just a minute. I'm not talking to my wife, am I? Céline knows better than to use that tone with me." He narrowed his eyes and sneered. "That you, Claréne? Another attempt at one of your twin-sister switcharoos to kick me while I'm down?

Dylan stood and stared down at her. "If you've come in here for a fight, I'm primed and ready. Come on, bitch, hit me with both barrels. We both know Cèline is incapable of a good old-fashioned yell-fest. Let's you and I duke it out once and for all. Who knows, Claréne, it might lead to the best roll in the hay *you've* ever had."

Céline stood, pushed Dylan away challenging his attempt to intimidate her with a defiant stare. "Oh no, dearest husband, this is all me, your beloved wife, in full Technicolor. Get used to it. I'm here specifically to warn you that your life is about to change — and not in a good way. In fact, a special group of people are about to join us. If I were you, I'd carefully listen to every word they have to say."

"I've had enough, Céline, go do what first ladies do. Plan a tea party, go to a museum, or read one of your damn books. Anything, but just leave me be. I need to work on my victory speech and don't have time for this shit."

Céline balled her fist and glared at her husband. "Victory speech?" She laughed. "You're awfully confident for a guy who's neck and neck in the polls with his opponent."

Dylan sneered at his wife, and then picked up the phone. "This is your last warning before I call security."

Céline yanked the receiver from his hand. "Elizabeth, send them in," she said to Dylan's assistant.

The door opened and Claréne, Mama Bea, Penelope Mills, and André Bélair filed into the Oval Office. They formed a half-circle in front of the president's desk.

"What's that bitch Mills doing here?" Dylan yelled. "She should be in jail."

Ignoring Dylan's outburst, Cèline walked over to the door and instructed her husband's assistant not to disturb the president for the next thirty minutes.

"This is outrageous," Dylan said pointing a finger at his wife, who had rejoined the others. "Even for you."

"I'm sure Burt Harrison would have been here, too," she said. "But, Harley Durham's flunky, Buck Broussard, ran him down like a stray dog and killed him, didn't he?"

"You're crazy," Dylan said. "I don't even know this Buck you're talking about. I'm telling you for the last time, get these people out of my office, or I'll have the secret service throw all of your asses in jail."

"And, *I'm* telling *you* for the last time," Céline warned, "you really don't have a choice but to listen. We literally hold your political career and reputation in our hands."

With reluctance, Dylan slid into the presidential throne.

"Mama Bea, you go first," Céline said.

Bea stepped forward; her eyes bored into Dylan. "You're an evil-man, Mr. President," she said as she pulled a hot pink diary from a gift bag. "This belonged to my sweet sister, until it was stolen. It was just returned to me today by the first lady. My Gabrielle poured her youthful soul onto these pages. Lord only knows why she declared her love for *you*." She sneered. "You and Harley Durham raped her and left her for dead."

Mama Bea set the book decorated with little pink hearts down on the presidential desk, and then stepped back.

"Wha... Where in the hell did you find that? It belongs..."

"Belongs, Dylan? Belongs to whom?" Céline asked.

The president quickly glanced away.

"I suggest you stop interrupting," the first lady warned once again. "We're just getting started."

Pepper Mills stepped forward.

Dylan's face turned red. "You, little lady, belong in a psyche ward." He mocked as he glared at her.

"A psych ward? Interesting choice of words," Pepper said with a touch of irony. "We all know how familiar *you* are with psych wards. Sherri Dee Durham certainly was. You *do* remember Sherri, don't you? Quite a colorful character, wouldn't you agree?"

Dylan sneered; shook his head and said, "You really don't know how to stop sensationalizing the facts, do you?"

"So, you *do* recall, Miss *Peezee*," Pepper said. "She was quite chatty. Before she died, she shared some *very* interesting facts about you and your... your... I'll be respectful and call them misguided, less than prudent college days."

Dylan slammed his fist on the desk. Of all the people standing in this room, *you* have no business being here."

Pepper stood her ground. "Trust me, this is the last place on earth I want to be. I'm only here because the first lady invited me. She convinced me of the importance of sharing the additional and mounting evidence we've all accumulated on you.

She smiled. "Unfortunately for you, I'm *not* finished. I have more," she said as she pulled two envelopes from her oversized Gucci bag.

Pepper placed a large envelope on his desk, and then slid a brass key from the smaller one. "This little gem was most likely bequeathed to me by Burt Harrison. When I first received the key, I refused to have anything to do with the contents of that safety deposit box. Mark Saderfield convinced me to give the information to the first lady."

"That son-of-a-bitch! I should have known he was a Benedict Arnold!" Dylan's eyes burned with contempt. He pointed a finger at her. "I'll make sure *neither* of you are in front of cameras, nor publish another word ever again."

"This is not a two-way conversation," Céline said interrupting his rant. "I suggest you shut up and listen. We've got a long way to go."

Pepper set the key down and placed her fingers on the larger envelope. "Inside this ticking bombshell are several photos from years of embarrassing baggage. I'm sure the tabloids would love to get their hands on them," she said.

Emboldened, the journalist reached into her pocket. This is one of my all time favorites," she said, as she presented a photo of Dylan and Harley wearing campaign hats. Their arms were wrapped around a scantily dressed, well-endowed woman. A bright, red, white and blue satin sash stretched across her naked breasts; she was kissing Dylan on the cheek.

Pepper handed the photo to the first lady for safekeeping. "We can only assume that these, and all the other items I'm providing today, were accumulated over the years by your old friend Harley Durham — his fingerprints are literally on everything."

She continued. "Still locked in that safety deposit box in New Orleans are more photographs, tape recordings, and thumb drives of suspected criminal activities by both you and Mr. Durham." Pepper touched the top of the envelopes one last time, and then stepped back from the president's desk. "It's a shame we'll never know how your campaign manager came into possession of all this information."

"This is bull-shit," Dylan scoffed. "What makes any of you think you have the right to challenge me with your theatrics?"

André tossed an envelope toward Dylan. It skipped across the desk and fell into the president's lap. "I have nothing to say to you," André said. "Unfortunately for me your disgusting DNA runs in my veins. That letter is certified proof you knew my biological mother *intimately* and possibly were responsible for her death."

Dylan tore the letter in half and threw it into the trash. He sneered at his accusers. "Anyone else? What about you, Claréne? So unlike you not to add your two bits."

"Oh no, nothing to add," she smiled with pleasure. "This overdue intervention is enough for me and quite entertaining — wish I had brought my camera. Just knowing that when the time is right, the good people of the United States will finally know what kind of man you really are."

Dylan pushed away from his desk and stood. He glared at the small entourage. "If you think your little attempt to try and intimidate me is working, you're dead wrong. Who in the hell do you think you're talking to? Now get out of my office," he ordered.

"Not so fast," Céline said. "I haven't had my turn."

Dylan threw up his hands and sat back down.

Céline pulled a chain from beneath her sweater. A key dangled on the end. "Ten days ago, you renewed your love vows and heartfelt devotion for me with a golden love-lock, and then handed me this key. You affirmed with a voice dripping in sincerity: *"You and you alone now hold the key to our happiness."*

She tucked the chain back inside her sweater, and then placed both hands on the desk and leaned forward. "I didn't fully come to appreciate those lovely words you pledged to me in front of all those people in New Orleans... all those words and pictures that were broadcast on every news channel throughout the United States — at least not until a few days ago," she said.

She managed a quick breath and continued. "Your past has finally caught up with you, Mr. President, and is nipping at your heels. Everyone standing here today now owns a piece of you. I literally hold the pivotal keys to whatever future you may or may not have left." She picked up the brass safety deposit key lying on the president's desk and tucked it in her pants pocket.

Céline stepped away from Dylan's desk, but her words kept flowing. "No one can predict the end result of the upcoming election. Just know the one variable the people standing in this room *can* control is how and where you go from this moment forward. Do we turn all this evidence we have against you over to the Department of Justice...the tabloids? Or, will you do the right thing and resign sparing this country from another unnecessary political crisis? The timing is up to you."

Dylan picked up the phone. "Get security in here now and throw these low-life Cajun's off the White House property... including my wife," he barked into the receiver.

Claréne, Mama Bea, André, and Pepper filed out of the Oval Office.

The first lady followed, but stopped. With one hand on the doorknob, she turned and said one last thing. "Tread lightly, Mr. President. Tread lightly. Karma is a bitch."

THE END

EXCERPT FROM

BOOK II – SONS OF CUBA – HOMECOMING

CHAPTER 1

"FIRING Squad ... *Atencíon* ..."

A dozen heels clicked together; the drum of boots tramped in unison against the sun baked soil. Felipe tugged and pulled against the tether securing him to the death post, but the rawhide cut into his wrist and ankles, holding fast.

The stench of death and haunted wails of ghosts from past executions swirled around Felipe. Memories of family ... lost love ... and battles in victory and defeat with his compatriots scrolled through his mind's eye at warp speed.

A soldier dressed in army green with a chest decorated with medals approached the prisoner; a smirk plastered across his face, the Colonel spat and laughed as spittle slid down Felipe's cheek.

The words *how could this be happening* spun out of control through Felipe's head. This had to be a mistake. It was *his* destiny to be Cuba's future.

A sneer twitched the corners of his mouth; certainly not the fraud veiled in the shadows of the observation tower. Who could he be? Who did he think he was killing ME, Felipe Cárdenas y Pérez?

Before the decorated soldier wrapped the black silk blindfold around Felipe's eyes, Felipe strained to catch a glimpse of his executioner. Even though the tall, muscular frame was cloaked in a dim light, there was something familiar about the man. If he didn't know better, he would swear he spotted a mirror image of himself.

A sword rattled as it was pulled from a scabbard; the swish of the blade cut through the air as the raspy voice of the Colonel bellowed, "Ready ... Aim ... Fire."

***

"Wake up, Felipe, wake up," panic laced Ileana's voice. "You're having a nightmare."

He jolted upright, snatched Ileana's wrist. "Wha ... what the hell ...?

"I'm sorry, I'm sorry," she exclaimed. "You ... you're screams frightened me. I thought we were under attack."

Felipe released Ileana's wrist then brushed the perspiration dripping from his brow. He took a deep breath and slowly exhaled; his hands still shook.

"Let me get you a cup of coffee," Ileana offered. "I could add some brandy if you like."

He glanced up at her and smiled, "Just coffee."

Ileana took a step, stopped reached back and placed a hand on Felipe's shoulder. "Are you okay?"

Without looking up, he patted her hand and nodded.

Ileana gave his shoulder one last squeeze and left the room.

Felipe couldn't shake the foreboding that gripped his insides tighter than a boa constrictor coiled around its prey. He shook his head and whispered to the ghosts in the room, "Trying to invade my dreams again Rafaela with your so called warnings?" he scoffed. "They become more absurd each time they occur."

He stood and snatched a jacket hanging over a dining chair and said to the vacant room, "Well, I don't buy your nonsense. Find another *idiota*."

As Felipe opened the cabin door, a gust of bitter wind rushed past. He buttoned his coat, reached over and picked up the binoculars lying on the veranda railing and scanned the horizon as daylight peeked over the mountains.

Cactus and rocks dotted the landscape, and ascended toward lush pine forests high in the *Sierra Madres Oriental.* Great columns of smoke from the snowcapped volcano, *Popocatépetl,* towered high into the clouds. The rugged terrain was the perfect training ground for the rebels, and it all was within a fifty-mile radius southeast of Mexico City.

He blew warm breath into his hands and returned to the ranch house shutting the door behind him. Cold air whistled and seeped through cracks and crevasses of the old structure and the wood-beamed ceiling creaked.

Felipe stumbled over a loose floor tile, caught his fall and said, "For Christ's sake I don't know whether the conditions are worse in here or out in the field."

He sat down at the long dining table and opened the account books; the numbers had not changed. Money was gushing out, little was coming in. Weapons, uniforms and other equipment needed to be purchased, not to mention the bare essentials such as food and living quarters. The men existed on eighty cents a day – which was less than Batista's army spent on their horses. Somehow, someway they needed to increase their intake, he thought, or their revolution would wither and die.

Ileana Calleri handed Felipe a steaming cup of coffee. Her shiny, raven hair was pulled back in a tight bun and accentuated her warm brown eyes and smooth golden skin. Her shoulders were wrapped in a royal blue and gold wool shawl. The hem of the Aztec patterned skirt covered the tops of her polished leather boots.

"Thank you," Felipe said, welcoming the cups warmth on his numb fingertips. "I needed this."

Ileana walked to the window and gazed out. "Did you see any sign of Emilio and the men?" She asked as she pulled the shawl tighter around her shoulders.

Felipe shook his head and closed the account books. "I need to be in the field with the men instead of searching these damn books for nonexistent funds."

She touched his shoulder, "In time you'll be with your comrades, Felipe … when it counts. Right now you're needed to make important political contacts and raise money."

He patted her cold hand. "Perhaps, but my heart is with my men."

"I still don't understand why you left the comfort of Mexico City to stay in this run down shack," Ileana shivered.

"Batista has spies everywhere," he said with a bitter scowl. "The city was getting too dangerous."

"True," Ileana said, "but at least in Mexico City you had access to modern communication and rich sympathizers."

"I'm needed here," Felipe insisted. "More men are arriving from Cuba weekly, and it is getting difficult to find safe houses for these recruits. More importantly, this area is similar to the Cuban Sierra and much easier to maintain discipline."

"Possibly," Ileana said, "but this old fortress couldn't possibly house more than a few dozen men."

Nonsense," Felipe said. "With the outlying barns and stables we can billet more than a hundred, if necessary. Need I remind you, we're not here to live in luxury? These ninety-six square miles of fields and mountains are similar to the Cuban Sierras and are perfect for forced marches, simulated combat and guard duty situations." He smiled, "What more could a rebel ask?"

Ileana bit her bottom lip and looked out the window. "But, Emilio has been gone for days. They took little food and water with them."

Felipe got up from the table and stood next to Ilena. He glanced down at her, "It is crucial guerrilla fighters walk for long periods in adverse conditions with very little food and water. They need to climb mountains and carry heavy packs. It's all part of the training. How did you think revolutionaries trained?

Ileana shrugged.

"Once we return to Cuba and join the main force, every soldier must be physically fit and resistant to fatigue."

"I know you're right," Ileana signed; her ample breasts tugged against her embroidered blouse, melancholy washed across her face. "I miss Emilio."

"What would your husband, Faustino, say to that?"

She looked down at the floor and tugged at her gold loop earrings. "He lives his life ... I live mine. Anyway, he's in Spain producing another movie and will be gone for months. I'm sure that Spanish harlot," a smiled played at the corner of her mouth, "I mean starlet keeps him company."

Felipe laughed. "Does he know his house in Mexico City has been a haven and shelter for a band of Cuban revolutionaries?"

"He doesn't ask and I don't offer the information," she said. "I'm proud of my Cuban heritage and will do whatever it takes to help the cause." Ileana stretched her five-foot two frame; flecks of gold blazed in her brown eyes, "Like I said, my husband doesn't monitor my life ... I don't question his. Besides, if your revolution is successful, I'm sure he'll produce a movie about it."

Ileana picked up the binoculars sitting on the dining table, went back to the window and searched the landscape.

Felipe followed her and wrapped his arm around her shoulders. "We truly appreciate everything you've done, Ileana. Cuban women like you will make our victory possible."

She looked up and smiled. "It's nothing. You're the one who makes a bigger sacrifice. Emilio told me you pawned your only heavy coat and used your entire meager monthly allowance to finance the printing of your latest manifesto."

"I'd sell my soul if I thought it would help get the message out. Monies flow in slowly ... if at all. The funds needed to come from somewhere."

Ileana smiled and looked up at Felipe. "Maybe it's time you accepted ex-president Prío Socarrás generous offer. He personally told me he'd meet you or Luis in McAllen, Texas with a check. It's that simple."

"No!" Felipe barked. "He's no better than Batista. The money he offers was also stolen from the Cuban people."

Ileana furrowed her, "Another consideration is Socarrás is returning a portion of the people's money and putting it to good use."

Felipe pushed back his rising annoyance. What did this woman know about rebellion? He took a cigar from his pocket and lit it. "If I take his money," he said, "Socarrás will expect something in return. Our goal is to rid Cuba of tyrants not replace them with another."

"Felipe, be realistic," Ilena said, "If you don't have an alternative financial plan, you need to consider his offer." She rubbed her hands together, "How can you stand this incessant cold?"

Felipe closed his eyes; bit back the words nipping his tongue. He grabbed two split logs and kindling and placed them over the dying embers. In moments the dry wood ignited into a blaze warming the chill in the air.

"As soon as my visa is approved," he said, "I'm going to the U. S. ... My American contacts have arranged speaking engagements in the Cuban communities up and down the eastern seaboard from New York to Miami. I have faith the expatriates won't fail me. Their support is an investment in their future – their children's future. Success will help them all eventually return to their homeland." A spark ignited in Felipe's eyes, "The donations will come, or I'll die trying."

The front door flew open and slammed against the cabin wall. A brisk breeze rushed in and fanned the flames in the fireplace. A tall, lean figure, mud and grime caked on his clothes and face, dropped his backpack on the floor. *"Buena's días! Qué pasa?"*

"Emilio!" Ileana exclaimed.

As they embraced, Felipe turned and looked into the fire giving Ileana and Emilio their private moment.

Emilio slapped Felipe on the back. "Great exercise, *mí amigo*. You would have been proud of the men. We get closer to our goals every day."

Felipe pulled a cigar from his pocket and handed it to Emilio. "Now all we need is more money and transportation back to Cuba."

"Luis should be returning soon with news about the PT cruiser," Emilio said. "If that option falls through, we're working another angle." He struck a match, touched the flame to the cigar tip and took several puffs. A twinkle glistened in his eyes. "We've come a long way these last several months since you've joined us in Mexico," Emilio said. "It won't be long now, my friend ... it won't be long."

Ileana handed Emilio a cup of hot coffee, "Bet you could use this?"

Emilio kissed the top of her head and said, "That, a belly full of food and your warm body next to mine."

CHAPTER 2

GENERAL Batista caressed the polished oak balustrade curving up the marble staircase leading up to the massive lobby of the Presidential Palace. He climbed the stairs; the musical sound of his steps against the shiny stone echoed throughout the foyer. He enjoyed this time of night the most when he could be alone with his thoughts. His family was in bed and the aides had been sent to their quarters. When he reached the top, he stopped and marveled, as he often did, at the mural ceiling and the opulence surrounding him. He was accustomed to this type of living and no one was going to take it away from him – especially not Felipe Cárdenas and his band of renegades.

A sour taste infested his mouth and irritated an already acidic stomach; this happened every time he thought of that troublesome rebel.

Batista cursed, "Incompetent Mexican intelligence sources. They'd let him down again. No one knew where Cardena's band of rebels had disappeared. They could be anywhere in Mexico.

The General's fiery temper simmered; he clenched his teeth. It was imperative he maintained self-control handling this latest problem – there could be no mistakes. If only he had been better informed, Cardena would never have gotten a visa to the United States. But now it was too late – he was already there, raising money for his cursed revolution. Batista heaved a disgusted sigh and headed toward his private and secured apartment hidden behind a secret door.

The area was smaller, cozier than his official living quarters, and reached only by a concealed elevator – a perfect escape route if he ever needed one. He switched on a small desk lamp and fell into the over-sized leather chair – it all but swallowed his small frame. Two family photographs - one of his black mother and Chinese father, and the other of his wife, Mirta, their four boys and sweet baby girl, stared back at him from the huge mahogany desk.

Batista tipped the lampshade revealing photos and memorabilia hanging on the mahogany paneled walls behind him. There was a picture of him when he first joined the army as a private. Next to it, he was in his General's uniform when he appointed himself Chief of the Military after the "Revolt of the Sergeants" in nineteen thirty-three. One of his favorite photos was with Frank Sinatra and mafia boss, Meyer Lansky, on the steps of the casino Montmartre Club.

He slammed the desk with his closed fist, the family photos danced across the smooth top. "Cardena, enough is enough! You'll not take this from me." He picked up the phone and dialed a private number.

"Yeah, what do you want?" A gruff voice asked on the other end.

"I need to speak with Joseph Nucci," Batista said.

"Who's askin'?"

"General Fulgencio Batista, the President of Cuba."

Batista could hear muffled voices exchanged in the background, followed by seconds of silence.

"This is Nucci," an Italian accent laced in doubt responded.

"Meyer Lansky told me I could call if I needed a special favor," the General said.

Nucci's tone switched from doubt to submissive in a flash, "What can I do for you?"

"I need you to take care of a problem for me."

"Go on."

"Felipe Cardena is in the United States. I'd like your boys to take care of him ... permanently."

"Well, I'll be a son-of-a bitch," Nucchi said. "The bad boy of Cuba is in my backyard. Where is he now?"

"For the last several months he's been in Mexico training revolutionaries. Military intelligence tells me he's attempting to raise funds in the U. S. for his so called Movement."

"Do you know his schedule?"

"No, but I believe he's in New York right now. I don't know how long he'll be there, but I'm sure he'll make several stops along the east coast, and then head to Florida; particularly since there are many sympathetic Cubans living in that area." Batista shifted in his chair, lowered his voice. "Cardena must be stopped! If his revolution is successful, we all will be out of business. The casinos will shut down permanently and tourist trade will be nonexistent."

"Say no more," Nucchi said. "Your man is as good as dead."

The mob boss cleared his voice and spoke softly, "General, who knows you called?"

"No one," Batista answered. "Our business is between you and me."

"Understood," Nucchi said. "Problem solved. Aside from this nuisance, how's the casino business?"

"Right now, it's booming," the General said. "We only have occasional unrest in Havana, but it's never enough to disrupt business … at least so far. We can't let a revolution ruin it for us, Señor Nucchi. Life is too good."

"Like I said, the rebel bastard is dead."

"I'm counting on you," Batista replied.

CPSIA information can be obtained
at www.ICGtesting.com
Printed in the USA
LVHW080010061121
702586LV00004B/6